The Everyman Wodehouse

T0333111

P. G. WODEHOUSE

Tales of Wrykyn and Elsewhere

Twenty-five Short Stories of School Life

EVERYMAN

Published by Everyman's Library
50 Albemarle Street
London W1S 4BD

Details of original publication of individual stories can be found at the back of
this volume.
This collection first published by Porpoise Books, Maidenhead, 1997
First trade edition published by Everyman's Library, 2014

Typography by Peter B. Willberg

ISBN 978-1-84159-179-7

Distributed by Penguin Random House UK,
20 Vauxhall Bridge Road, London SW1V 2SA

Typeset by AccComputing, Wincanton, Somerset

Printed and bound in Germany
by CPI books GmbH, Leck

Tales of Wrykyn
and Elsewhere

CONTENTS

WRYKYN

ELSEWHERE

WRYKYN

The story of how Wrykyn beat Ripton at cricket

The Ripton match was fixed for July the second, on the Ripton ground.

Wrykyn was more anxious than usual to beat Ripton this year. Wrykyn played five schools at football, and four at cricket, and at both games a victory over Ripton would have made up for two defeats in other games.

Every public school which keeps the same fixtures on its card year after year sooner or later comes to regard a particular match as *the* match to be won. Sometimes this is because the other school has gained a long run of victories, or it may be because neither can get far ahead in its score of wins, but wins and loses every other year.

This was the case with Wrykyn and Ripton.

Last year Ripton had won by eleven runs. In the year before that Wrykyn had pulled it off by two wickets. Three years back the match had ended in a draw. And so on, back to the Flood.

Wrykyn had another reason for wanting to win this year. A victory over Ripton would make the season a record one, for each of the other three schools had been defeated, and also the MCC and Old Wrykynians. Wrykyn had never won both these games and all its school matches too. Twice it had beaten the schools and the old boys, only to fall before what was very nearly a county team sent down by the MCC. That is the drawback to a successful season. The more matches a school wins the stronger is the team sent against it from Lord's.

This year, however, the match had come on early, before the strength of the school team had got abroad, and Wrykyn, having dismissed the visitors before lunch for ninety-seven, had spent a very pleasant afternoon running up three hundred for six wickets.

It was in this match that Jackson, of Spence's, had shown the first sign of what he was going to do during the season. He made a hundred and eighteen without giving a chance. A week later he scored fifty-four against the Emeriti; and after that his career, with the exception of two innings of three and nought respectively, had been a series of triumphs. Wrykyn rubbed its hands, and wondered what would happen at Ripton.

Now Jackson, apart from his cricket, did not shine in school. He was one of those cheerful idiots without one atom of prudence in his whole composition. If he were bored by anything he could not resist from showing the fact. He would instantly proceed to amuse himself in some other way. Form-work always bored him, and he was, as a result, the originator of a number of ingenious methods of passing the time.

Fortunately for him, Mr Spence – who was the master of his form as well as of his house – was the master who looked after the school cricket. So, where other masters would have set him extra lessons on half-holidays, Mr Spence, not wishing to deprive the team of its best man, used to give him lines to write. Jackson would write them in preparation the same evening, and all would be joy and peace.

But, unhappily, the staff was not entirely composed of masters like Mr Spence.

There were others.

And by far the worst of these others was Mr Dexter.

It was not often that Jackson saw Mr Dexter, being neither in his house nor his form. But he did so once. And this is what happened:

The Ripton match was fixed, as I have stated, for July the second. On the afternoon of June the thirtieth, Henfrey, of Day's, who was captain of cricket, met Jackson on his way to the nets.

'Oh, I say, Henfrey,' remarked Jackson, as if he were saying nothing out of the common, 'I shan't be able to play on Saturday.'

'Don't be more of an ass than you can help,' pleaded Henfrey. 'Go and get your pads on.'

'I'm not rotting. I'm in extra.'

If you had told Henfrey that the Bank of England had smashed he would have said: 'Oh!'

If you had told him that the country was on the brink of war he would have replied: 'Really! After you with the paper.' But tell him on the eve of the Ripton match that his best batsman was in extra lesson, and you really did interest him.

'What!' he shouted.

'Sorry,' said Jackson.

'Who's put you in?'

'Dexter.'

'What for?'

'Ragging in French.'

'Idiot you are to go and rag!'

'What else *can* you do in French?' asked Jackson.

'Go on,' said Henfrey, with forced calm; 'you may as well tell me all about it.'

And Jackson did.

'For some reason or other,' he began, 'old Gaudinois couldn't turn up today – got brain fag or something.'

M. Gaudinois was the master to whom the Upper Fifth, Jackson's form, was accustomed to go for their bi-weekly French lesson.

'Well?' said Henfrey.

'So I'm hanged if the Old Man didn't go and send Dexter to take the Upper Fifth French. Bit low, don't you know, sending a man like that. You know what Dexter is. He's down on you for every single thing you do. It's like eight hours at the seaside to him if he catches you at anything. I do bar a man like that. I don't mind a man being strict; but Dexter doesn't play the game.'

'Well, buck up!' said Henfrey impatiently; 'don't be all night. I know all about Dexter. What happened?'

The injured youth resumed, in the injured tone of one who feels that he has been shamefully used.

This was the burden of his story:

From his earliest years he had been in the habit of regarding French lessons as two hours specially set apart in each week for pure amusement. His conduct in the form room was perfect compared with what he did in French.

'And it didn't occur to me somehow,' said he, 'that one couldn't rag with Dexter as one can with Gaudinois. I always thought it my right, so to speak, to rag. But the other chaps in the form lay low when they saw Dexter, and chucked rotting for the afternoon. That's why he spotted me, I suppose.'

This was indeed the case. Their exemplary behaviour had formed a background for Jackson. His conduct, which in a disorderly room might have passed without notice, became now so apparent that, exactly a quarter of an hour after his entrance, he was sent out of the room, and spent the rest of afternoon school in the passage.

So far all was well. It was no novelty for him to be sent out of that room. Indeed, he had come to look upon being sent out as the legitimate end to his afternoon's amusement, and, as a rule, he kept a book in his pocket to read in the passage. A humble apology to M. Gaudinois at four o'clock always set him free.

But with Mr Dexter it was different. Apologies were useless. He attempted one, but got by it nothing but a severe snub. It now became clear that the matter was serious.

One of Mr Dexter's peculiarities was that, while he nearly always sent a boy whom he had fallen foul of into extra lesson – which meant spending from two to four o'clock on the next half-holiday doing punishment work in a form room – he never told him of his fate. With a refinement of cruelty, he liked to let him linger on in the hope that his sins had been forgotten until, on the afternoon before the fatal half-holiday, the porter copied the names of the victims out of the extra-lesson book and posted them up outside the school shop.

Jackson, therefore, though Mr Dexter had not said a word to him about it, was pretty sure that he was a certainty for the 'black list' on the following Saturday, and would thus be unable to go with the team to Ripton.

Henfrey, having heard the story, waxed bitter and personal on the subject of lunatics who made idiots of themselves in school and lost Ripton matches by being in extra on the day on which they were played.

He was concluding his bright and instructive remarks on Jackson's character when O'Hara, of Dexter's, another member of the eleven, came up.

'Hwhat's the matter?' enquired he.

O'Hara, as his name may suggest, was an Irish boy. In the matter of wildness he resembled Jackson, but with this difference that, while the latter sometimes got into trouble, he never did.

He had a marvellous way of getting out of scrapes and quite a reputation for helping other people out of them.

Five years' constant guerrilla warfare with Dexter, who regarded his house as a warder might a gang of convicts, and treated them accordingly, had rendered him a youth of infinite resource. Henfrey went away to bat at the nets, leaving Jackson to tell his tale over again to O'Hara. 'So you see how it is,' he concluded: 'he's said nothing about it yet, but I know he means to stick me down for extra.'

'Dexter always does,' said O'Hara. 'I know the man. There's no getting away from him if you give him an opening. I suppose you tried apologising?'

'Yes. No good – rot, I call it. Gaudinois always takes an apology.'

'Well, I'll try and think of something. There's bound to be some way out of it. I've got out of much tighter places.'

Jackson departed with an easier mind. He felt that his affairs were in the hands of an expert.

After he had had his innings at the nets O'Hara strolled off to the porter's lodge. He wished to see whether Jackson's fears had been realised. The porter offered no objection to his inspecting the extra-lesson book. Old Bates was always ready to oblige the genial O'Hara.

O'Hara turned the pages till he came to the heading 'Saturday, July 2nd.' One of the first items was 'Jackson: gross misbehaviour. R. Dexter.' He thanked Bates, closed the book, then walked thoughtfully back to his house.

'Well?' asked Jackson when they met next morning.

'Has Dexter said anything about it yet?' said O'Hara.

'Not a word. But that doesn't mean anything.'

'It means a lot. I think I've got it now.'

'Good man! 'What is it?'

'I can't tell you. I wish I could. Ye'd be amused. But the whole point of it is that ye can say, if they ask afterwards, that ye knew nothing about it at all. But anyhow, go with the team tomorrow.'

'But, if my name's up for extra?'

'That's all right. Never mind that.'

'But, I say, you know' (simply to cut extra lesson was a feat more daring than even he had ever dreamed of), 'there'll be a ghastly row.'

'I've allowed for that. What you've got to do is to keep clear of Dexter today and go to Ripton tomorrow. I give ye my word 'twill be all right.'

Jackson breathed heavily, struggled with his timidity, and gave his decision.

'Right!' he said. 'I'll go.'

'Good!' said O'Hara. 'Now, there's one other thing. How much will ye give not to be in extra tomorrow? Oh, it's not for me, ye know, it's necessary expenses. Will ye give me half-a-crown?'

'Half-a-crown! Rather! Like a bird!'

'Hand it over, then.'

'You might tell me what it's all about,' complained Jackson as he produced the coin. 'I bar mysteries.'

But O'Hara would not say a word. Tombs were talkative compared with him.

That afternoon the extra-lesson list went up, with Jackson's name on it; and at 8.30 the following morning the Wrykyn team, Jackson amongst them, started for Ripton.

When Wrykyn played away from home two telegrams were always sent to the school, one at the luncheon interval, the other when the match was over. The first of these telegrams read as follows:

'Ripton, one-six-eight for five. Lunch.'

A hundred and sixty-eight for five wickets! It was a good start. The Wrykyn team would have to do all they knew, the school felt, when their turn came to bat.

At seven o'clock Mr Dexter, returning to his house for dinner, looked in at the school shop to buy some fives-balls. Fives was his one relaxation.

As he waited to be served his eyes were attracted by two telegrams fixed to the woodwork over the counter. The first was the one that had been sent at the luncheon interval.

The other was the one that had caused such a sensation in Wrykyn. And it created a considerable sensation in the mind of Mr Dexter. The sensation was a blend of anger, surprise, and incredulity.

This was the telegram:

> 'Ripton 219. Wrykyn 221 for 2. Trevor 52; Henfrey 20; Jackson 103 not; O'Hara 41 not.'

Only that and nothing more!

Mr Dexter, having made sure, by a second perusal, that he was not mistaken, went straight off to the Headmaster.

'I sent Jackson into extra lesson this afternoon, and he did not go.' That was the gist of a rather lengthy speech.

'But, Mr Dexter,' said the Head, 'surely you are mistaken. Jackson was in the extra lesson today – I saw him.'

'Jackson in the cricket team?'

'I was referring to a younger boy, W. P. Jackson, who is in your house. Was he not the boy you sent into the extra lesson?'

Mr Dexter's face darkened. Like the celebrated M.P., 'he smelt a rat; he saw it floating in the air'.

'This is a trick,' he said. 'I will see Jackson.'

He saw Jackson – W. P. Jackson, that is to say; aged fourteen; ordinary fag; no special characteristics.

'What is this I hear, Jackson?' he said.

Jackson gaped.

'You were in extra lesson this afternoon?'

'Yes, sir.'

'Who told you to go?'

'Please, sir, I saw my name on the list.'

'But you knew you had done nothing to deserve this.'

'Please, sir, I thought I might have done.'

This was so true – the average fag at Wrykyn did do a good many things for which he might well have received extra lesson – that Mr Dexter was baffled for the moment. But he suspected there was more in this than met the eye, and he was resolved to find out who was the power behind Jackson.

'Did anybody tell you that you were in extra?' he asked.

'Please, sir, O'Hara.'

A gleam of triumph appeared in the master's eye. The aroma of the rat increased. O'Hara and he were ancient enemies.

'Tell O'Hara I wish to see him.'

'Yes, sir.'

Exit W. P. Jackson, and, later, enter O'Hara.

'O'Hara, why did you tell Jackson that he was in the extra lesson this afternoon?'

'I saw his name on the list, sir.'

'And, may I ask, O'Hara, if it is your custom to inform every boy on these occasions?'

'No, sir,' said O'Hara stolidly.

'Then why did you tell Jackson?'

'I happened to meet him in the house, and mentioned it casually – in a joking way,' added O'Hara.

'Oh, in a joking way?'

Silence for two minutes.

'You may go, O'Hara,' said Dexter finally. 'You will hear more of this.'

O'Hara made no comment; but Mr Dexter was wrong – he heard no more of the matter. It dawned on the Housemaster by degrees that he had no case. A second conversation with the Head strengthened this view.

'I have been speaking to Jackson,' said the Head, 'and he says that you did not tell him to go into detention.'

'But,' added Mr Dexter, 'his name was on the list for extra lesson.'

'I have examined the list, and I find that you omitted to insert any initials before Jackson's name. You wrote "Jackson", and nothing more. That explains this somewhat ludicrous situation, I think,' said the Head. 'If no particular Jackson is specified it is naturally the Jackson with the guiltier conscience who accepts the punishment. It is a curious miscarriage of justice; but I do not see that there is anything to be done.'

And that was the end of the affair.

It was an accident, of course – a very curious – and lucky – accident.

And, of course, it was simply a guilty conscience that induced the younger Jackson to go into extra lesson that Saturday. However, it would be interesting to know how it came about that that worthy, who was notoriously penniless on the Thursday, was able to spend exactly half-a-crown at the school shop on the Friday.

In most of the houses at Wrykyn boys who had been at the school two years, and who were consequently in a sort of transition stage between fags and human beings, shared studies in couples. The fags 'pigged' in a body in a common room of their own.

This rule was pleasant enough, provided you got a study-companion of tastes and habits similar to your own. But it often happened that, once in your study, an apparently perfect individual developed some deadly trait, such as a dislike for 'brewing' or a taste for aesthetic furniture, and then life on the two-in-a-study system became troubled.

Liss and Buxton shared study eight at Appleby's. For some time all went well. They had much in common with one another. It is true that they were not in the same form, which is what usually cements alliances of this sort, Liss being in the Upper Fourth and Buxton in the Lower Fifth.

But otherwise the understanding seemed perfect. Both did a moderate amount of work, and both were perfectly willing to stop at a moment's notice, in order to play stump cricket or 'soccer' in the passage. Liss collected stamps; so did Buxton. Buxton owned a Dr Giles's crib to the play of Euripides, which the Upper Fourth were translating that term. Liss replied with a Bohn's Livy, Book One. Livy, Book One, was what the Lower

Fifth were murdering. In short, all Nature may be said to have been at first one vast substantial smile.

An ideal state of things, but one that was not destined to last.

Liss came back from school one afternoon, entered his study, and threw his books down on the table. Then he sniffed in a startled manner. The first sniff proving unsatisfactory, he encored himself. He was embarking on a third, when Buxton came in. It seemed to Liss that the aroma became stronger on his entry.

'Why, I believe it's you!' he cried.

'What's up now?' asked Buxton.

'Beastly smell somewhere. I was trying to find where it came from.'

'Oh, *that!*' said Buxton, 'that's all right. It's only some stuff I've got on my handkerchief. The man at the shop called it *Simpkins Idle Moments*. Don't you like it?'

Liss flung open the window, and leaned out as far as he could with safety, breathing hard.

'It's not bad when you get used to it,' said Buxton. Liss, having fortified himself with a stock of fresh air, wriggled back into the study and directed an indignant glance at his friend.

'It's beastly,' he said. 'It's the sort of stuff an office-boy out for Bank Holiday uses.'

'Oh, no,' said Buxton deprecatingly, 'I think it's rather pleasant myself.'

'But what do you want to do it *for?*' enquired Liss. 'You make me sick.'

'Sorry for that. The man I want it to do that to is Day.'

Mr Day was the master of the Lower Fifth.

'The fact is,' proceeded Buxton, in the manner of the man who says to the hero of the melodrama, 'sit down, and I will tell ye the story of me life', 'I've been having rather a row with Day.

He shoved me into extra last Wednesday for doing practically nothing. It wasn't *my* fault that the bit of paper hit him; I was aiming at Smith, and he strolled into the zone of fire just as I shot. I told him I was sorry, too. Well, anyway, he jammed me in extra and yesterday he slanged me about my Latin prose before the whole form, so I thought this was getting a bit too thick, so I thought something had got to be done. So I thought it over a good time, and at last I thought it would be a sound idea if I came into the form room with some scent on me. Day bars scent awfully, you know.'

'So do I,' said Liss coldly.

'Calls it clarified fat,' continued Buxton, 'and that kind of thing, and says using it's a filthy and effete habit only worthy of a degenerate sybarite!'

'So it is,' said Liss.

'Well, it acted splendidly. I sat tight, you know, waiting for developments. I could see him getting restive, and peering round the room over his spectacles, and then he spotted me. I don't know how.

'He glared at me for a second; then he said, "Buxton".

'"Yes, sir," I said.

'He beckoned me solemnly and I went up. When I got to his desk he took me by the tip of the ear and examined me.

'"Boy," he said, "what – *what* is this abomination on your handkerchief?"

'"*Simpkins Idle Moments*, sir," I said.

'The chaps yelled.

'"A scent, I presume?"

'"Yes, sir."

'"And will you kindly inform me, Buxton, for what reason you have adopted this clarified fat?"

'I told him that it was for the good of my health. I said doctors recommended it.

'"Boy," he said, "your story leaves me sceptical. I do not credit it. Go to your seat. Pah! Throw open the door and all the windows. Buxton, translate from Ille tamen – and do not dare to enter this room in such a state tomorrow."

'I went on to translate, and got ploughed, of course. He gave me the lesson to write out.'

'Serve you jolly well right,' said Liss.

'I don't think it would be safe,' said Buxton, 'to try him again with *Simpkins* after what he said.'

'I should think not,' said Liss.

'So,' continued Buxton triumphantly, 'I'm going to appear tomorrow in—' (here, regardless of his friend's look of disgust, he drew a small bottle from his pocket and examined the label) '—in *Riggles's Rose of the Hills*. That'll make him sit up. And, curiously enough, doctors say it's very nearly as good for you as *Simpkins* would be.'

When the somewhat searching perfume of Riggles's masterpiece reached Mr Day on the following morning, he stiffened in his chair.

'Boy!' he shouted. With the natural result that all the form except Buxton looked up. Buxton was apparently too busy with his work to spare a moment.

'Come *here*, Buxton,' added Mr Day.

Buxton advanced to the desk with the firm step that tells of an easy conscience.

'In spite of what I said to you yesterday, you have The Audacity,' began Mr Day, speaking in capitals, 'to Come Here *Again* in this DISGUSTING State.'

'Si-i-r!!' interjected Buxton, moaning with righteous indignation.

'Well, boy?'

'I don't see what I've done, sir.'

'You-Don't-See-What-You've-Done? Did I not tell you yesterday that I would not have you enter my form room with *Simpkins* – er – I forget the precise name of the abomination – on your handkerchief?'

'Oh, but, sir,' said Buxton, in the pleased tone of one who sees exactly where he and a bosom friend have misunderstood one another, and sees also his way to put matters right, 'This isn't *Simpkins Idle Moments*. It's *Riggles's Rose of the Hills*.'

Mr Day raved. What did it matter whether the abomination he affected were manufactured by Riggles, or Diggles, or Biggles, or Robinson? *WHAT* did it matter what name its degraded patentee had applied to it? The point was that it was scent, and-he-would-not-*have*-scent in his form room. So-kindly-remember-that-once-and-for-all-and-go-to-your-seat-and-don't-let-me-have-to-speak-to-you-again.

Buxton protested. Was he a slave? That was what Buxton would like to know. He was sure that there was no school rule against the use of scent as a precaution against germs. He didn't want germs. He was certain that his mother would not like it if he had germs. It was a shame that you were sent to schools where you were made to have germs.

The situation was at a deadlock. Much as he disliked scent, Mr Day was obliged to admit to himself that the law was not on his side. He was a serious man without a spark of humour in his composition, and with a tremendous enthusiasm for fairness, and he did not wish to do anything tyrannical. If the boy really was afraid of germs, he had no right to prevent him doing his best to stave them off.

He gave up the struggle in despair. Buxton walked back to his seat, and two days later entered the form room with a cold which not only made it necessary for him to use eucalyptus, but also to speak unintelligibly through his nose. Mr Day spent the morning with his handkerchief to his face, a pathetic figure which would have softened the heart of a less vengeful person than Buxton.

Public opinion was divided on the subject of Buxton's manœuvres. The Lower Fifth, glad of anything to relieve the tedium of school-time, hailed him as a public benefactor. Liss openly complained that life was not worth living, and that he might just as well spend his time in a scent-factory. Greenwood, the prefect of Buxton's dormitory, took a stronger line.

Having observed without preamble that he was not going to be asphyxiated for the amusement of Buxton or anyone like him, he attached himself to the scruff of that youth's neck, and kicked him several times with much vigour and enthusiasm. He said, that if Buxton came into the dormitory like that again, he would have much pleasure in wringing his neck and chucking him out of the window.

In this delicate position, Buxton acted in statesmanlike fashion. Scented as before during the day, he left his handkerchief in the study on retiring to rest. So that, with the exception of Mr Day and Liss, everyone was satisfied.

Liss brooded darkly over his injuries. At last, struck with an idea, he went across to the Infirmary to see Vickery. Vickery, a noted man of resource, was an Applebyite member of the Upper Fourth, and he had been down for a week or two with influenza. He was now convalescent, and visitors were admitted at stated intervals.

'I say, Vickery,' began Liss, taking a seat.

'Hullo!'

'When are you coming back to the house?'

'Oh, soon. Next Monday, I believe.'

'Well, look here.' And Liss set forth his grievance. Vickery was amused.

'It's all very well to laugh,' said Liss, complainingly, 'but it's beastly for me. I say, what I really wanted to see you for was to ask if you'd mind swopping studies for a bit.' (Vickery owned study three, one of the smaller rooms, only capable of accommodating one resident.) 'You see,' pursued Liss hurriedly, in order to forestall argument, 'it wouldn't be the same for you. I don't suppose you can smell a thing after the 'flu, can you?'

'It would have to be pretty strong to worry me,' agreed Vickery.

'Then will you?' said Liss. 'You'll find Buxton a good enough sort of chap when he isn't playing rotten games of this sort. And he's got Giles's crib to the *Medea*.'

This was Liss's ace of trumps, and it settled the matter. Vickery agreed to the exchange instantly, and gave his consent to the immediate removal of his goods and chattels from study three and the substitution of those of Liss. Liss went over to the house and spent the evening shifting furniture, retiring to his dormitory grubby, but jubilant, at 'lights-out'.

On the following Monday, Vickery was restored to Appleby's, with a doctor's certificate stating that he was cured.

Buxton welcomed him with open arms, explained the state of the game to him, and assured him that he was an improvement upon Liss.

'*You* don't mind this scent business, do you?' he said.

'Rather not,' said Vickery, 'I love scent. I use it myself.'

'Good man,' said Buxton.

But he altered his opinion next day.

'Great Caesar,' he cried, as he came into the study after a pleasant afternoon with Mr Day. He rushed to the window, and opened it. Vickery surveyed him with amused surprise.

'What's up?' he asked.

'Can't you smell it, you ass?' said Buxton, wildly.

'Smell it?' repeated Vickery. A light seemed to dawn upon him. 'Oh,' he said, 'you mean the stuff I've got on my handkerchief. Don't you like it? Doctors say it's awfully good for keeping off germs.'

Buxton, in a voice rendered nasal by a handkerchief pressed tightly over his face, replied that he did not. He hung out of the window again. Vickery grinned broadly, but became solemn as his companion turned round.

'Well, I didn't think *you* would have minded,' he said, in a reproachful voice, 'I thought you rather liked scent.'

'Scent! Do you call it a scent! What on earth is the muck?'

'It's only sulphuretted hydrogen. The doctor recommended it, to keep off any bad effects after the 'flu. I can't smell it much, but it seems rather decent. You wouldn't like some, would you?'

'Look here,' said Buxton, 'how long is this going on?'

'I couldn't say exactly, till I'm quite fit again. Two or three weeks, probably.'

'Weeks! Did you say weeks?'

'Yes. Not longer, I shouldn't think. A month at the outside. Hullo, you aren't off?'

Buxton left the room, and went down the passage to number three.

'Get out,' said Liss briefly. 'I don't want this study—'

'Then would you mind swopping with me?' put in Buxton

eagerly. 'I don't think I shall quite hit it off with Vickery. He's much more a pal of yours than mine.'

'Oh, hang it,' said Liss, 'I can't always be changing about. I've got all my things fixed up here. It's too much fag to move them again.'

'I'll do that. You needn't worry about it. I'll shift your things into number eight tonight, if you'll swop. Will you?'

'All right,' said Liss, 'don't go breaking any of my pictures.'

'Rather not,' said Buxton. 'Thanks awfully. And, I say, you can keep that Giles, if you like.'

'Thanks,' said Liss, 'it'll come in useful.'

'What made Buxton clear out like that?' he asked Vickery, as they brewed their first pot of tea after the exchange. 'Did you have a row?'

'No. It was only that he didn't like the particular brand of scent I used.'

Liss's jaw dropped.

'Great Scott,' he said, 'you don't use scent, too, do you?'

'Only when Buxton's there,' said Vickery. He related the story briefly.

'I thought it would be better for us two together than having to share the study with Buxton,' he concluded; 'so I laid in a little scent, as he was so fond of it. I chucked it away yesterday.'

'What a ripping idea,' said Liss. 'I hope it made him feel jolly ill. Anyway, it paid him back for the time he gave me.'

'Yes, scent per scent,' murmured Vickery; and, the last round of toast being now ready, and the kettle boiling over, study number eight proceeded to keep the wolf from the door.

'What they want, of course,' said Clowes, 'is exercise.'

'They get out of that with their beastly doctor's certificates,' said Trevor. 'That's the worst of this place. Any slacker who wants to shirk games goes to some rotten doctor in the holidays, swears he's got a weak heart or something, and you can't get at him. You have to sit and look on while he lounges about doing nothing, when he might be playing for the house. I bet Bellwood and Davies would both make good enough forwards if one could only get them on to the field. They're heavy enough.'

'I don't wonder, considering the amount they eat and the little exercise they take. I should say there was about twice as much of Bellwood as there ought to be. And he's the sort of chap you don't want more of than's absolutely necessary.'

Study sixteen was under discussion, not for the first time. Bellwood and Davies, its joint occupants, had been a thorn in Trevor's side ever since he had become captain of football. It was bad enough that two such loafers should belong to the school. That they should be in his own house was almost more than he could bear.

It was his aim to make Donaldson's the keenest and most efficient house at Wrykyn, and in this he had succeeded to a great extent. They had won the cricket cup, and were favourites for the football cup. Everyone in Donaldson's was keen except Bellwood and Davies. They, sheltered behind doctor's certificates, took life in their own slack way, and refused to exhibit any interest whatever in the doings of the house.

'It's a rummy thing about that study,' said Clowes, 'it's always been like that. I believe anybody who's a slacker or a bad lot goes there naturally; wouldn't be happy anywhere else. Do you remember, when we first came to the house, Blencoe and Jones had it? They got sacked at the end of my first term. After that it was Grant and Pollock. They didn't get sacked, but they ought to have been. Now it's these two. Let's hope they'll keep up the tradition and get turfed out at their earliest convenience!'

'It makes me so sick,' said Trevor poking the fire viciously, 'to think of two heavy chaps like that being wasted. They might make all the difference to the house second. We want weight in the scrum.'

In addition to the inter-house challenge cup there was a cup to be competed for by the second fifteens of the houses. Donaldson's had a good chance of this, but were handicapped by a small pack of forwards. Seymour's, their only remaining rival, were big and weighty. Clowes got up and stretched himself.

'Well,' he said, 'I don't think you'll get much help from Bellwood and pard. They remind me of the man who slept well and ate well but who, when he saw a job of work, was all of a tremble. They won't do a stroke if they can help it, and I don't see how you can get them in the teeth of their certificates. Well, I must go and work. I like to do a Greek book unseen if possible, but the *Agamemnon* is too tricky. I shall have to prepare it. By the way, have you got a copy to spare? I left mine over at school.'

'I'm afraid I've only got one, and I shall be wanting that. You can have it if you'll give it up at half past nine sharp.'

'No, it's all right, thanks. I'll borrow one from Dixon. He's sure to have one. I believe he's got every Greek play ever written.'

Clowes went off to Dixon's study. Dixon was a mild, spectacled youth who did an astonishing amount of work, and was about as much of a hermit as anyone can be in a public-school house. He was nervous and anxious to oblige when he was not too deep in his own thoughts to understand what your request was.

'Hullo,' said Clowes, as he entered Dixon's room, 'this door seems pretty wobbly. What have you been doing to it?'

He moved it to and fro by way of illustration.

It was very rickety indeed. It was, in fact, almost off its hinges.

'I'm afraid it *is* a little,' assented Dixon. 'The fact is, fellows have been running against it, and I think that has made it a little shaky.'

'Running against it!' said Clowes. 'What did you do?'

'I – er – well, the fact is, I didn't do anything. You see it was an accident. They told me themselves that it was.'

'It only happened once then? Must have taken a good strong chap to rush a door almost off its hinges at one shot.'

'No. They stumbled against it rather often.'

'Stumbled is good,' said Clowes. 'I suppose they didn't say how they came to stumble?'

'Oh, yes, they did. They tripped.'

'And you mean to say you believed that?'

'I couldn't very well doubt their word,' expostulated Dixon.

Clowes smiled pityingly.

'I didn't want to hurt their feelings,' Dixon went on.

Clowes smiled again.

'Who are the sensitive trippers?' he asked.

'Well, I don't know that I ought to say, but I suppose it will be all right. They were Davies and Bellwood.'

'So I should have thought,' said Clowes. 'How do you find that sort of thing affects your work?'

'Well the fact is,' said Dixon eagerly, 'I *do* find it a little hard to concentrate myself when I am continually interrupted by bangs on the door.'

'So should I. I think you'd get on better if you didn't study Bellwood's feelings so much. Do you mind if I borrow this *Agamemnon* for a couple of hours? I've left mine over at the school, and we've got a beastly hard chorus to prepare for tomorrow.'

'Oh, certainly, do,' said Dixon. 'Splendid play, isn't it?'

'Not bad. I prefer *Charley's Aunt* myself. Matter of taste, though. Thanks. I'll return it before I go to bed.'

And he went back to his own study.

It was in the afternoons, after school, that Bellwood and his companion Davies found time hang so heavily on their hands. To lounge in one's study and about the passages was pleasant for a while, but it was apt to pall in time, and then it was difficult to know how to fill in the hours.

On the afternoon following Clowes's conversation with Dixon, Bellwood found things particularly slow. In ordinary circumstances he and Davies would have been at the school shop eating a heavy, crumpety tea. But today an unfortunate passage of arms with his form-master had led to that youth's detention after school; and he was not yet out. Bellwood was one of those people who do not like to tea alone.

Besides, it was Davies's turn to pay; and to go and have a meal at his own expense would have been so much dead loss.

So Bellwood haunted the house, feeling very much out of humour.

After wandering up and down the passage a few times and reading all the notices on the house notice-board, it occurred to him that the half hour before the return of Davies might be well spent by ragging Dixon. It was for the purpose of keeping their betters from becoming dull, that people like Dixon were put into the world; and Dixon would in all probability be working – which would add a spice to the amusement.

He collected half a dozen football boots from the senior day-room. The rule of the house being that football boots were not to be brought into that room, there was always a generous supply there. Then he lounged off to Dixon's study.

The door, as he had expected, was closed. He took a boot and flung it with accurate aim at one of the panels. There was a loud bang, and he grinned as he heard a chair pushed back inside the study and somebody jump up. That was all right, then. Dixon was at home.

He was stooping to pick up another missile, when the door opened. It was only when the second boot got home on the shin of the person who stood in the doorway, that he recognised in that person not Dixon, but Trevor. It was just here that he wished he had tried some other form of amusement that afternoon.

And, indeed, the situation was about as unpleasant as it could be. Even in moments of calm Trevor was a cause of uneasiness to Bellwood. And here he was, unmistakably angry. It so happened that Bellwood's boot had found its billet on the exact spot on which a muscular forward from Trinity College, Cambridge, had kicked Trevor in the match of the previous Saturday.

'Oh, I say, sorry,' gasped Bellwood.

'What the blazes are you playing at?' asked Trevor.

'I'm frightfully sorry,' said the demoralised Bellwood; 'I thought you were Dixon.'

'And why should you fling boots at Dixon?'

Bellwood, not feeling equal to the explanation that it was the mission in life of people like Dixon to have football boots thrown at them, remained silent; and Trevor, having summed up Bellwood's character in an address in which the words 'skunk, worm', and 'disgrace to the house', occurred with what seemed, to the recipient of the terms, unnecessary frequency, dragged him into the study, produced a stick, and taught him in two minutes more about the folly of throwing football boots at other people's doors than he would have learned in a month of verbal tuition.

Bellwood slunk away down the passage, and half-way to his own study met Davies, released from the form room and full of his grievances.

To judge from his remarks, Davies did not think highly of Mr Grey, his form-master. Mr Grey in his opinion, was a person of the manners-none-and-customs-horrid type. He had a jolly good mind, had Davies, to go to the Headmaster about it.

In a word, Davies was savage. Bellwood, eyeing his wrathful friend, was struck with an idea. Trevor's stick had stung like an adder.

'Beastly shame,' he agreed, as Davies paused for breath. 'It was jolly slow for me, too. I've been putting in the time having a lark with old Dixon. I can't get him to come out, though I've been flinging boots. And his door won't open. I believe he's locked it.'

'Has he, by Jove!' muttered Davies, 'we'll soon see about that. Stand out of the way.'

He retired a few paces, and charged towards the door. Bellwood took cover in study twelve, the owner of which happened to be out, and listened.

He heard the scuffle of Davies's feet as he dashed down the passage. Then there was a crash as if the house had fallen. He peeped out. Davies's rush had taken the crazy door off its hinges, and he had gone with it into the study. He had a fleeting view of an infuriated Trevor springing from the ruins. Then, with Davies's howl of anguish ringing in his ears, he closed the door of study twelve softly, and sat down to wait till the storm should have passed by.

At the end of a couple of minutes somebody limped past the door. The remnants of Davies, he guessed. He gave him a few moments in which to settle down. Then he followed, and found him in a dishevelled state in their study.

'Hullo,' he said artlessly, 'what's up? What happened? Did you get the door open?'

Davies glared suspiciously, scenting sarcasm, but Bellwood's look of astonishment disarmed him.

'Where did you go to?' he enquired.

'Oh, I strolled off. What happened?'

Davies sat down, only to spring up again with a cry of pain. Bellwood recognised the symptoms, and felt better.

'I took the beastly door clean off its hinges. I'd no idea the thing was so wobbly.'

'Well, we ragged it a bit the other night, you remember. It was a little rocky then. Was Dixon sick?'

'Dixon! Why, Dixon wasn't in there at all. It was Trevor – of all people! What the dickens was he doing there, I should like to know?'

Bellwood's look of amazement could not have been improved upon.

'Trevor!' he exclaimed. 'Are you sure?'

'Am I sure! Oh, you—!' words failed Davies.

'But what was he doing there?'

'That's what I should like to know.'

It was really quite simple. Clowes had told the head of the house of Dixon's painful case, and suggested that if he wished to catch Bellwood and his friend 'on the hop', as he phrased it, an excellent idea would be to change studies secretly with Dixon. This Trevor had done, with instant and satisfactory results. The ambush had trapped its victims on the first afternoon.

Study sixteen continued to brood over its misfortunes.

'Beastly low trick changing studies like that,' said Davies querulously.

'Beastly,' agreed Bellwood.

'That worm Dixon must have been in it. He probably suggested it to Trevor. And now he'll be grinning over it.'

This suspicion was quite unfounded. Dixon had probably never grinned in his life.

'I tell you what,' said Bellwood suddenly, 'if they've changed studies, Dixon must be in Trevor's den now. He's always in the house at this time. He starts swotting directly after school. What's the matter with going and routing him out and ragging him now? He wants it taken out of him for letting us down like that. Come on.'

'We'll heave books at him,' said Davies with enthusiasm.

And the punitive expedition started.

Trevor's study was in the next passage. They advanced stealthily to the door and listened. Somebody coughed inside the room. That was Dixon. They recognised the cough.

'Now,' whispered Davies, 'when I count three!'

Bellwood nodded, and shifted a Hall and Knight's algebra from his left hand to his right.

'One, two, three.'

He turned the handle sharply, and flung open the door. At the same moment Bellwood discharged his algebra. It was a snapshot, but Dixon, sitting at the table outlined against the window, made a fine mark.

'Oh, I say!' cried Dixon, as the corner of the projectile took him on the ear.

'Go on,' shouted Davies from behind the door, as Bellwood paused with Victor Hugo's *Quatre-vingt-treize* poised. 'Sling it in!'

But Bellwood did not throw. The book dropped heavily to the floor. Just as his first shot found its mark he had caught sight of Trevor, seated in a deck-chair by the window, reading a novel.

Finding Dixon's study somewhat uncomfortable after Davies had removed the door, he had taken his book to his own den, where he could read in peace (so he thought) without disturbing Dixon's work.

This third attack was the last straw. The matter had become too serious for summary treatment. He must think out a punishment that would fit the crime.

It flashed upon him almost immediately.

'Look here,' he said, 'this is getting a bit too thick. You two chaps think you can do just as you like in the house. You're going to find that you can't. You're no good to Donaldson's. You shirk games. You do nothing but eat like pigs and make bally nuisances of yourselves. So you can just choose. I'm going out for a run in a few minutes. You can either come too, and get into training and play for the house second against Seymour's, or you can take a touching-up in front of the whole house after tea.'

Davies and Bellwood looked blankly at one another. Could these things be? For three years they had grown up together like two daisies of the field: they had toiled not, neither had they spun. For three years the only form of exercise they had known had been the daily walk to the school shop. And here was Trevor offering them, as the sole alternative to a house licking, a beastly violent run. And Trevor was celebrated for the length of his runs when he trained, and also for the rapidity of the same. The thing was impossible. It couldn't be done at any price. Davies bethought him of the excuse which had stood by him so well for the past three years. This was just one of those emergencies for which it had been especially designed. But even as he spoke he could not help feeling that Trevor was not in just the proper frame of mind for medical gossip.

'But,' said Davies, 'our doctor's certificates. We aren't allowed to play footer.'

'Doctor's certificates! Rot! You'd better burn them. Well, are you coming for the run?'

Bellwood clutched at a straw.

'But we've no footer clothes,' he said.

'You'd better borrow some, then. If you aren't back in this study, changed, by half past five, you'll get beans. Now get out.'

At ten minutes past five a tentative knock sounded on the door. Trevor opened it. There stood the owners of study sixteen garbed in borrowed football shirts and shorts.

Of the details of that run no record remains. The trio started off in a south-easterly direction, along the road which led to Little Poolbury. From this it may be deduced that the spin was not a short one. Whenever Trevor had chosen this direction for one of his training runs on previous occasions he had worked round through Little Poolbury to Much Wenham by road, then across difficult country (ploughed fields, brooks, and the like) to Burlingham, and then back to the school along the high road, the whole distance being between four and five miles. There is no reason for supposing him to have chosen another route on this occasion.

At any rate, as six struck from the college clock, a procession of three turned the corner of the road which ran past the school.

Bellwood headed the procession. He was purple, moist, and muddy, and he breathed in heavy gasps. A yard behind him came Davies in a similar condition, if anything, a shade worse. At the tail of the procession came Trevor, who looked as fresh as when he had started. He wore a pleasant smile. They passed in at Donaldson's gate, and were lost to view.

Study sixteen was subdued that night, but ate an enormous tea, and looked ninety per cent fitter than it had done for years.

And in the last paragraph of the one hundred and eighteenth page of the eleventh volume of the *Wrykynian*, you will find these words to be written: 'Inter-House Cup (second fifteens), Final. Donaldson's v. Seymour's – This match was played on Saturday, March 10th, and resulted in a win for the former, after a good game by one goal and two tries to a penalty goal. For the winners Kershaw played well at half, and Smith in the centre. The pick of the forwards were Bellwood and Davies. The latter's try was a clever piece of play. For Seymour's . . .' But that's all.

Tales of Wrykyn

I

There was not a great deal of Master Reginald Rankin, of Seymour's – he weighed seven stone three – but his acquaintances objected very strongly to all that there was. Reginald, indeed, did not court popularity. He had not that winsome, debonair manner which characterises the Social Pet. He was small and ugly. His eyes, which were green, wore a chronic look of suspicion and secretiveness. In fact, the superficial observer, who judged only by appearances, would have summed him up without further trouble as a little brute.

The superficial observer would have been quite right. He was.

Reginald's hobby was Revenge. I hope the printer will not fail to use a capital R for that word. A small letter might send the reader away with the impression that the Revenges of Reginald were of the same hasty, unscientific kind as those affected by the average boy. If the average boy is kicked on the shin by an enemy, he kicks back, and goes on his way rejoicing, and the episode is closed. Not so Reginald. One of his most treasured possessions was a small leather-covered diary of the sort one's aunt gives one at Christmas. In this he entered the important events of each day, and, unlike most people, he did not grow tired of it on January the third, and leave the rest of the year blank. He went conscientiously through the whole three hundred and sixty-five days; and, read as a consecutive story, it was not uninteresting. Thus, if one had been privileged to probe its mysteries, one would have found on March the sixth the following entry:

'*Got up. Washed. Said my prayers.*' (The last two statements rest on the unsupported word of the author. Neither feat produced any noticeable result.)

Continuing:

'*After breakfast Smith said I was a little beast and smacked my head. Got turned in Livy. Templar gave me the lesson to write out.*'

The next entry of interest is March the eighth, where we see Mr Templar rewarded for his trouble: '*Ragged a lot in form.*'

All this while Nemesis has been hovering over the too truthful Smith. The incident of Mr Templar has been a parenthesis. Honour, as far as Smith is concerned, remains unsatisfied. A whole week elapses before our hero gets his own back. All that while one imagines him dogging his victim's footsteps remorselessly. At last, on March the thirteenth, this item leaps to the eye:

'*Got up. Washed. Said my prayers. Hid Smith's boots, and he was late for school and got two hundred lines. Beef for dinner, and some muck that looked like plum pudding. Wrote home for money. Said my prayers. Went to bed.*'

Exit Smith, properly punished.

With which excursus on the manners and customs of the ruthless one, we can begin our story.

Rankin fagged for Rigby, of the Sixth. In this he was fortunate; for Rigby, as a rule, when he was not wrestling with some obstinate set of iambics or elegiacs, was of a placid nature, and rarely fell foul of those who fagged for him. And when he did, he merely relieved his feelings with sarcasm, the same passing over

Rankin's head so completely that he generally imagined that he was being complimented. Yet even Rigby got into Rankin's black book.

It happened in this way.

The architect who had built Mr Seymour's house was a man with a quiet, but strongly marked, sense of humour. The place was full of quaint surprises. One of his original effects was to cause the partition wall between Rigby's study and the one adjoining it to stop short of the ceiling by a couple of feet. How he hoped to benefit his fellow man by this is not known. Probably, he reflected that the used-up air of one study would be enabled to escape into the other, and vice versa, a healthy and incessant ventilation being thus secured. At any rate, there the opening was, and it had never been filled up.

When Rigby got his study he lodged a complaint. Two chatty persons, named Dent and Hammond, dwelt next door, and when three consecutive nights' work had been spoiled by the conversation which flowed over the wall in an unceasing stream, he flung down his Liddell and Scott and bounded off to the Housemaster. Since when the next-door study had been empty.

But even then his troubles had not ceased altogether. Time sometimes hung heavy on the hands of the senior day-room, and when this happened it was the custom with the gay sparks who led the revels in that den of disorder to adjourn to the vacant study (having first ascertained that Rigby was at home and hard at work) and make weird noises there. When the goaded worker finally plunged in to investigate with a stick, he found the room bare and empty, while the sound of receding footsteps in the distance told him that the revellers, much refreshed, were returning to their own quarters. These little things irritated Rigby.

Now it chanced one evening that Linton and Menzies, of the senior day-room, prowling the passages in search of adventure, came upon Rankin near Rigby's door.

'Hullo,' said Linton, 'lost anything?'

'No,' replied Rankin, edging away suspiciously.

'You look as if you were looking for something. Do you want to find Rigby?'

'No,' said Rankin, essaying a flanking movement.

'Don't you be an ass,' said Menzies kindly. 'You must want to see Rigby. You're fagging for him, and if you don't go to him you'll get into trouble. I'm sure he wants you now. Come on.'

The procession passed into the empty study. From the other side of the wall heavy breathing could be heard. The sound of a great soul struggling with a line that would not 'come out'.

'Let go, you cads!' shrilled Reginald.

'Stop that beastly row there!' shouted Rigby from the other study. 'Is that you, Rankin? Come here. I want you.'

'I told you so,' whispered Menzies. 'Come along. Better go by the short cut.'

He grabbed Rankin by the knees.

'Saves time,' agreed Linton, attaching himself to Rankin's shoulders. 'One, two, three – go!'

'Do you hear, Rankin?' said Rigby. 'Come here.'

And Reginald came.

What followed was distinctly a miscarriage of justice. When Rigby had picked up – in the following order – himself, his table, his chair, his books, his pen, and his ink-pot, and mopped up the last drop of ink on his waistcoat with his last sheet of blotting-paper, he proceeded to fall upon the much-enduring Reginald with the stick which he took with him to church on Sundays. Long before the interview concluded, Reginald had reason to regret that it had not been left behind in the pew on the previous Sabbath.

In the case of another hero in similar circumstances we read that 'Corporal punishment produced the worst effect upon Eric. He burned not with grief and remorse, but with rage and passion.' Or words to that effect. Just so with our Reginald. His symptoms were identical. In his diary for that day the following entry appears:

'*Got up. Washed. Said my prayers. After school two cads, Linton and Menzies, heaved me over the partition wall bang on to Rigby's table, and Rigby licked me when it wasn't my fault at all. He is a beast. Said my prayers. Went to bed.*'

After preparation that night Linton and Menzies, talking it over, came to the conclusion that the sequel to the affair must be a confession. They had little sympathy with Rankin, but the code of etiquette at Wrykyn demanded that he who got another into trouble should own up, and take all that was going in the matter of consequences. So Linton and Menzies went to Rigby's study. Rigby was immersed in some work which was apparently disturbing him a little. His hair was rumpled, and he was turning over the pages of his lexicon with feverish rapidity.

'Get out,' he said, when the pair made their appearance. 'What do you want?'

'It's only about this afternoon,' said Linton.

'What about this afternoon?' said Rigby, putting in a spell of rapid finger-work with the pages of the lexicon. 'What does— oh, it's all right, I've got it. Well, go on. Don't be all night.'

'About Rankin,' said Menzies, gently, as one explaining to a lunatic.

'Pushing him over, you know,' said Linton.

'We did it,' said Menzies.

'Did what?' said Rigby, from the depths of the lexicon.

'Shoved him over the wall,' said Menzies patiently.

'Yes?' said Rigby, in an absent tone of voice. 'I wonder what—oh, here it is. Now, what do you chaps want? If you can't come to the point and talk sense, get out. Can't you see I'm busy?'

'We thought you ought to know that it was us who shoved Rankin over the wall on to your—' He stopped. Rigby's head was bent over the lexicon.

'Good-night, Rigby,' said Menzies.

'Good-night,' said Rigby.

And the pair departed. They had done their best. It was not their fault if the man refused to listen to their chivalrous explanations.

Rigby worked on till the gas went out suddenly, as was its habit. Then he went to bed, and in the small hours the purport of Menzies' visit dawned upon him, and he realised that for all practical purposes he had been the Beetle-Browed Bully that afternoon, ill-treating the innocent small boy without cause or excuse. His was a genial nature, when not roused, and he resolved to make it all right with Rankin on the following morning.

After breakfast, accordingly, he summoned him to his study, made what was, in the circumstances – from prefect to fag – a handsome apology, and then dismissed the matter from his mind in favour of the second book of Thucydides, satisfied that the *Entente Cordiale* was sealed.

II

But in the black depths of Reginald's soul the desire for Vengeance still remained. Apologies are good enough in their way, but there are some things which cannot be wiped out by apologies. Reginald was not yet able to sit down with any comfort.

A lesser injury might have been repaid by the burning of toast or the over-boiling of an egg, but for a special case such as this Reginald scorned these obvious modes of retaliation as inadequate. This was an occasion for really drastic measures. Rigby thus escaped punishment for a season. And then, while the avenger was halting irresolutely between the various modes of retribution open to him, Fate, by the medium of a mild illness, removed his intended victim to the secure retreat of the Infirmary. Reginald felt as those Homeric warriors must have felt who, when they had, after great trouble, succeeded in rattling an opponent, had the mortification of seeing him rescued by some local god of unsportsmanlike nature, and conveyed to a place of safety in a special cloud.

One afternoon, however, he received a message from the invalid. Rigby wanted to see him at the Infirmary. It was important, said the message.

Reginald went to the Infirmary, where he found his foe lying on a sofa, reading an old volume of *Punch*. There was a pleasant fire blazing in the grate, and the whole aspect of the room, with its air of snugness and luxury, deepened his sense of injury. Not only had Rigby been permitted to evade his rightful punishment, but he was, in addition, being Pampered.

'Come in, Rankin,' said the sufferer. 'Look here, I've got something for you to do. My uncle and aunt are coming down tomorrow, and they'll want to see my study after they've looked me up here. So you might do the honours. And there's another thing. On the second shelf of my book-case you'll find a crib to the *Agamemnon*. You'd better cart that away and hide it till they've gone. My uncle's a bishop, and he has views of his own on cribs. Thinks they're deceitful. See? You'll know the book. It's blue, and it's one of Bohn's series. Don't forget. And mind the study's tidy. Thanks. Shut the door.'

Reginald shut the door gently. A sudden thought had come,

> 'like a full-blown rose,
> Flushing his brow.'

He meant to make that study very tidy. If ever there was a tidy study on the face of the earth, this tidy study was going to be that tidy study. But with respect to details he intended to exercise a certain licence.

There lived in the town of Wrykyn one J. Mereweather Cooke, a day-boy. Having been associated with him in dark deeds, Reginald had formed an alliance with him. Cooke's father was a sporting doctor. To the *maison* Cooke Reginald therefore made his way after leaving the Infirmary.

'I want to borrow some books,' he said. 'Can you bag any of your pater's?'

'What sort of books?'

'Oh, anything. Let's have a look, and I'll choose.'

He chose.

III

This was the letter.

THE STATION HOTEL,
WRYKYN

My Dear George (Rigby's name was George) – I am both grieved and disappointed. I have no wish to be unduly harsh with you at a time when you are laid up, but my duty compels me to speak out.

It seems incredible, I know, but I regret to say that my dear George's impression after reading so far was that his uncle had been lunching.

He read on.

That you were not wholly free from the failings of boyhood I was aware. I knew you to be in a measure deficient in reverence for your elders, and thoughtless. But I did not dream that you were also deceitful. My visit to your study today convinces me that I was wrong. Escorted to the room by a small lad, who was throughout most polite, I found on your shelves such an array of Dr Bohn's *English Translations of the Classics* as I could not have believed (but for ocular evidence) to have existed at one of our public schools. Nor is that all. Seeing me glancing at these volumes, the small boy to whom I have alluded uttered an irrepressible cry of mental distress. 'Oh,' he said, piteously, 'please do not look at those. *He told me to hide them, and said he would beat me if I did not.*' I have underlined these words, George. That you should so corrupt the mind of one of your juniors (to whom you ought to set a good example) is bad; but that you should force him with blows to carry out an act offensive to his conscience is worse, far worse. This petty tyranny did not, however, avail you, for I observed the books. In addition to these deceitful aids to study, I regret to say that I noticed other evidence of a perverted taste not often to be found in one so young. Of a dozen or more yellow-covered novels (so-called) I can recall the titles of but two, *Jenny, the Girl Jockey*, by Hawley Gould, and *A Tale of the Stableyard*, by Nat Smart. That you might have no more money to waste on such trash, I decided to give the sovereign with which I had intended to present you, to the small lad of whom I have made mention. I shall hope to see you when you return home for your holidays. Meanwhile,

I am, your uncle,
PETER PECKHAM

Ten minutes later Rigby, having pondered deeply over the matter, and traced his misfortunes to the right source, asked the Infirmary matron if she would be good enough to send for

Rankin, as he had something very particular and important that he wished to say to him.

The reply came back, per messenger.

Master Reginald Rankin presented his compliments to Mr Rigby, and very much regretted that one of those unfortunate previous engagements rendered it impossible for him to accept his kind invitation to come and listen to something very particular and important.

Two days after breaking-up day Rigby came out of hospital.

When the school re-assembled on the last night of the holidays, Rigby smiled a glad smile, and sought out the Seymour's matron.

'Oh, has Rankin come back yet?' he asked winningly. 'I've got something rather particular and important to say to him.'

'Rankin?' said the matron. 'Oh, Rankin. No, he's left the house. His parents have come to live in the town, and he is a day-boy now.'

'Oh,' said Rigby.

And he moved away disappointedly, feeling that some considerable time would probably have to elapse before he got square with Master Reginald Rankin.

The painful case of G. Montgomery Chapple, bachelor, of Seymour's house, Wrykyn. Let us examine and ponder over it.

It has been well said that this is the age of the specialist. Everybody, if they wish to leave the world a better and happier place for their stay in it, should endeavour to adopt some speciality and make it their own. Chapple's speciality was being late for breakfast. He was late not once or twice, but every day. Sometimes he would scramble in about the time of the second cup of coffee, buttoning his waistcoat as he sidled to his place. Generally he would arrive just as the rest of the house were filing out; when, having lurked hidden until Mr Seymour was out of the way, he would enter into private treaty with Herbert, the factotum, who had influence with the cook, for Something Hot and maybe a fresh brew of coffee. For there was nothing of the amateur late-breakfaster about Chapple. Your amateur slinks in with blushes deepening the naturally healthy hue of his face, and, bolting a piece of dry bread and gulping down a cup of cold coffee, dashes out again, filled more with good resolutions for the future than with food. Not so Chapple. He liked his meals. He wanted a good deal here below, and wanted it hot and fresh. Conscience had but a poor time when it tried to bully Chapple. He had it weak in the first round.

But there was one more powerful than Conscience – Mr

Seymour. He had marked the constant lateness of our hero, and disapproved of it.

Thus it happened that Chapple, having finished an excellent breakfast one morning some twenty minutes after everybody else, was informed as he sat in the junior day-room trying, with the help of an illustrated article in the boys' paper, to construct a handy model steam-engine out of a reel of cotton and an old notebook – for his was in many ways a giant brain – that Mr Seymour would like to have a friendly chat with him in his study. Laying aside his handy model steam-engine, he went off to the Housemaster's study.

'You were late for breakfast today,' said Mr Seymour, in the horrid, abrupt way housemasters have.

'Why, yes, sir,' said Chapple, pleasantly.

'And the day before.'

'Yes, sir.'

'And the day before that.'

Chapple did not deny it. He stood on one foot and smiled a propitiating smile. So far Mr Seymour was entitled to demand a cigar or coconut every time.

The Housemaster walked to the window, looked out, returned to the mantelpiece, and shifted the position of a china vase two and a quarter inches to the left. Chapple, by way of spirited repartee, stood on the other leg and curled the disengaged foot round his ankle. The conversation was getting quite intellectual.

'You will write out—'

'Sir, please, sir—' interrupted Chapple in an 'I-represent-the-defendant-m'lud' tone of voice.

'Well?'

'It's awfully hard to hear the bell from where I sleep, sir.'

Owing to the increased numbers of the house this term

Chapple had been removed from his dormitory proper to a small room some distance away.

'Nonsense. The bell can be heard perfectly well all over the house.'

There was reason in what he said. Herbert, who woke the house of a morning, did so by ringing a bell. It was a big bell, and he enjoyed ringing it. Few sleepers, however sound, could dream on peacefully through Herbert's morning solo. After five seconds of it they would turn over uneasily. After seven they would sit up. At the end of the first quarter of a minute they would be out of bed, and you would be wondering where they picked up such expressions.

Chapple murmured wordlessly in reply. He realised that his defence was a thin one. Mr Seymour followed up his advantage.

'You will write a hundred lines of Virgil,' he said, 'and if you are late again tomorrow I shall double them.'

Chapple retired.

This, he felt, was a crisis. He had been pursuing his career of unpunctuality so long that he had never quite realised that a time might come when the authorities would drop on him. For a moment he felt that it was impossible, that he could not meet Mr Seymour's wishes in the matter; but the bull-dog pluck of the true Englishman caused him to reconsider this. He would at least have a dash at it.

'I'll tell you what to do,' said his friend, Brodie, when consulted on the point over a quiet pot of tea that afternoon. 'You ought to sleep without so many things on the bed. How many blankets do you use, for instance?'

'I don't know,' said Chapple. 'As many as they shove on.'

It had never occurred to him to reckon up the amount of bed-clothes before retiring to rest.

'Well, you take my tip,' said Brodie, 'and only sleep with one. Then the cold'll wake you in the morning, and you'll get up because it'll be more comfortable than staying in bed.'

This scientific plan might have worked. In fact, to a certain extent it did work. It woke Chapple in the morning, as Brodie had predicted; but it woke him at the wrong hour. It is no good springing out of bed when there are still three hours to breakfast. When Chapple woke at five the next morning, after a series of dreams, the scenes of which were laid mainly in the Arctic regions, he first sneezed, then he piled upon the bed everything he could find, including his boots, and then went to sleep again. The genial warmth oozed through his form and continued to ooze until he woke once more, this time at eight-fifteen. Breakfast being at eight, it occurred to him that his position with Mr Seymour was not improved. While he was devoting a few moments' profound meditation to this point the genial warmth got in its fell work once again. When he next woke, the bell was ringing for school. He lowered the world's record for rapid dressing, and was just in time to accompany the tail of the procession into the form room.

'You were late again this morning,' said Mr Seymour, after dinner.

'Yes, sir. I overslebbed myselb, sir,' replied Chapple, who was suffering from a cold in the head.

'Two hundred lines.'

'Yes, sir.'

Things had now become serious. It was no good going to Brodie again for counsel. Brodie had done for himself, proved himself a fraud, an idiot. In fine, a rotter. He must try somebody else. Happy thought, Spenlow. It was a cold day, when Spenlow got left behind. He would know what to do. *There* was a chap for you, if you liked! Young, mind you, but what a brain! Colossal!

'What *I* should do,' said Spenlow, 'is this. I should put my watch on half an hour.'

'What 'ud be the good of that?'

'Why, don't you see? You'd wake up and find it was ten to eight, say, by your watch, so you'd shove on the pace dressing, and nip downstairs, and then find that you'd really got tons of time. What price that?'

'But I should remember I'd put my watch on,' objected Chapple.

'Oh, no, probably not. You'd be half asleep, and you'd shoot out of bed before you remembered, and that's all you'd want. It's the getting out of bed that's so difficult. If you were once out, you wouldn't want to get back again.'

'Oh, shouldn't I?' said Chapple.

'Well, you might want to, but you'd have the sense not to do it.'

'It's not a bad idea,' said Chapple. 'Thanks.'

That night he took his Waterbury, prised open the face with a pocket-knife as if he were opening an oyster, put the minute hand on exactly half an hour, and retired to bed satisfied. There was going to be no nonsense about it this time.

I am sorry to disappoint the reader, but facts are facts, and I must not tamper with them. It is, therefore, my duty to state, however reluctantly, that Chapple was not in time for breakfast on the following morning. He woke at seven o'clock, when the hands of the watch pointed to seven-thirty. Primed with virtuous resolutions, he was just about to leap from his couch, when his memory began to work, and he recollected that he had still an hour. Punctuality, he felt, was an excellent thing, a noble virtue, in fact, but it was no good overdoing it. He could give himself at least another half hour. So he dozed off. He woke again with something of a start. He seemed to feel that he had been asleep for a considerable time. But no. A glance at the watch showed the hands pointing to twenty-five to eight. Twenty-five minutes more. He had a good long doze this time. Then, feeling that now he really must be getting up, he looked once more at the watch, and rubbed his eyes. It was still twenty-five to eight.

The fact was that, in the exhilaration of putting the hands on, he had forgotten that other and even more important operation, winding up. The watch had stopped.

There are few more disturbing sensations than that of suddenly discovering that one has no means of telling the time. This is especially so when one has to be in a certain place by a certain hour. It gives the discoverer a weird, lost feeling, as if he had stopped dead while all the rest of the world had moved on at the usual rate. It is a sensation not unlike that of the man who arrives on the platform of a railway station just in time to see the tail-end of his train disappear.

Until that morning the world's record for dressing (set up the day before) had been five minutes, twenty-three and a fifth seconds. He lowered this by two seconds, and went downstairs.

The house was empty. In the passage that led to the dining-room he looked at the clock, and his heart turned a somersault. *It was five minutes past nine.* Not only was he late for breakfast, but late for school, too. Never before had he brought off the double event.

There was a little unpleasantness in his form room when he stole in at seven minutes past the hour. Mr Dexter, his form-master, never a jolly sort of man to have dealings with, was rather bitter on the subject.

'You are incorrigibly lazy and unpunctual,' said Mr Dexter,

towards the end of the address. 'You will do me a hundred lines.'

'Oo-o-o, sir-r,' said Chapple. But he felt at the time that it was not much of a repartee. After dinner there was the usual interview with Mr Seymour.

'You were late again this morning,' he said.

'Yes, sir,' said Chapple.

'Two hundred lines.'

'Yes, sir.'

The thing was becoming monotonous.

Chapple pulled himself together. This must stop. He had said that several times previously, but now he meant it. Nor poppy, nor mandragora, nor all the drowsy syrups of the world should make him oversleep himself again. This time he would try a combination of schemes.

Before he went to bed that night he put his watch on half an hour, wound it up, and placed it on a chair at his bedside. Then he seized his rug and all the blankets except one, and tore them off. Then he piled them in an untidy heap in the most distant corner of the room. He meant to put temptation out of his reach. There should be no genial warmth on this occasion.

Nor was there. He woke at six feeling as if he were one solid chunk of ice. He put up with it in a torpid sort of way till seven. Then he could stand it no longer. It would not be pleasant getting up and going downstairs to the cheerless junior day-room, but it was the only thing to do. He knew that if he once wrapped himself in the blankets which stared at him invitingly from the opposite corner of the room, he was lost. So he crawled out of bed, shivering, washed unenthusiastically, and he proceeded to put on his clothes.

Downstairs it was more unpleasant than one would have

believed possible. The day-room was in its usual state of disorder. The fire was not lit. There was a vague smell of apples. Life was very, very grey. There seemed no brightness in it at all.

He sat down at the table and began once more the task of constructing a handy model steam-engine, but he speedily realised, what he had suspected before, that the instructions were the work of a dangerous madman. What was the good of going on living when gibbering lunatics were allowed to write for weekly papers?

About this time his gloom was deepened by the discovery that a tin labelled mixed biscuits, which he had noticed in Brodie's locker, was empty.

He thought he would go for a stroll. It would be beastly, of course, but not so beastly as sitting in the junior day-room.

It is just here that the tragedy begins to deepen.

Passing out of Seymour's gate he met Brooke, of Appleby's. Brooke wore an earnest, thoughtful expression.

'Hullo, Brooke,' said Chapple, 'where are you off to?'

It seemed that Brooke was off to the carpenter's shop. Hence the earnest, thoughtful expression. His mind was wrestling with certain pieces of wood which he proposed to fashion into photograph frames. There was always a steady demand in the school for photograph frames, and the gifted were in the habit of turning here and there an honest penny by means of them.

The artist soul is not always unfavourable to a gallery. Brooke said he didn't mind if Chapple came along, only he wasn't to go rotting about or anything. So Chapple went along.

Arrived at the carpenter's shop, Brooke was soon absorbed in his labours. Chapple watched him for a time with the interest of a brother-worker, for had he not tried to construct handy model steam-engines in his day? Indeed, yes. After a while, however, the role of spectator began to pall. He wanted to *do* something.

Wandering round the room he found a chisel, and upon the instant, in direct contravention of the treaty respecting rotting, he sat down and started carving his name on a smooth deal board which looked as if nobody wanted it. The pair worked on in silence, broken only by an occasional hard breath as the toil grew exciting. Chapple's tongue was out and performing mystic evolutions as he carved the letters. He felt inspired.

He was beginning the A when he was brought to earth again by the voice of Brooke.

'You *are* an idiot,' said Brooke, complainingly. 'That's my board, and now you've spoilt it.'

Spoilt it! Chapple liked that! Spoilt it, if you please, when he had done a beautiful piece of carving on it!

'Well, it can't be helped now,' said Brooke, philosophically. 'I suppose it's not your fault you're such an ass. Anyhow, come on now. It's struck eight.'

'It's what?' gasped Chapple.

'Struck eight. But it doesn't matter. Appleby never minds one being a bit late for breakfast.'

'Oh,' said Chapple. 'Oh, doesn't he!'

Go into Seymour's at eight sharp any morning and look down the table, and you will see the face of G. M. Chapple – obscured every now and then, perhaps, by a coffee cup or a slice of bread and marmalade. He has not been late for three weeks. The spare room is now occupied by Postlethwaite, of the Upper Fourth, whose place in Milton's dormitory has been taken by Chapple. Milton is the head of the house, and stands alone among the house prefects for the strenuousness of his methods in dealing with his dormitory. Nothing in this world is certain, but it is highly improbable that Chapple will be late again. There are swagger-sticks.

The house cricket cup at Wrykyn has found itself on some strange mantelpieces in its time. New talent has a way of cropping up in the house matches. Tail-end men hit up fifties, and bowlers who have never taken a wicket before except at the nets go on fifth change, and dismiss first-eleven experts with deliveries that bounce twice and shoot. So that nobody is greatly surprised in the ordinary run of things if the cup does not go to the favourites, or even to the second or third favourites. But one likes to draw the line. And Wrykyn drew it at Shields'. And yet, as we shall proceed to show, Shields' once won the cup, and that, too, in a year when Donaldson's had four first-eleven men and Dexter's three.

Shields' occupied a unique position at the school. It was an absolutely inconspicuous house. There were other houses that were slack or wild or both, but the worst of these did something. Shields' never did anything. It never seemed to want to do anything. This may have been due in some degree to Mr Shields. As the Housemaster is, so the house is. He was the most inconspicuous master on the staff. He taught a minute form in the junior school, where earnest infants wrestled with somebody's handy book of easy Latin sentences, and depraved infants threw cunningly compounded ink-balls at one another and the ceiling. After school he would range the countryside with a pickle-bottle in search of polly woggles and other big game, which he subsequently transferred to slides and examined through a microscope till an advanced hour of the night. The curious part of the matter was that his house was never riotous. Perhaps he was looked on as a non-combatant, one whom it would be unfair and unsporting to rag. At any rate, a weird calm reigned over the place; and this spirit seemed to permeate the public lives of the Shieldsites. They said nothing much and they did nothing much and they were very inoffensive. As a rule, one hardly knew they were there.

Into this abode of lotus-eaters came Clephane, a day-boy, owing to the departure of his parents for India. Clephane wanted to go to Donaldson's. In fact, he said so. His expressions, indeed, when he found that the whole thing had been settled, and that he was to spend his last term at school at a house which had never turned out so much as a member of the gym six, bordered on the unfilial. It appeared that his father had met Mr Shields at dinner in the town – a fact to which he seemed to attach a mystic importance. Clephane's criticism of this attitude of mind was of such a nature as to lead his father to address him as Archibald instead of Archie.

However, the thing was done, and Clephane showed his good sense by realising this and turning his energetic mind to the discovery of the best way of making life at Shields' endurable. Fortune favoured him by sending to the house another day-boy, one Mansfield. Clephane had not known him intimately before, though they were both members of the second eleven; but at Shields' they instantly formed an alliance. And in due season – or a little later – the house matches began. Henfrey, of Day's, the Wrykyn cricket captain, met Clephane at the nets when the drawing for opponents had been done.

'Just the man I wanted to see,' said Henfrey. 'I suppose you're captain of Shields' lot, Clephane? Well, you're going to scratch as usual, I suppose?'

For the last five seasons that lamentable house had failed to put a team into the field. 'You'd better,' said Henfrey, 'we haven't overmuch time as it is. That match with Paget's team has thrown us out a lot. We ought to have started the house matches a week ago.'

'Scratch!' said Clephane. 'Don't you wish we would! My good chap, we're going to get the cup.'

'You needn't be a funny ass,' said Henfrey in his complaining voice, 'we really are awfully pushed. As it is we shall have to settle the opening rounds on the first innings. That's to say, we can only give 'em a day each; if they don't finish, the winner of the first innings wins. You might as well scratch.'

'I can't help your troubles. By rotten mismanagement you have got the house matches crowded up into the last ten days of term, and you come and expect me to sell a fine side like Shields' to get you out of the consequences of your reckless act. My word, Henfrey, you've sunk pretty low. Nice young fellow Henfrey was at one time, but seems to have got among bad companions. Quite changed now. Avoid him as much as you can. Leave me, Henfrey. I would be alone.'

'But you can't raise a team.'

'Raise a team! Do you happen to know that half the house is *biting* itself with agony because we can't find room for all? Shields gives stump-cricket soirées in his study after prep. One every time you hit the ball, two into the bowl of goldfish, and out if you smash the microscope.'

'Well,' said Henfrey viciously, 'if you want to go through the farce of playing one round and making idiots of yourselves, you'll have to wait a bit. You've got a bye in the first round.'

Clephane told the news to Mansfield after tea. 'I've been and let the house in for a rollicking time,' he said, abstracting a copy of Latin verses which his friend was doing, and sitting on them to ensure undivided attention to his words. 'Wanting to score off old Henfrey – I have few pleasures – I told him that Shields' was not going to scratch. So we are booked to play in the second round of the houses. We drew a bye for the first. It would be an awful rag if we could do something. We *must* raise a team of some sort. Henfrey would score so if we didn't. Who's there, d'you think, that can play?'

Mansfield considered the question thoughtfully. 'They all *play*, I suppose,' he said slowly, 'if you can call it playing. What I mean to say is, cricket's compulsory here, so I suppose they've all had an innings or two at one time or another in the eightieth game or so. But if you want record-breakers, I shouldn't trust to Shields' too much.'

'Not a bit. So long as we put a full team into the field, that's all I care about. I've often wondered what it's like to go in first and bowl unchanged the whole time.'

'You'll do that all right,' said Mansfield. 'I should think Shields' bowling ran to slow grubs, to judge from the look of 'em. You'd better go and see Wilkins about raising the team. As head of the house, he probably considers himself captain of cricket.'

Wilkins, however, took a far more modest view of his position. The notion of leading a happy band of cricketers from Shields' into the field had, it seemed, small attractions for him. But he went so far as to get a house list, and help choose a really representative team. And as details about historic teams are always welcome, we may say that the averages ranged from 3.005 to 8.14. This last was Wilkins's own and was, as he would have been the first to admit, substantially helped by a contribution of nineteen in a single innings in the fifth game.

So the team was selected, and Clephane turned out after school next day to give them a little fielding-practice. To his surprise the fielding was not so outrageous as might have been expected. All the simpler catches were held, and one or two of the harder as well. Given this form on the day of their appearance in public, and Henfrey might be disappointed when he came to watch and smile sarcastically. A batting fiasco is not one half so ridiculous as maniac fielding.

In the meantime the first round of the house matches had been played off, and it would be as well to describe at this point the positions of the rival houses and their prospects. In the first place, there were only four teams really in the running for the cup: Day's (headed by the redoubtable Henfrey), Spence's, who had Jackson, that season a head and shoulders above the other batsmen in the first eleven – he had just wound up the school season with an average of 51.3, Donaldson's, and Dexter's. All the other house teams were mainly tail.

Now, in the first round the powerful quartette had been diminished by the fact that Donaldson's had drawn Dexter's, and had lost to them by a couple of wickets.

For the second round Shields' drew Appleby's, a poor team. Space on the Wrykyn field being a consideration, with three house matches to be played off at the same time, Clephane's men fought their first battle on rugged ground in an obscure corner. As the captain of cricket ordered these matters, Henfrey had naturally selected the best bit of turf for Day's v. Dexter's. That section of the ground which was sacred to the school second-eleven matches was allotted to Spence's v. the School House. The idle public divided its attention between the two big games, and paid no attention to the death struggle in progress at the far end of the field. Whereby it missed a deal of quiet fun.

I say death struggle advisedly. Clephane had won his second-eleven cap as a fast bowler. He had failed to get into the first eleven because he was considered too erratic. Put these two facts together, and you will suspect that dark deeds were wrought on the men of Appleby in that lonely corner of the Wrykyn meadow.

The pitch was not a good one. As a sample of the groundsman's art it was sketchy and amateurish; it lacked finish. Clephane won the toss, took a hasty glance at the corrugated turf, and decided to bat first. The wicket was hardly likely to improve with use.

He and Mansfield opened the batting. He stood three feet out of his ground, and smote. The first four balls he took full pitch. The last two, owing to a passion for variety on the part of the bowler, were long hops. At the end of the over Shields' score was twenty-four. Mansfield pursued the same tactics. When the first wicket fell, seventy was on the board. A spirit of martial enthusiasm pervaded the ranks of the house team. Mild youths with spectacles leaped out of their ground like tigers, and snicked fours through the slips. When the innings concluded, blood had been spilt – from an injured finger – but the total was a hundred and two.

Then Clephane walked across to the school shop for a vanilla ice. He said he could get more devil, as it were, into his bowling after a vanilla ice. He had a couple.

When he bowled his first ball it was easy to see that there was truth in the report of the causes of his inclusion in the second eleven and exclusion from the first. The batsman observed somewhat weakly, 'Here, I *say!*' and backed towards square leg. The ball soared over the wicket-keeper's head and went to the boundary. The bowler grinned pleasantly, and said he was just getting his arm in.

The second ball landed full pitch on the batsman's right thigh. The third was another full pitch, this time on the top of the middle stump, which it smashed. With profound satisfaction the batsman hobbled to the trees, and sat down. 'Let somebody else have a shot,' he said kindly.

Appleby's made twenty-eight that innings.

Their defeat by an innings and fifty-three runs they attributed subsequently to the fact that only seven of the team could be induced to go to the wickets in the second venture.

'So you've managed to win a match,' grunted Henfrey. 'I should like to have been there.'

'You might just as well have been,' said Clephane, 'from what they tell me.'

At which Henfrey became abusive, for he had achieved an 'egg' that afternoon, and missed a catch; which things soured him, though Day's had polished off Dexter's handsomely.

'Well,' he said at length, 'you're in the semi-final now, of all weird places. You'd better play Spence's next. When can you play?'

'Henfrey,' said Clephane, 'I have a bright, open, boyish countenance, but I was not born yesterday. You want to get a dangerous rival out of the way without trouble, so you set Shields' to smash up Spence's. No, Henfrey. I do not intend to be your cats-paw. We will draw lots who is to play which. Here comes Jackson. We'll toss odd man out.'

And when the coins fell there were two tails and one head; and the head belonged to the coin of Clephane.

'So, you see,' he said to Henfrey, 'Shields' is in the final. No wonder you wanted us to scratch.'

I should like this story to end with a vivid description of a tight finish. Considering that Day's beat Spence's, and consequently met Shields' in the final, that would certainly be the most artistic ending. Henfrey batting – Clephane bowling – one to tie, two to win, one wicket to fall. Up goes the ball! Will the lad catch it!! He fumbles it. It falls. All is over. But look! With a supreme effort – and so on.

The real conclusion was a little sensational in its way, but not nearly so exciting as that.

The match between Day's and Shields' opened in a conventional enough manner. Day's batted first, and made two hundred and fifty. Henfrey carried his bat for seventy-six, and there were some thirties. For Shields' Clephane and Mansfield made their usual first-wicket stand, and the rest brought the total up to ninety-eight. At this point Henfrey introduced a variation on custom. The match was a three days' match. In fact, owing to the speed with which the other games had been played, it could, if necessary, last for four days. The follow-on was, therefore, a matter for the discretion of the side which led. Henfrey and his team saw no reason why they should not have another pleasant spell of batting before dismissing their opponents for the second time and acquiring the cup. So in they went again, and made another two hundred and fifty odd, Shields' being left with four hundred and twelve to make to win.

On the morning after Day's second innings, a fag from Day's brought Clephane a message from Henfrey. Henfrey was apparently in bed. He would be glad if Clephane would go and see him in the dinner-hour. The interview lasted fifteen minutes. Then Clephane burst out of the house, and dashed across to Shields' in search of Mansfield.

'I say, *have* you heard?' he shouted.

'What's up?'

'Why, every man in Day's team, bar two kids, is in bed. Ill. Do you mean to say you haven't heard? They thought they'd got that house cup safe, so all the team except the two kids, fags, you know, had a feed in honour of it in Henfrey's study. Some ass went and bought a bad rabbit pie, and now they're laid up. Not badly, but they won't be out for a day or two.'

'But what about the match?'

'Oh, that'll go on. I made a point of that. They can play subs.'

Mansfield looked thoughtful.

'But I say,' he said, 'it isn't very sporting, is it? Oughtn't we to wait or something?'

'Sporting! My dear chap, a case like this mustn't be judged by ordinary standards. We can't spoil the giant rag of the century because it isn't quite sporting. Think what it means – Shields' getting the cup! It'll keep the school laughing for terms. What do you want to spoil people's pleasure for?'

'Oh, all right,' said Mansfield.

'Besides, think of the moral effect it'll have on the house. It may turn it into the blood house of Wrykyn. Shields himself may get quite sportive. We mustn't miss the chance.'

The news having got about the school, Clephane and Mansfield opened their second innings to the somewhat embarrassed trundling of Masters Royce and Tibbit, of the junior school, before a substantial and appreciative audience.

Both played carefully at first, but soon getting the measure of the bowling (which was not deep) began to hit out, and runs came quickly. At fifty, Tibbit, understudying Henfrey as captain of the side, summoned his young friend Todby from short leg, and instructed him to 'have a go' at the top end.

It was here that Clephane courteously interfered. Substitutes, he pointed out, were allowed, by the laws of cricket, only to field, not to bowl. He must, therefore, request friend Todby to return to his former sphere of utility, where, he added politely, he was a perfect demon.

'But, blow it,' said Master Tibbit, who (alas!) was addicted to the use of strong language, 'Royce and I can't bowl the whole blessed time.'

'You'll have to, I'm afraid,' said Clephane with the kindly air of a doctor soothing a refractory patient. 'Of course, you can take a spell at grubs whenever you like.'

'Oh, darn!' said Master Tibbit.

Shortly afterwards Clephane made his century.

The match ended late on the following afternoon in a victory for Shields' by nine wickets, and the scene at the school shop when Royce and Tibbit arrived to drown their sorrows and moisten their dry throats with ginger beer is said by eyewitnesses to have been something quite out of the common run.

The score sheet of the match is also a little unusual. Clephane's three hundred and one (not out) is described in the *Wrykynian* as a 'masterly exhibition of sound yet aggressive batting'. How Henfrey described it we have never heard.

This story deals with an earlier phase of the career of the ruthless Rankin, before he left Seymour's. The events narrated covered a period of some weeks, and the beginning and the end of it were divided by the Easter holidays.

Shoeblossom began it. J. R. Leather-Twigg, of Seymour's, frequently did begin trouble. It happened in this way. Towards the end of the Easter term there were sports. Not only the school sports, but also form sports. For the last three weeks of term you could not move in any direction on the school grounds without being warned off because you were in the track of some miserable race that was being or was going to be run. The sky was obscured by people high-jumping. Every now and then you walked within range of some putter of the shot, and narrowly escaped taking the same in the small of the back. Avoiding this danger, you were seized upon to hold the tape for the heats of the Lower Second Modern hundred yards or the Eighth Engineers half-mile. In fact, the only really safe place was the school shop. Even there you ran the risk of meeting someone who would place a bare foot beside your plate, and ask you whether you would put Elliman's on it or not. It was a stirring, hustling time, and for one who was not an athlete it was a little boring.

Shoeblossom found it more than a little boring. He had never run a race in his life. And he hoped he never should. If he wanted exercise, he went into Seymour's senior day-room, and upset the table. Rankin, on the other hand, was an enthusiast. The beauty of these form sports was twofold. In the first place, the events were all handicaps; and such was the insignificance and general weediness of the diarist that he hoped to be limit man in every race for which he entered. In the second place, the prizes were in cash. Solid. None of your pen-knives and flasks and leather ink-pots, but hard coin. Everyone in the form subscribed a certain sum; the form-master gave of his plenty a further ten shillings; and the nett result was divided up as prizes. Theoretically, you were supposed to buy with the money you won a suitable trophy. On the other hand, nobody stood over you to see that you did it; and, as a rule, the money went into the school treasury across the counter of the shop.

Reginald loved cash. He had never had enough of it. The more he got, the more he wanted. So he put his name down for all the races and half the other events, and started to train.

It was, I believe, an agreeable sight to see Reginald training. Before you saw him at it you thought that twenty yards was too much to give anybody in the hundred. After you had feasted your eyes on the spectacle for a few minutes, you thought what a shame it was not giving him more.

Shoeblossom watched him one morning, and wished somebody had told him of it earlier. People are so thoughtless. Here was this gorgeous feast of comic relief going on day after day, and until now he had missed it. He saw it every morning after that, and it never staled. He was fascinated. He brought Barry and Drummond to watch. And Reginald, oblivious of everything, toiled on.

Shoeblossom was one of those youths who are never really

happy unless they are promoting some demoniacal rag. He felt that he must base a rag on Reginald's passion for training, or life would be hollow. So he conceived a deadly snare for the athlete.

'What you want to do,' he said to him sympathetically one night, as they were undressing in their dormitory, 'is to rub yourself with stuff at nights. It keeps the muscles from getting stiff.'

'I do,' said Reginald, with some haughtiness; 'I use Elliman's.'

'I've got some stuff that's better than that,' said Shoeblossom. 'It's called Capsicum Vaseline. It's hot stuff.'

'What's it do?' enquired Reginald, examining the saucer which Shoeblossom held up for his inspection.

'Sends a gentle glow all over you, and makes you supple. You'd better have some tonight.'

'All right,' said the deluded athlete.

They rubbed it on then and there. Capsicum Vaseline, according to the printed label on each packet, is 'a tincture of the finest red pepper taken on to Vaseline'. It is generally used as a substitute for mustard-plaster, over which it has this advantage, that, though a 'powerful counter-irritant', it does not blister the skin.

About five minutes after the dastard Shoeblossom had helped his friend to rub this specific well in, a sharp howl broke from his victim.

'Stop that noise,' said Mill, the prefect of the dormitory.

'*Oo!*' said Reginald.

'Don't be an ass,' whispered Shoeblossom. 'What's up?'

'I'm burning.'

'You're all right,' said Shoeblossom consolingly. 'That's the gentle glow.'

'Gentle glow!'

'Stop – that – noise!' said Mill again. 'Here, who's that going out? Come back.'

The lights were out by this time, and he could just detect through the darkness a small figure racing out of the door. The next moment distant sounds of running water came from the bathroom. Reginald was taking a cold tub.

Mill shook the bathroom door, but it was locked.

'Come out of that, you little beast,' he hissed.

'Ow,' said the little beast, 'Oo.'

Vigorous sounds of splashing from within. Mill retired baffled.

By the time the cooling-off process was complete, both Mill and Shoeblossom were sleeping like angels. With even his passion for retaliation quenched, Reginald clambered into bed, and on the following morning got up early, being wishful to keep out of Mill's way as far as possible. But he was not in such a hurry to leave the room that he forgot to abstract Shoeblossom's studs – a feat which led to the humorist being late for breakfast and getting a hundred lines in lieu of porridge. But Reginald did not consider this Revenge. It was simply an earnest of more to come, a little on account, as it were. Nor, when he positively won the second prize in the form quarter-mile, did Shoeblossom's statement that it was all due to the Capsicum Vaseline, and that he, Shoeblossom, ought to have a commission on the prize, soothe him. If ever a look spoke, Reginald's look at that moment said, 'Aha! a time will come, and then—!'

The Easter term ended without event; and he came back at the conclusion of the holidays full of stern resolve. The entry in his diary:

'Got up. Washed. Said my prayers. Trained. That beast Leather-Twigg rubbed some stuff on to me which burnt like anything and hurt awfully,'

still lacked a corresponding entry on the credit side.

* * *

Early in the summer term, the weather being fine, it being a Saturday, and, finally, it being the day of the School v. Regiment match, Shoeblossom, who had no soul for cricket, slid softly away in the direction of the town. He meant to have a long afternoon on the river. Wrykyn is on the Severn, which, in parts, is a very jolly river, affording much pleasure to the not over-energetic oarsman. Shoeblossom was perhaps the laziest oarsman in existence. He hated rowing. If he could have got to the spot he wished to reach in a steam-launch, he would have done it. Having no launch, he was obliged to set to and pull.

His destination was a small, wooded island up-stream. It was not known to many of the school, as most Wrykynians got aboard at the school boat-house, which was further downstream past the town, and went the other way. Owing to various regrettable encounters between Wrykyn fags and the young bloods of the town, which had in one instance culminated immediately opposite the Mayor's house in a naval battle of a kind that made Trafalgar seem like the effort of a band of amateurs, rules and regulations had been issued by the Headmaster to the effect that the school must keep to its own waters. On the occasion referred to, three boats had been sunk, and ten fags from Dexter's and the School House had returned dripping to their quarters. Shoeblossom was therefore out of bounds. But did his dauntless spirit reck of that? No, indeed it did not.

Half an hour's rowing brought him to the island. He pulled in, tied up his Argo to the branch of a willow, and disembarked. Then he proceeded to haul from the seat, in the following order, a vast bag of cherries, a bottle of ginger beer, sixpennyworth of plain chocolate, a copy of *Many Cargoes*, and, by way of a variant, a shilling paper-covered volume entitled *The Montresors of the Grange*. This done, he placed them under a tree, and started on a round tour of the island to see if the scenery and the local flora and fauna generally had altered at all since his last visit – a year ago now.

The island was oval in shape, and about seventy yards long by twenty wide. It was densely wooded, and the vegetation might have been described as rank. The stinging-nettles in places, for instance, had to be felt to be realised. Also there were brambles. But apart from these disadvantages, it was as romantic, satisfactory an island as you could wish to find, and Shoeblossom, who had a romantic nature, was fond of it. He liked to fancy that he owned it.

The distance from the island to the banks on either side was in each case from ten to fifteen yards. The water was deep, and ran strongly. Not that Shoeblossom minded that. Like most Wrykynians, he could swim well. As at Eton, before going on the river you had to pass an examination in swimming.

Having reached the upper end of the island, Shoeblossom worked his way back along the coast, as it were, to the spot where he had left his books and provisions, which he proceeded to carry inland. Being out of bounds, it was necessary that he should not be seen by passing boats or by strollers on the bank. One never knew when a master might not take it into his head to scull up-stream instead of down, and petty discussions with masters on the subject of bounds revolted Shoeblossom. He disappeared, therefore, into the interior, whence presently came a musical pop, as the ginger-beer bottle was broached.

Now, while Shoeblossom was making the tour of the island, he had been observed, though he did not know it. There was another member of Seymour's who had no soul for cricket. To wit, Reginald Rankin. And Reginald, wearying of the monotony of the lower and lawful part of the river – which he knew by heart – and caring as little as did Shoeblossom for the prejudices of the Head-master respecting bounds, had hired a boat at the town landing-stage and set off up-stream to spend a happy afternoon.

He was rounding a bend in the river when, looking over his shoulder, he caught sight of the island and of Shoeblossom dis-appearing into the jungle. His first impulse was to turn back. The earth was barely big enough to hold the two of them since the Vaseline incident. The island would be a good deal too small. Then he reflected that so far the river had been pretty dull, and that once past this island he might come on some pleasant spot where he could moor his vessel, and read, and brood over his wrongs.

So he sculled slowly and painfully up on the right of the island; and, when he had gone a little way, he came upon Shoeblossom's boat tied to its willow. And something seemed to whisper to him, 'Cut her adrift'.

He gazed at the island. No sign of Shoeblossom. Somewhere within the recesses of the bushes that wanderer lurked; but he was not in sight.

Very cautiously Reginald paddled in till he could reach the rope. The knot was loosely tied and it was an easy task to undo it. He did not wish to cut it. Shoeblossom must be led to believe that accident, not design, was at the bottom of his misfortunes. He did not send the captured boat spinning down-stream, as had been his intention at first. It would be better, he reflected, simply to borrow it for a time, and restore it when it was certain that Shoeblossom had missed roll-call. It was now half past two all but a few minutes, and roll-call was at four. To be in time, Shoeblossom would have to start for home at a quarter past three. He himself had arranged that little matter of roll-call. The master on duty had to call four hundred names in something under seven minutes, and, so long as a name was answered, never made particular enquiries as to who had answered it. So Reginald had arranged that Renford, of Seymour's, should perform that kind office. Renford liked watching cricket, and would be on the ground the whole afternoon.

So he tied the boat on to the stern of his own, and continued his pull up-stream. He was prepared at any moment to be accosted in abusive terms by the bereaved proprietor, but no wail of anguish cleft the air, and he got out of sight round another bend in safety. Here he moored his boat, and, howbeit a trifle blistered about the hands from rowing, felt on the whole satisfied with life.

Shoeblossom, meanwhile, was too absorbed in his book to pay attention to anything else. The march of time did not trouble him. Curiously enough, he, too, had arranged the question of roll-call in precisely the same way. His understudy was Barry, who, though reviling him as unpatriotic for not watching the school match, nevertheless consented to answer his name. So on the subject of roll-call Shoeblossom's mind was at rest.

It was only when he had finished *The Montresors of the Grange*, and also the cherries, and had begun to find the ground a little hard as a couch, that he fancied another stroll would do him good.

He then discovered the flight of his boat.

If Reginald could have seen him at that moment, he would have felt that his toil had not been in vain.

It was certainly a staggerer. He stood at the water's edge breathing heavily.

It occurred to him that the boat might have drifted in again, and be stuck lower down the island. As he made his way in that direction, the sound of oars striking the water made him dive into the bushes once more.

Somebody was coming up-stream.

He listened. Voices made themselves heard.

'Oh, Rupert, what a pretty island!'

'Not bad. Shall we land?'

Hope and anxiety in this query. Rupert had been rowing against the stream, and wanted a rest.

'Oh, let's.'

Sounds of boat crushing through a willow-branch.

'Look out for your dress, Effie. I'm going to ship oars. *Now*, where's that painter? Right ho.'

They passed within a couple of yards of Shoeblossom. 'Effie' stopped and looked round her.

'It's splendid,' she said.

She was a handsome girl, with lovely hair, and she made a pretty picture standing with her profile towards him; but nevertheless Shoeblossom wished she would move on. He wished very much that she would move on.

She did at last.

'I'm going to explore,' she said, and walked away, followed by the attentive Rupert.

Shoeblossom was sorry for them, but it had to be. After all, they had only to shout, and someone was bound to hear them. They didn't want the thing half so much as he did. Besides, they ought to be glad of a good excuse for over-staying their time on the island together by an hour or two.

In short . . .

Exactly one hour and a half after this event Reginald thought that the time had come to restore Shoeblossom's boat. He got out the sculls, and drifted lazily down to the island.

He was fastening the painter noiselessly to a tree when a large hand suddenly swooped down from nowhere on his neck, and a voice observed, apparently from between somebody's teeth:

'*Now*, you young brute, what – do – you – mean – by – it?'

Rankin gasped helplessly.

The young man shook him with some violence. Things had been happening on the island. Tempers were not so angelic as they had been earlier in the afternoon. Effie had been stating icily that it was Rupert's fault, and that had not brightened Rupert up.

'*What* the— what do you mean, you little *beast*, by collaring our boat! And having the infernal cheek to bring it back and tie it up, too! What you *want*—'

People who insist on telling us what we *want* are always a nuisance. So Reginald found in this case. So far from being what he wanted, it was particularly painful and unpleasant.

'Now,' said the young man, more calmly, 'having got that off to the right address, we can talk business. I see you're at the school. Seymour's, I notice. Don't look surprised. I'm an O.W. myself. And I know the rules about the school and this part of the river. Your name is—'

He removed Reginald's cap, looked at the interior, and replaced it.

'—Rankin. Thanks. I'll drop a line to Mr Seymour tonight. One oughtn't to keep a funny joke like this to one's self. Goodbye.'

And perhaps the bitterest part of it all, reflected Reginald after his interview with Mr Seymour on the following day, was that he did not know the man's name or where he lived. It was monstrous that such a criminal should go scot-free, but there was nothing to be done.

He could not even poison the wedding cake. As for Shoe-blossom, he lived happily ever after.

Once, on an average, in every four years, there comes to most public schools such a season of athletic prosperity that many who would, in ordinary years, have been certain of places in the first eleven or fifteen have to be content with second caps. This happened at Wrykyn in the year when Trevor was captain of football and Henfrey captain of cricket. The fifteen won all their school matches and most of the club games, and, which only happened at very rare intervals, beat Ripton twice. The cricket team did, if anything, better. All the four schools they played went down before them. The MCC, who brought a poor team, were positively massacred; and the OWs were beaten, though including in their ranks three county men, one of whom had been in the last English eleven to Australia.

It may be imagined, therefore, that there was some competition for places in the team. There were eight old colours, which left only three caps for the twenty odd second- and third-eleven men who wanted them.

At the beginning of the summer term it was found that Strachan had not returned, and news came that he was ill at home with scarlet fever. Strachan, who played back for the school fifteen, was a reckless, hard-hitting bat and a useful field. He had got one of the last places in the team of the previous year, and was the eighth of the eight old colours mentioned above. Henfrey bore his loss philosophically enough, having such magnificent material to his hand with which to fill the vacant place, wrote him a letter of sympathy, telling him to come back as soon as he could, and in the list for the first school match, against the Emeriti, included Ellison and Selwicke, both of Donaldson's.

In an ordinary season both of them would have been high up in the team on their form of that year. Three years later they were playing for Oxford together. They were good, stylish bats, curiously alike in method, and they fielded beautifully, Ellison at third man, Selwicke at cover. Out of the cricket-field they were inseparable. Wrykynians as a class were rather inclined to hunt in couples, but Selwicke and Ellison lowered all records. For years, since the days when they had been fags, they had walked to school together, sat next to one another in form, gone for afternoon strolls together on Sundays, boated together, and prepared their work together. They were now in the Sixth together, and house prefects. They did not share one study, but they were so constantly in each other's dens that it amounted to that. In the holidays it was believed, they visited each other's homes. The school knew curiously little of them except the fact that they were good at games. It was said that they were good sorts, but the firm was so self-sufficient that it did not recognise the necessity of knowing anybody outside it. They were very quiet, and not even Trevor or Clowes, who had gone up the school with them and been in the same house for five years, could remember an occasion on which they had let themselves go, and plunged into any public escapade. There were single hermits at Wrykyn, though not many, fellows who seemed to know nobody and to want to know nobody, but the Ellison-Selwicke combination was the only case of a firm of hermits.

The match against the Emeriti resulted in a fairly easy win

for the school. Ellison and Selwicke were at the wickets together towards the middle of the innings, and scored respectively twenty-nine and thirty-one. Ellison caught a couple of catches at third man, Selwicke held a nice one at cover. Each came out of the ordeal, therefore, with credit, and, as might have been expected, with equal credit. One could not imagine either of the two making a century to the other's duck. One expected a neat twenty or thirty from both. Clowes and Trevor talked the match over that night after tea. Both were certain to be in the eleven at the end of the season. Trevor was an old colour, and, after Jackson and Henfrey, perhaps the best bat on the side. Clowes, though not a great bat, was sure of his place as wicket-keeper.

'What did you think of Ellison's innings?' asked Clowes.

'Good,' said Trevor.

'And what did you think of Selwicke's?'

'Good' said Trevor again.

'Not much to choose between them, was there? And there never will be, either. You see. As long as Henfrey goes on playing them they'll each make exactly the same number of runs in exactly the same sort of way, and they'll each field exactly as well as the other. I tell you what, Trevor, and that is that there's brain-fag waiting for our popular and energetic skipper. He can put it off, but he's got to have it. What would you do in his place? I should cry, I think.'

'But there are three places,' said Trevor.

'Nothing escapes you,' said Clowes admiringly. 'On the other hand, in my modest way I had already bagged one of the said three for myself. At any rate, if they don't have me – and I shall bring an action if they try to turn me out – that won't affect Ellison and pard. Because they've got to have a wicket-keeper, and, if it's not me, it'll be Dunstable or someone in the third.'

'Yes, you're right there.'

'I'm always right,' said Clowes. 'They call me Archibald the All Right, for I am infallible. Then there's Milton. He must get one of the vacant places for his bowling. You must have a fast bowler in the team. And if Milton didn't get in, which he will, that, again, wouldn't let in Ellison or Selwicke. They'd give the place to some other bowler. Clephane, perhaps; only he's too erratic. So, however you look at it, there's only one place for the two of them. And I tell you what, if this doesn't smash up the firm, I shall be surprised. I could imagine David quarrelling with Jonathan if they both wanted the same place in a cricket team.'

'I hope it won't,' said Trevor. 'I rather like seeing two chaps pals like that. They don't interfere with anybody, and they give the house a leg-up whenever they can.'

The house was Trevor's hobby.

'So do I hope it won't,' said Clowes. 'Who said they hoped it would? I used to be sick with them at one time, but it amuses me now. Still, it'll be interesting watching the effect of this on them. If anybody came between me and that cap for which I hope shortly to write to Devereux, I should feel it my painful duty to blot him off the face of the globe. I should feel that he wasn't wanted, that he didn't fit into the general scheme of utility. And I bet that's what Ellison and Selwicke 'll be feeling before long. You watch 'em. And, in the meanwhile, lest we become rusty in the noble language of old Greece, make a long arm and hoik down yon *Prometheus Vinctus*, and let's do a little work for a change. For slackness,' said Clowes, opening his Bohn's English translation, 'I can't abear.'

Clowes was right. Slowly but surely the rivalry began to have its effect on Selwicke and Ellison. There was something almost

ludicrous in the way they kept together in their cricket performances. Against the Gentlemen of the County Ellison made
twenty-five. Selwicke replied with twenty-four. In the first of
the school matches Selwicke had made nine and Ellison ten,
when Henfrey declared the innings closed. Without inflicting
upon the reader their full scores in every match, it may be said
that three-quarters of the way through the term there were not
a dozen runs between them. They had played in every match,
and neither had failed nor yet achieved a big success. Useful
twenties and thirties stood to their names in the score sheets of
every match.

Henfrey was not disturbed. As far as he was concerned, all
was well. He had not to decide on the final composition of his
team till after the return match against Ripton, three weeks away.
And, meanwhile, he had two absolutely reliable men to go in
sixth or seventh and knock up a nice little score as a background
to the scintillations of Jackson, Trevor, O'Hara, or himself earlier
in the innings. He was not going to worry himself yet about
which of the two must have his cap. 'Sufficient unto the day' –
he felt. He gave Milton his colours after the MCC match, and
Clowes his after the game against the Old Wrykynians. But the
last place remained open; and Selwicke and Ellison grew more
silent than ever. They avoided one another now. It had started
in a small way, by Ellison omitting to come to his friend's study
to work, but it grew till sometimes they barely spoke half a dozen
times to one another in the day. Like the heroes of Mr Gilbert's
Etiquette,

> At first they didn't quarrel very openly, I've heard.
> They nodded when they met, and now and then exchanged a word.
> The word grew rare, and rarer still the nodding of the head,
> And when they meet each other now, they cut each other dead.

It was a pity. But when two dogs want the same bone, there is always unpleasantness.

'What did I tell you?' said Clowes to Trevor.

'Fools – they are,' growled Trevor. 'What's it *matter*, when you come to think of it! In another five years nobody'll remember they were at the school.'

'It's all very well to say that,' said Clowes, 'and thank you very much for the moral reflection, but I should like to see *you* if somebody tried to bag your place in the first.'

A fortnight before the Ripton match the situation was further complicated by the reappearance of Strachan, who turned up at the school thin but cheerful. There was one match before the game which would settle the team for good and all, for, as in the case of the fifteen, it was a school tradition that the eleven which played against Ripton in the return match should be the official Wrykyn eleven. This last remaining fixture before Ripton was against the Incogniti, and took place a week after Strachan's return. All through that week the ex-invalid had been practising hard at the nets, and it was certain that he would play against the Incogs. The excitement in the school was great now that it seemed that Henfrey must make his choice between the two rivals. Selwicke and Ellison went about looking gaunt and anxious.

And after all the choice was not made. When the list went up on the Friday morning the school, crowding round the notice-board, saw that the two names still figured on the list. Strachan's was there also. Examination revealed that O'Hara was not playing. And presently authoritative information came (through the fags of the house) that O'Hara had bruised his right hand, and that, in order to ensure its being serviceable against Ripton, he intended to rest it for a few days.

There must have been a bigger gathering at that Incogs match than at any other match on the school grounds for years. Not even the Ripton matches had aroused such interest. There was a sporting flavour about this long-drawn-out duel between the Damon and Pythias of Donaldson's which appealed to the school.

By five o'clock the match was in a most exciting state. The Incogs had batted first. They had brought down a sound side, with a Middlesex man who had scored a double century against Essex during the previous week, in command, and quite a number of well-known players in the ranks. The Incogniti did not intend to make the mistake the MCC had made. They recognised that the Wrykyn team this year was an uncommonly good one. Starting on a good wicket, the earlier batsmen had helped themselves freely off the school bowling. At lunch time a hundred and forty was on the board, and only three wickets were down. But lunch had had its effect on the eye of the visiting team. Milton, in the course of a couple of very destructive overs immediately after the start, had disposed of three men, including a dangerously adhesive gentleman who had made seventy before the interval. After this the game settled down. The tail wagged comfortably, and the total score when Clowes whipped the last man's bails off at a moment when that impulsive player had gone out of his ground to the extent of a couple of yards in order to hit one of Allardyce's slows into the pavilion, was two hundred and eighty-one.

The Wrykyn ground was made for fast scoring. The turf was hard and dry, and the ball travelled beautifully, like a red streak along the green. The school went in at three o'clock confidently. Eighty an hour is quick work, but on just such a day as this, in the Masters' Match, runs had come at the rate of ninety an hour and more. Wrykyn never played for a draw, and today they meant to win, even if it entailed the taking of risks.

And so at five o'clock it came about that, with four wickets down, the school had one hundred and sixty-three runs to its name. So far the rate of scoring had been exactly right. Some good men had gone in the amassing of those hundred and sixty-three runs. Henfrey was out: lbw 31. Worse still, Jackson was out: clean bowled 54. Trevor had knocked up a beautiful seventy before being caught in the slips; but Strachan, after scratching about miserably for a few minutes, had been yorked for six. Allardyce was in at one end. At the other was Clowes. Neither had scored.

For some overs the scoring was slow. Then Clowes got the fast bowler away for a couple of fours. Off the next ball he was caught at third man.

Ellison came in. He played the last ball of the over, but half-way through the next Allardyce's leg stump was knocked askew by a lovely length-ball from the slow bowler. The score was now one hundred and seventy-nine, and six wickets were down.

Selwicke was the next man. There was a stir of excitement round the ropes as he walked down the pavilion steps. The school clapped encouragingly. The interest was twofold. Would Wrykyn save the match? And would Selwicke do better than Ellison, or vice versa?

Selwicke took guard amidst a profound silence, and played the remaining balls of the over carefully. Both he and Ellison were always slow starters.

Soon it began to be apparent that they had played themselves in. The rot was stopped. Selwicke hit the fast bowler twice past cover, scoring seven by the strokes. Ellison took eight off the slow bowler. Two hundred went up on the board. Ellison had made eleven, Selwicke ten.

Selwicke glanced the fast bowler to the boundary. It looked as if the two were going to knock off the runs. The opinion of the school was that each would make forty not out and that Henfrey would get brain fever.

But the very next ball the gruesome thing happened. It was a short, fast ball. Selwicke got well over it and cut it crisply to third man. Third man just reached it. For a moment Ellison thought he had let it pass him.

'Come on,' he shouted. Then in the same breath, in an agonised yell, 'No, go back, go back.'

But Selwicke was already half-way up the pitch. Back came the ball, and off went the bails. The wicket-keeper looked a query at the umpire. The umpire's hand went up, and Selwicke, white as a sheet, turned sharply off to the pavilion. There was a dead silence all round the ground.

'Hard lines, sir,' said the wicket-keeper consolingly. Selwicke made no reply.

Ellison stood where he was, as if he had been frozen. There seemed to be lead in his chest. The sun seemed to have gone in, and a chill wind to have begun to blow. He walked down the pitch, and tapped a worn spot mechanically with his bat. He felt as if he were in a dream. He could feel vaguely that somebody had just committed the most stupendous act of folly on record, and he seemed to know the fellow and be sorry for him. The suddenness of the thing had stunned him.

'Man in!' said somebody.

He looked up, and saw Milton walking to the crease. His first impulse was to get himself out, to knock his wicket down, as a sort of atonement. But he realised in time that he must do his best to win the match for the school. But he longed to hear the rattle of the stumps behind him. If only they would get him out before he could make any more!

But somehow no bowling he had ever played had seemed so absurdly easy. How could a fellow be expected to get out against such stuff! Soon he began to feel a sort of dull fury at the feebleness of it. He hit out viciously. There were roars from the school on the ropes. The incident of the run-out was forgotten in this brilliant display of hitting. Every over the ball skimmed along the turf and flew under the ropes. It's your fault, Ellison kept saying to himself; you shouldn't bowl such muck. And yet the bowling was fully as good as it had been during the earlier part of the innings, and Milton, at the other end, was in considerable trouble whenever he had to face it.

Two hundred and fifty went up. Another over from the slow man, and two hundred and sixty succeeded it. There was a brief consultation among the authorities. Then the field spread out like a fan. Ellison laughed savagely to himself. What was the good of lobs?

The lob-bowler's name was Saintsbury. If you look at the analysis of that match in the *Wrykynian* you will find:

	Overs	Maidens	Runs	Wickets
Saintsbury, E. J.	1	0	24	0

Ellison hit every single ball full-pitch over the boundary, and the Incogniti helped to chair him into the pavilion.

'The man's a lunatic!' said Henfrey, some hours later that evening, as he read the letter Ellison's fag had brought him.

Dear Henfrey [it ran] – It is very good of you to offer me my colours for the first, but I'm afraid I cannot accept them. I would much rather you played Selwicke against Ripton. He was quite set when I ran him out, and but for my folly would have made a century.

Yours faithfully,
G. B. ELLISON

'He's off his dot,' said Henfrey. 'Of course, he feels raw about that run-out; but Selwicke couldn't play an innings like that if he tried all the summer. And yet Selwicke's a jolly good bat. I wish— but it can't be helped.'

It was to be proved, however, that it could. As Henfrey was going to his dormitory that night, he was stopped by Strachan. Strachan was very calm and business-like.

'Made out the list for Ripton yet, Henfrey?'

'Not written it yet. But of course Ellison gets the place. Chap who can make an eighty-three like that—!'

'Half a second,' said Strachan, 'I just wanted to speak to you about that. Put in Ellison, of course. And put in Selwicke, too. I'm not going to play.'

'Not going to play!'

In spite of himself Henfrey could not help feeling pleased. He had not even thought of such a solution of his difficulty, but it was the very best possible. Poor old Strachan was dead out of form. Selwicke was worth two of him at present.

'No,' said Strachan, 'I thought I'd make this afternoon's game a test, and I found I'd lost all my hitting powers. No nerve either. So I'm no good. Be all right next year, I suppose. So count me out. See?'

'Well, if you really—' said Henfrey.

'That's all right,' said Strachan. 'Good-night.'

'One minute. I see how we'll manage it. You'll keep your cap, of course. It'll be quite in order, you know, as you've been ill. "Not placed". There'll be twelve caps instead of eleven this year.'

'All right. So long as you get Ellison and Selwicke in, I don't care what you do. Good-night.'

'Good-night. I say, Strachan.'

'Hullo?'

'Er – you're a good chap,' said Henfrey gratefully.

Next day it was noticed by the observant that the firm of Selwicke and Ellison was once more doing business at the old stand.

I

The whole thing may be said to have begun when Mr Oliver Ring of New York, changing cars, as he called it, at Wrykyn on his way to London, had to wait an hour for his train. He put in that hour by strolling about the town and seeing the sights, which were not numerous. Wrykyn, except on Market Day, was wont to be wrapped in a primeval calm which very nearly brought tears to the strenuous eyes of the man from Manhattan. He had always been told that England was a slow country, and his visit, now in its third week, had confirmed this opinion: but even in England he had not looked to find such a lotus-eating place as Wrykyn. He looked at the shop windows. They resembled the shop windows of every other country town in England. There was no dash, no initiative about them. They did not leap to the eye and arrest the pedestrian's progress. They ordered these things, thought Mr Ring, better in the States. And then something seemed to whisper to him that here was the place to set up a branch of Ring's Come-One Come-All Up-to-date Stores. During his stroll he had gathered certain pieces of information. To wit, that Wrykyn was where the county families for ten miles round did their shopping, that the population of the town was larger than would appear at first sight to a casual observer, and, finally, that there was a school of six hundred boys only a mile away. Nothing could be better. Within a month he would take to himself the entire trade of the neighbourhood.

'It's a cinch,' murmured Mr Ring with a glad smile, as he boarded his train, 'a lead-pipe cinch.'

Everybody who has moved about the world at all knows Ring's Come-One Come-All Up-to-date Stores. The main office is in New York. Broadway, to be exact, on the left as you go down, just before you get to Park Row, where the newspapers come from. There is another office in Chicago. Others in St Louis, St Paul, and across the seas in London, Paris, Berlin, and, in short, everywhere. The peculiar advantage about Ring's Stores is that you can get anything you happen to want there, from a motor to a macaroon, and rather cheaper than you could get it anywhere else. England had up to the present been ill-supplied with these handy paradises, the one in Piccadilly being the only extant specimen. But now Mr Ring in person had crossed the Atlantic on a tour of inspection, and things were shortly to be so brisk that you would be able to hear them whizz.

So an army of workmen invaded Wrykyn. A trio of decrepit houses in the High Street were pulled down with a run, and from the ruins there began to rise like a phoenix the striking building which was to be the Wrykyn Branch of Ring's Come-One Come-All Up-to-date Stores.

The sensation among the tradesmen caused by the invasion was, as may be imagined, immense and painful. The thing was a public disaster. It resembled the advent of a fox in a fowl-run. For years the tradesmen of Wrykyn had jogged along in their comfortable way, each making his little profits, with no thought of competition or modern hustle. And now the enemy was at their doors. Many were the gloomy looks cast at the gaudy building as it grew like a mushroom. It was finished with incredible speed, and then advertisements began to flood the local papers. A special sheaf of bills was despatched to the school.

Dunstable got hold of one, and read it with interest. Then he went in search of his friend Linton to find out what he thought of it.

Linton was at work in the laboratory. He was an enthusiastic, but unskilful, chemist. The only thing he could do with any real certainty was to make oxygen. But he had ambitions beyond that feat, and was continually experimenting in a reckless way which made the chemistry master look wan and uneasy. He was bending over a complicated mixture of tubes, acids, and Bunsen burners when Dunstable found him. It was after school, so that the laboratory was empty, but for them.

'Don't mind me,' said Dunstable, taking a seat on the table.

'Look out, man, don't jog. Sit tight, and I'll broaden your mind for you. I take this bit of litmus paper, and dip it into this bilge, and if I've done it right, it'll turn blue.'

'Then I bet it doesn't,' said Dunstable.

The paper turned red.

'Hades,' said Linton calmly. 'Well, I'm not going to sweat at it any more. Let's go down to Cook's.'

Cook's is the one school institution which nobody forgets who has been to Wrykyn. It is a little confectioner's shop in the High Street. Its exterior is somewhat forbidding, and the uninitiated would probably shudder and pass on, wondering how on earth such a place could find a public daring enough to support it by eating its wares. But the school went there in flocks. Tea at Cook's was the alternative to a study tea. There was a large room at the back of the shop, and here oceans of hot tea and tons of toast were consumed. The staff at Cook's consisted of Mr Cook, late sergeant in a line regiment, six foot three, disposition amiable, left leg cut off above the knee by a spirited Fuzzy in the last Sudan war; Mrs Cook, wife of the above, disposition similar, and possessing the useful gift of being able to listen to five people at one and the same time; and an invisible menial, or menials, who made toast in some nether region at a perfectly dizzy rate of speed. Such was Cook's.

'Talking of Cook's,' said Dunstable, producing his pamphlet, 'have you seen this? It'll be a bit of a knock-out for them, I should think.'

Linton took the paper, and began to read. Dunstable roamed curiously about the laboratory, examining things.

'What are these little crystal sort of bits of stuff?' he asked, coming to a standstill before a large jar and opening it. 'They look good to eat. Shall I try one?'

'Don't you be an idiot,' said the expert, looking up. 'What have you got hold of? Great Scott, no, don't eat that stuff.'

'Why not? Is it poison?'

'No. But it would make you sick as a cat. It's Sal Ammoniac.'

'Sal how much?'

'Ammoniac. You'd be awfully bad.'

'All right, then, I won't. Well, what do you think of that thing? It'll be rough on Cook's, won't it? You see they advertise a special 'public-school' tea, as they call it. It sounds jolly good. I don't know what buckwheat cakes are, but they ought to be decent. I suppose now everybody'll chuck Cook's and go there. It's a beastly shame, considering that Cook's has been a sort of school shop so long. And they really depend on the school. At least, one never sees anybody else going there. Well, I shall stick to Cook's. I don't want any of your beastly Yankee invaders. Support home industries. Be a patriot. The band then played God Save the King, and the meeting dispersed. But seriously, man, I am rather sick about this. The Cooks are such awfully good sorts, and this is bound to make them lose a tremendous lot. The school's simply crawling with chaps who'd do anything to get a good tea cheaper than they're getting now. They'll simply scrum in to this new place.'

'Well, I don't see what we can do,' said Linton, 'except keep on going to Cook's ourselves. Let's be going now, by the way. We'll get as many chaps as we can to promise to stick to them. But we can't prevent the rest going where they like. Come on.'

The atmosphere at Cook's that evening was heavily charged with gloom. Ex-Sergeant Cook, usually a treasury of jest and anecdote, was silent and thoughtful. Mrs Cook bustled about with her customary vigour, but she too was disinclined for conversation. The place was ominously empty. A quartette of School House juniors in one corner and a solitary prefect from Donaldson's completed the sum of the customers. Nobody seemed to want to talk a great deal. There was something in the air which

> said as plain as whisper in the ear,
> 'The place is haunted,'

and so it was. Haunted by the spectre of that hideous, new, glaring red-brick building down the street, which had opened its doors to the public on the previous afternoon.

'Look there,' said Dunstable, as they came out. He pointed along the street. The doors of the new establishment were congested. A crowd, made up of members of various houses, was pushing to get past another crowd, which was trying to get out. The 'public-school tea at one shilling' appeared to have proved attractive.

'Look at 'em,' said Dunstable. 'Sordid beasts! All they care about is filling themselves. There goes that man Merrett. Rand-Brown with him. Here come four more. Come on. It makes me sick.'

'I wish it would make *them* sick,' said Linton.

'Perhaps it will ... By George!'

He started.

'What's up?' said Linton.

'Oh, nothing. I was only thinking of something.'

They walked on without further conversation. Dunstable's brain was working fast. He had an idea, and was busy developing it.

The manager of the Wrykyn Branch of Ring's Come-One Come-All Up-to-date Stores stood at the entrance to his shop on the following afternoon spitting with energy and precision on to the pavement – he was a free-born American citizen – and eyeing the High Street as a monarch might gaze at his kingdom. He had just completed a highly satisfactory report to headquarters, and was feeling contented with the universe and the way in which it was managed. Even in the short time since the opening of the store he had managed to wake up the sluggish Britishers as if they had had an electric shock.

'We,' he observed epigrammatically to a passing cat, which had stopped on its way to look at him, 'are it.'

As he spoke he perceived a youth coming towards him down the street. He wore a cap of divers colours, from which the manager argued that he belonged to the school. Evidently a devotee of the advertised 'public-school' shillingsworth, and one who, as urged by the small bills, had come early to avoid the rush. 'Step right in, mister,' he said, moving aside from the doorway. 'And what can I do for *you*?'

'Are you the manager of this place?' asked Dunstable – for the youth was that strategist, and no other.

'On the bull's eye first time,' replied the manager with easy courtesy. 'Will you take a cigar or a coconut?'

'Can I have a bit of a talk with you, if you aren't busy?'

'Sure. Step right in.'

'Now, sir,' said the manager, 'what's *your* little trouble?'

'It's about this public-school tea business,' said Dunstable. 'It's rather a shame, you see. Before you came barging in, everybody used to go to Cook's.'

'And now,' interrupted the manager, 'they come to us. Correct, sir. We *are* the main stem. And why not?'

'Cook's such a good sort.'

'I should like to know him,' said the manager politely.

'You see,' said Dunstable, 'it doesn't so much matter about the other things you sell; but Cook's simply relied on giving fellows tea in the afternoon—'

'One moment, sir,' said the man from the States. 'Let me remind you of a little rule which will be useful to you when you butt into the big, cold world. That is, never let sentiment interfere with business. See? Either Ring's Stores or your friend has got to be on top, and, if I know anything, it's going to be We. We! And I'm afraid that's all I can do for you, unless you've that hungry feeling, and want to sample our public-school tea at twenty-five cents.'

'No, thanks,' said Dunstable. 'Here come some chaps, though, who look as if they might.'

He stepped aside as half a dozen School House juniors raced up.

'For one day only,' said the manager to Dunstable, 'you may partake free, if you care to. You have man's most priceless possession. Cool Cheek. And Cool Cheek, when recognised, should not go unrewarded. Step in.'

'No thanks,' said Dunstable. 'You'll find me at Cook's if you want me.'

'Kindness,' said he to himself, as Mrs Cook served him in the depressed way which had now become habitual with her, 'kindness having failed, we must try severity.'

II

Those who knew and liked Dunstable were both pained and disgusted at his behaviour during the ensuing three days. He suddenly exhibited a weird fondness for some of Wrykyn's least deserving inmates. He walked over to school with Merrett, of Seymour's, and Ruthven, of Donaldson's, both notorious outsiders. When Linton wanted him to come and play fives after school, he declined on the ground that he was teaing with Chadwick, of Appleby's. Now in the matter of absolute outsiderishness Chadwick, of Appleby's, was to Merrett, of Seymour's, as captain is to subaltern. Linton was horrified, and said so.

'What do you want to do it for?' he asked. 'What's the point of it? You can't like those chaps.'

'Awfully good sorts when you get to know them,' said Dunstable.

'You've been some time finding it out.'

'I know. Chadwick's an acquired taste. By the way, I'm giving a tea on Thursday. Will you come?'

'Who's going to be there?' enquired Linton warily.

'Well, Chadwick for one, and Merrett and Ruthven and three other chaps.'

'Then,' said Linton with some warmth, 'I think you'll have to do without me. I believe you're mad.'

And he went off in disgust to the fives-courts.

When on the following Thursday Dunstable walked into Ring's Stores with his five guests, and demanded six public-school teas, the manager was perhaps justified in allowing a triumphant smile to wander across his face. It was a signal victory for him.

'No free list today, sir,' he said. 'Entirely suspended.'

'Never mind,' said Dunstable, 'I'm good for six shillings.'

'Free list?' said Merrett, as the manager retired. 'I didn't know there was one.'

'There isn't. Only he and I palled up so much the other day that he offered me a tea for nothing.'

'Didn't you take it?'

'No. I went to Cook's.'

'Rotten hole, Cook's. I'm never going there again,' said Chadwick. 'You take my tip, Dun, old chap, and come here.'

'Dun, old chap,' smiled amiably.

'I don't know,' he said, looking up from the tea-pot, into which he had been pouring water; 'you can be certain of the food at Cook's.'

'What do you mean? So you can here.'

'Oh,' said Dunstable, 'I didn't know. I've never had tea here before. But I've often heard that American food upsets one sometimes.'

By this time, the tea having stood long enough, he poured out, and the meal began.

Merrett and his friends were hearty feeders, and conversation languished for some time. Then Chadwick leaned back in his chair, and breathed heavily.

'You couldn't get stuff like that at Cook's,' he said.

'I suppose it is a bit different,' said Dunstable. 'Have any of you . . . noticed something queer . . . ?'

Merrett stared at Ruthven. Ruthen stared at Merrett.

'I . . .' said Merrett.

'D'you know . . .' said Ruthven.

Chadwick's face was a delicate green.

'I believe,' said Dunstable, 'the stuff . . . was . . . poisoned. I . . .'

'Drink this,' said the school doctor, briskly, bending over Dunstable's bed with a medicine-glass in his hand, 'and be ashamed of yourself. The fact is you've over-eaten yourself. Nothing more and nothing less. Why can't you boys be content to feed moderately?'

'I don't think I ate much, sir,' protested Dunstable. 'It must have been what I ate. I went to that new American place.'

'So *you* went there, too? Why, I've just come from attending a bilious boy in Mr Seymour's house. He said he had been at the American place, too.'

'Was that Merrett, sir? He was one of the party. We were all bad. We can't all have eaten too much.'

The doctor looked thoughtful.

'H'm. Curious. Very curious. Do you remember what you had?'

'I had some things the man called buckwheat cakes, with some stuff he said was maple syrup.'

'Bah. American trash.' The doctor was a staunch Briton, conservative in his views both on politics and on food. 'Why can't you boys eat good English food? I must tell the Headmaster of this. I haven't much time to look after the school if all the boys are going to poison themselves. You lie still and try to go to sleep, and you'll be right enough in no time.'

But Dunstable did not go to sleep. He stayed awake to interview Linton, who came to pay him a visit.

'Well,' said Linton, looking down at the sufferer with an
expression that was a delicate blend of pity and contempt, 'you've
made a nice sort of ass of yourself, haven't you! I don't know if
it's any consolation to you, but Merrett's just as bad as you are.
And I hear the others are, too. So now you see what comes of
going to Ring's instead of Cook's.'

'And now,' said Dunstable, 'if you've quite finished, you can
listen to me for a bit . . .

'So now you know,' he concluded.

Linton's face beamed with astonishment and admiration.

'Well, I'm hanged,' he said. 'You're a marvel. But how did you
know it wouldn't poison you?'

'I relied on you. You said it wasn't poison when I asked you in
the lab. My faith in you is touching.'

'But why did you take any yourself?'

'Sort of idea of diverting suspicion. But the thing isn't finished
yet. Listen.'

Linton left the dormitory five minutes later with a look of a
young disciple engaged on some holy mission.

III

'You think the food is unwholesome, then?' said the Headmaster
after dinner that night.

'Unwholesome!' said the school doctor. 'It must be deadly.
It must be positively lethal. Here we have six ordinary, strong,
healthy boys struck down at one fell swoop as if there were a
pestilence raging. Why—'

'One moment,' said the Headmaster. 'Come in.'

A small figure appeared in the doorway.

'Please, sir,' said the figure in the strained voice of one speaking a 'piece' which he has committed to memory. 'Mr Seymour says please would you mind letting the doctor come to his house at once because Linton is ill.'

'What!' exclaimed the doctor. 'What's the matter with him?'

'Please, sir, I believe it's buckwheat cakes.'

'What! And here's another of them!'

A second small figure had appeared in the doorway.

'Sir, please, sir,' said the newcomer, 'Mr Bradfield says may the doctor—'

'And what boy is it *this* time?'

'Please, sir, it's Brown. He went to Ring's Stores—'

The Headmaster rose.

'Perhaps you had better go at once, Oakes,' he said. 'This is becoming serious. That place is a positive menace to the community. I shall put it out of bounds tomorrow morning.'

And when Dunstable and Linton, pale but cheerful, made their way – slowly, as befitted convalescents – to Cook's two days afterwards, they had to sit on the counter. All the other seats were occupied.

THE DESERTER

The story of a stolen game of cricket

Jackson, of Spence's house, Wrykyn, was a great and many-sided man. He was at the head of the Wrykyn averages in a season when the team contained six members who subsequently, when years had rolled by, played for their Varsities at Lord's. He was the only Wrykynian who ever got three centuries in first-eleven matches and five extra lessons in the same term. He was the only Wrykynian who ever got a double century in a house match and four hundred lines in the same week.

The fact was that Jackson on the cricket-field was a different person from Jackson off it. On the field he was a genius. Off it he was not.

The consequence was that life for him was apt to be a little feverish, and he made it more so by a confirmed recklessness and love of adventure, which qualities, though they may have made us Englishmen what we are, are somewhat unpopular among the authorities at a public school.

It was the hour of the evening meal; and Jackson, returning to his house after a long afternoon at the nets, found on his plate when he entered the dining-room a letter, which he saw by the writing was from one Neville-Smith. This sportsman had been in the Wrykyn eleven, and had left at the end of the previous summer for Cambridge. He had been at Spence's while at school, and he and Jackson were close allies.

Jackson sawed off a foot or so of the loaf in front of him, bit a semi-circular section out of it, and turned his attention to the letter, with a view to ascertaining what Neville-Smith had got to say for himself.

It was a letter of some import. Neville-Smith, it seemed, home for the long vacation, was getting up a match between his village and the one next to it on the map. That is to say – for there is nothing like accuracy – between Bray Lench and Chalfont St Peter's.

To the uninitiated it will seem, perhaps, that this was not exactly a Test match. But mark! Round about Chalfont St Peter's there lived certain of the nobility and gentry. These had sons. And many of the sons knew how to play cricket. There would, to use the imagery of Jackson's correspondent, be no flies on the Chalfont St Peter's eleven.

It behoved Neville-Smith to collect a hot side in order to beat them. The local curate was an old Blue, a bowler; and Neville-Smith himself had got his cap at Wrykyn as a bowler. So there would be nothing wrong with Bray Lench as far as that department of the game was concerned.

It was batsmen that Neville-Smith wanted.

He had two King's men staying with him who had done well for the college, and he could get a few more moderate performers. But he wanted a touch of Class to set off the side, so would Jackson come down and play?

The match was fixed for the following Wednesday. Now, there was no school match on that day; but Jackson knew very well that it was impossible to hope for leave to go and play in a village game twenty miles away. There would be nothing wrong or dangerous in it, but it would be unusual, and to the Wrykyn authorities everything unusual was anathema.

Jackson, however, determined not to refuse the invitation off-hand. He would sleep on it in case there might be some way of accepting it which was not apparent to the casual observer. He had not found one by the morning. All he got by sleeping on it was a nightmare, in which he dreamed that he was just scoring heavily at Bray Lench when the opposition wicket-keeper suddenly turned into the Headmaster, and denounced him in full field.

But going over to school he met O'Hara, of Dexter's. And, as O'Hara had frequently made useful suggestions in crises, he showed him Neville-Smith's letter, and intimated that all contributions in the way of counsel would be thankfully received.

O'Hara read the letter through, and turned back to the first page to read it again.

'Ye're all right,' he said, handing it back.

'Why? How?' said Jackson.

'Ye're in the corps?'

'What's that got to do with it?'

'Why, look at the address on the letter. Bray something or other, station Ealesbury. There's a field day at Ealesbury on Wednesday.'

'Great Scott! So there is. And I was thinking of cutting it. But, half a second. I don't quite see how it works out. I get to Ealesbury with the corps all right sometime in the morning, I suppose – about half past eleven. Then what happens?'

'Do ye know the country round there? Find your way all right to Neville-Smith's?'

'Oh, yes.'

'That's all you want then. You'll easily find a chance of falling out and cutting away. Then you nip off, have your match, and meet the corps at the station. You'll have to take your chance of being spotted.'

'Oh, that'll be all right,' said Jackson. 'There's always such a dickens of a crush and confusion at the station after a field day getting the chaps into the train that I shan't be noticed. Thanks awfully, O'Hara. I'll write to Smith tonight. He'll have to lend me some things to play in, but I suppose he'll be able to manage that.'

'If only I were in the corps,' said O'Hara, 'I'd come too.'

'See what you miss,' said Jackson.

An answer to Neville-Smith's letter left Wrykyn that evening. It set forth fully the difficulties and perils which must be encountered by flood and field, laid stress, however, on the fact that the master who acted as lieutenant in the school corps was astigmatic, and might be relied on not to notice a defection from the ranks, and strictly enjoined the recipient to render all possible help to the scheme. Above all, to meet the train at Ealesbury.

When the corps detrained on the following Wednesday they found waiting outside the station two other school corps, a detachment of the local volunteers, and Neville-Smith, wearing flannels and sitting in a neat dog-cart.

'We're playing in our field,' said Neville-Smith to Jackson in the interval which took place between the departure of the train and the forming of the corps into a workable unit of the attacking force. 'I got your letter. I've got some things for you to wear. Isn't it a ripping day? There'll be tea in the afternoon. It's a big match. Everybody's coming.'

Jackson grinned expansively. The word 'tea' always stirred chords within his bosom.

'We've only got ten men at present,' continued Neville-Smith. 'The curate's promised to rout out another, though. Oh, by the way, you'll go down on the score-sheet as Johnson. T. W.

Johnson. Don't forget. And I've told my people you're a college friend of mine, and you're just breaking your journey to London to play in the match.'

'Great Scott!' said Jackson plaintively. 'I can't remember all that. Say it again. Where did I start the journey I've broken?'

At this moment the excited voice of the Wrykyn sergeant-major was heard.

'Cum'ny – *shun*! Farm-farrs-'s-you-were-smartly-now-at-the-word-of-command-farm-*farrs-kick-arch*,' said the sergeant-major.

Jackson dived into his place, and the column moved off.

'I say,' said Neville-Smith, as Jackson left him, 'I'll follow you in the cart till you leave the road. Fall out as soon as you can, and you'll find me waiting for you.'

It appeared that the army of which the Wrykyn corps formed a part was to trek across country in the direction of Chalfont St Peter's, which, for reasons of their own, the opposing force had occupied, and was resolved to hold. Chalfont St Peter's lay between Ealesbury and Bray Lench.

For half a mile the corps advanced down the road in fours, followed by Neville-Smith, or, to be sensational, Dogged by a Dog-cart! Then they turned through a gate into a wide gorse-covered common.

Jackson was in the rear-rank four, so that when he sat down and observed 'Ow!' in a melancholy voice, he did not excite a great deal of attention. 'Something in my boot,' he explained, beginning to unlace his foot-gear.

Jackson sat where he was till the column had passed out of sound and sight. Then he made his way cautiously into the road. At the same moment a vigorous fusillade began in the woods at the far end of the common. The corps were in action.

'So *they've* got something to occupy their minds,' said Jackson, trotting down the road. 'Now, where's Smith got to?'

Neville-Smith was waiting a hundred yards from the gate. 'Hop in,' he said. 'Give us the rifle. Shove it against the seat. Good man, getting away so soon. We shall just be in time for the start. Now, then, Pickford,' he added encouragingly to the pony, 'bustle about, and show what you're made of.'

'I say,' said Jackson; 'about this uniform: I mustn't be seen. We can't go in the front way. What shall we do?'

'That's all right,' said Neville-Smith, 'I thought of that. Reach behind you, and you'll find a long dust-coat. I brought it on purpose; and there's a King's straw there, too. Put 'em on, and nobody 'll spot your uniform. Shove your hat in the pocket of the coat.'

'You're a genius,' said Jackson joyfully, as he wriggled into the coat. 'You think of everything. You're a sort of— what's the man's name?'

'How should I know?' said Neville-Smith. 'I tell you what you'll be like if you spring about in this cart, and that is a man with a broken neck. You'll be tumbling out if you aren't careful.'

A drive of five miles through pleasant lanes brought them to the lodge gates of the Neville-Smith residence, and through the trees to the left Jackson caught an occasional cheering glimpse of white flannels, and heard the sound of bat meeting ball, as the two teams knocked about before the game.

Neville-Smith drove round to the back of the house, and they made their way to his bedroom by mysterious back stairs.

Having arrived at the room, Neville-Smith produced flannels and boots, and Jackson was soon out of his uniform, which had long since begun to be hot and uncomfortable, and arrayed in garments more suitable to the boiling day. He was lacing his last boot, when there was a grating of wheels on the drive outside.

Neville-Smith looked out.

'It's the curate,' he said. 'Good, he's brought a man with him all right. Now the side's complete. Come on.'

The sun was still shining gloriously, and it may be said at once that Jackson enjoyed his afternoon. It was an ideal day for cricket; the wicket was not terribly bad, and a gentle breeze tempered the heat sufficiently to make run-getting a pleasing occupation. Bray Lench won the toss, and Jackson accompanied Neville-Smith to the wickets. The bowling was of the sort usual at country-house cricket matches.

There was a long fast bowler and a short slow bowler. The fast bowler had four men in the slips, took a run of twenty yards, and sent down three full pitches to leg in his first three balls. Jackson, praising his luck, steered each of the trio to the extreme limit of the ground, to the marked discomfort of certain pheasants that were nesting in that neighbourhood.

With the slow bowler, who spent several minutes in arranging his field, and several more in sending down preliminary balls to the wicket-keeper, and then gave Jackson an innocuous long hop wide of the off-stump, he also took tea. The applause from the tent was soft and decorous, but frequent. Jackson had made a century off good bowling a week before, and was inclined to take liberties with the deliveries of Chalfont St Peter's.

Neville-Smith ran himself out, but Jackson, partnered by the curate, continued to worry the nesting pheasants. The eighth wicket fell with the score at sixty-one. By the exercise of immense care the last two men continued to stay in for a few overs, until Jackson had compiled eighty-three; then they succumbed, leaving Jackson not out with a very pretty innings to his credit.

He felt, as he walked back to the tent, that this was life as it should be lived. He had enjoyed his afternoon.

On Chalfont St Peter's going in to bat, the demon curate, the ex-Blue, performed prodigies with the ball. Jackson held a nice catch on the boundary; and wickets began to fall rapidly. A stand half-way through the innings caused some trouble, but once more Jackson held a lofty drive, and the one dangerous batsman of the enemy left with fifty-two to his credit.

It was now late in the afternoon, and Jackson, who, in his usual casual way, had hitherto not given the matter a thought, began to wonder when and how he was to rejoin his wandering fellow Wrykynians. As far as he could remember from previous field-days, the train by which the corps returned was a late one. But it would not do to run the thing too fine. He would have to leave the field shortly.

Just as the Chalfont St Peter's innings came to an end, a good twenty-five runs behind the Bray Lench total, there was borne on the breeze the noise of battle. The combatants were working round in the direction of the Neville-Smiths' territory.

Jackson was eating a soothing ice apart from the crowd when a scrap of conversation between a new arrival and his hostess reached him.

'. . . Yes, isn't it? Awfully exciting. It's a sham fight. And there are ever so many boys in blue waiting in that wood over there. We saw them. It's an ambush, somebody said. And the other boys will march into the wood, and these boys will pounce out, and then the other boys will have lost. At least, Captain Main-waring said so. I'll get him to explain. He does it so *well*, you know. He was in South Africa, you know. Captain *Main*-waring. Mr Neville-Smith wants to know . . .'

Five minutes later Jackson was in Neville-Smith's room, doing a rapid change of costume.

'You always say that Jackson is such a fool off the cricket-field,' said Mr Templar, the lieutenant of the Wrykyn corps to another member of the staff in the common-room on the following day, when they were donning their gowns before prayers, 'but you should have been with us yesterday. I tell you that boy can use his brains.'

Incredulous murmur from colleague.

'Yes, he can. He thinks for himself; and acts, too. It was the smartest bit of scouting I've ever seen,' continued Mr Templar enthusiastically, for his heart was bound up with the corps. 'But for him we should have been wiped out.

'It was like this. We were advancing. Main body of enemy here where this ink-pot is. We were coming along here. This pen-holder shows our route. Well, just where I've put this box of nibs was a wood, and in it were hiding a large force of the enemy. We were just going to plump straight into the ambush when up comes Jackson, salutes, and gives the information of the whereabouts of the trap. How he got it without being captured I can't think. They were hidden completely. He must have stalked them like an Indian.

'The curious thing is that he is not one of our regular scouts. In fact, I can't remember sending him to scout at all. I must have done it, and forgotten. Anyhow, being prepared for the ambush, we moved up carefully, outflanked them, and captured every one of them. There were about two hundred. Of course, after that it was a walk-over. I tell you that boy is not such a fool as he looks.'

'Hang it, Templar,' protested his colleague, 'I never went so far as to accuse him of being *that*.'

Merrett junior said he wished he had a banjo. He went further. He said he wished Merrett senior would give him one.

'Do you know what banjos cost, Theodore?' enquired Merrett senior, who was in the City, and knew with a certain exactitude the value of money.

They were walking home from an afternoon concert when Merrett junior made his request. At the concert a man in a frock-coat and a yellow tie, a man, that is to say, entirely without claim to the respect of a right-thinking public, had dealt so dexterously with an instrument of the kind in question that Theodore's vague yearnings for fame had swollen within him and crystallised. Hitherto he had wished to distinguish himself, without settling on any specific channel for his talents. He wanted to sit in an atmosphere of envy and congratulation, but he did not go so far as to say exactly how he proposed to do it. The concert weed's rendering of *Dixie*, closely followed by *The Mosquitoes' Parade*, had decided the matter. He would learn the banjo and play it to awed audiences when he got back to school. If a man in a frock-coat and yellow tie − bright yellow − could do it as well as that, how much better after earnest practice, couldn't he do it? The general consensus of opinion at Seymour's house, Wrykyn, of which house and school Merrett was a member, up to the present, was that he was a bit of an ass. His banjo would remove this impression.

The only objections were that he had not a banjo, and that his father, though a man of wealth, was not taking to the idea of giving him one with that jovial eagerness which ought to be the leading trait in a parent's character.

'Do you know what these things cost, my boy?' asked Mr Merrett, returning to his original suit.

'Yes. I know a place where you can get one for a quid. We're just coming to it now. Look there!'

They stopped before a pawnbroker's. In the window was an undeniable banjo, and the price, marked on a card in fair, round letters, was one pound.

'Well?' said Mr Merrett, rattled.

'Shall I go in and order it?'

'Certainly not, certainly not. I shall give the matter a great deal more thought than I have had time to do up to the present before I buy you this instrument. *Palmam qui meruit ferat*, my boy. You must earn it, Theodore, you must earn it.'

Theodore's reply was spoken under his breath, and escaped notice.

And so home.

On the following morning Merrett junior's school report arrived. His father read it over his second cup of coffee. Coffee is supposed to have a soothing effect on the system. If this is so, we can only suppose that this was one of the beverage's off-days. It seemed from this document that his form-work was poor. 'Lacks energy and concentration,' wrote his form-master nastily, 'without which qualities his undeniable talents avail him little.'

'This report is disgraceful,' said his father. 'I see that the average age of boys in your form is fifteen. You are sixteen and a half.

Your French, I note is weak. How is that, when only last summer you spent a fortnight with your Aunt Elizabeth at St Malo?'

Theodore muttered something wordless through a jungle of toast and marmalade, and was asked not to speak with his mouth full.

The Serious Talk which was the sequel to the battle at breakfast ended in a sort of informal treaty. All was to be forgiven if Theodore should show a marked improvement during the forthcoming term. Meanwhile, for the remainder of the holidays, he would spend his mornings reading Greek and Latin authors on alternate days in order to give his Undeniable Talents a fair show. In the evenings, when he returned from business, Mr Merrett would examine him on the day's portion (with the help, though he did not mention this detail, of a Dr Giles' crib).

In this strenuous fashion the holidays drew to a close. By the time his boxes were packed, locked, and corded, and placed in the hall in readiness for the cab on the last afternoon, what Theodore did not know about the first three hundred lines of Euripides' *Medea* and the first two books of Horace's *Odes* was not knowledge. As for Merrett senior, he was beginning quite to enjoy those classics, and his opinion of Dr Giles as an author was of the highest. On Theodore, on the other hand, the thought of those wasted mornings bore heavy. His air in the cab was one of gloom.

His father noted this melancholy, and not unnaturally set it down to grief at leaving the ancestral home. He was touched. When not impressed with the idea of doing his duty as a parent, Mr Merrett was not a hard-hearted father. After all, he reflected, the boy had worked well for the last fortnight. He deserved some reward. (What the boy would have done if he had had a word to say in the matter, he did not ask himself.)

'Theodore, my boy,' he said, as they got out at the station, 'I have come to a decision. Some time ago you mentioned a desire for a banjo.'

Sudden alertness on the part of Merrett junior.

'You shall have it.'

'Oh, thanks awfully.'

'If you bring back a prize with you at the beginning of the summer holidays.'

Return of dejected expression to the face of Theodore. What was the good of making a condition like that? What earthly chance had he of landing a prize? As regarded the form prize, he was in the position of a distant relative of a peer with a number of healthy lives between himself and the title. That trophy would fall to one of half a dozen or more Frightful Swots who were going up the school at a perfectly indecent pace. He had often felt that there ought to be some sort of a speed limit for this type of person.

He felt it again as the train moved on its way. The form prize was out of the question. Mathematics? He barred mathematics. Never had liked them. Couldn't do a sum for nuts unless he consulted the Answers at the end of the book first. French? Ah, now what *about* French? What was the matter with that?

Two minutes later Theodore had decided to win the French prize.

It was Theo's misfortune that in the same form as himself there happened to be one Tilbury. Now, Tilbury also wanted the French prize, and he meant to get it. The other members of the form had not the slightest desire even to see it. It happened, therefore, that while thirty of the Lower Fifth entirely overlooked Merrett's manoeuvres, his thirty-first rival regarded them with the deepest suspicion and discontent. He confided his woes to Linton, that Lower-Fifth ornament, during the interval one day. Linton was a cheery individual who rather led the Lower Fifth life and thought. He was promising at all games, and worked hard in form – making up for this expenditure of effort by creating disturbances whenever possible.

'I say, Linton, I call it a bit thick,' said Tilbury.

'What is?' asked Linton.

'That bounder, Merrett,' explained Tilbury. 'He's given up full marks in French six times running.'

'Why shouldn't he? Amuses him, and doesn't hurt anyone else.'

'But there's the prize.'

'You don't mean to tell me that you want it! I wouldn't have it as a gift. If you're so keen, your best dodge is to give up full marks, too.'

'Thanks. That's a jolly good idea,' said Tilbury. 'I will.'

(I do not defend Linton's moral outlook. I merely record it.)

The system on which French was conducted at Wrykyn needs a little explanation. Etiquette did not demand honesty from you save in the examinations. At the end of the hour everyone corrected his neighbour's 'slip', and handed it back to him. The marks were then given up to M. Gaudinois. Most people gave up something near full marks. It pleased M. Gaudinois, and hurt nobody else. At the end of term the term's marks were added to examination marks, and the winner got away with the prize. With Merrett, therefore, giving up full marks every time, it will be seen that Tilbury's grievance was well-founded. Tilbury had not that wealth of imagination which is so necessary to success in French. He was in the habit of giving up only about seventy-five per cent. In the exams, of course, everybody played fair.

This was a curious point of French etiquette at Wrykyn. Cribbing might run riot during the term. In fact, the better you did it, the more of a sportsman you were considered. But by unwritten law it ceased absolutely as soon as the examination began. It had frequently puzzled M. Gaudinois, the disastrous falling-off in the standard. Boys who had scored ninety-five per cent throughout the term on questions of grammar, would amass totals of fifteen and twenty-one in the time of crisis. He put it down to brain-fag.

So Tilbury went his way, and proceeded to adopt a system of Retaliation. As for Merrett, he went on from strength to strength. Looking at his marks, the casual observer would have said that here was that rare prodigy, the English boy who was brilliant at French.

And in due course the end of the term came, bringing with it the examinations.

Tilbury came up to Linton as the Lower Fifth streamed out of the room, and foamed with indignation. His hands revolved in the air.

'Oh, chuck it,' said Linton; 'you aren't a semaphore. What's up?'

'It's that bounder, Merrett.'

'What's he been doing to you?'

'He was swindling. He swindled all the time. I saw him. I was watching him.'

Linton looked serious.

'Are you certain?' he said.

'Absolutely. I was watching him. I saw him. He had a book under the desk. Old Gaudinois couldn't see him because the top of his desk was in the light, but I could. I was watching him. And now he'll get the prize.'

'Don't you worry. He hasn't got it yet,' said Linton. 'Look here, did anyone else see him?'

'I don't know. Firmin might have done. He was sitting near him.'

'All right. I'll ask Firmin. And don't go gassing about it till you hear from me, or you'll be getting into trouble. See!'

Tilbury saw.

Linton consulted Firmin. Firmin supported Tilbury.

'Yes, he'd certainly got a book under the desk. Rather rot, I call it, even in French. Not that one wants the prize of course,' he added hastily, lest he should be misjudged.

'Of course not. Still—'

'In an exam—' said Firmin.

'It's not quite—'

'The game, is it?'

'Better not say anything to anybody, Firmin. I'll look after this.'

That night Merrett wrote to his father. He was, he said, in excellent health, and hoped his father was the same. He added that he had hopes of bringing back the French prize.

And when at the prize-giving, two days later, the Headmaster read out, without excitement (for he was beginning to get a little tired of the business), 'French prize, Lower Fifth – T. Merrett', these hopes would have appeared to the majority of people to have been realised. As Merrett walked down the hall with his handsomely bound copy of *Les Misérables* in his hand, he saw himself as in a vision, playing 'Lumberin' Luke' to enthusiastic audiences.

The Lower Fifth had assembled in force in their form room to collect their books when Merrett arrived. Linton was standing by the master's desk. He seemed to be waiting for something.

'Hullo, Merrett,' he said. 'Is that the prize? Let's have a look.'

Possessing himself of the gleaming volume, he cleared a space for himself among the ink-pots and papers on the desk, and sat down. Merrett noticed that a certain hush of expectancy had fallen on the room.

'Look here, Merrett,' said Linton, turning over the leaves of the book, 'you probably don't know it, but you were seen cribbing in the exam. What about that?'

'Fat lot of right you've got to talk about cribbing,' said Merrett.

'We all crib during the term, so it's all right. But it's an understood thing that we don't do it during exams. So you don't seem to have much claim to this rotten book, do you?'

'Give it back.'

'Wait a second. You'll get your share all right. This is going to be done perfectly fairly. Now, some forms would have touched you up for this, wouldn't they, you chaps?'

'Rather,' said the form.

'But we aren't going to. You ought to be grateful. Only, as we've all got just as much right to the prize as you, we're going to divide it.'

'I say—' said a voice of protest. Tilbury had come out second in the French order, and he had not looked for this Communistic arrangement.

'Dry up,' said Linton. 'And if you come any nearer, Merrett, you'll get it hot. Follow? There are five hundred and sixteen pages [*sic*] of this book. How much is that each, someone?'

A pause.

'Thirteen, exactly,' said Firmin.

'Thanks. Here's your lot, Firmin,' said Linton. 'Don't mind them being a bit torn, do you?'

'Not a bit,' said Firmin. 'Thanks.'

'You can have the cover, Merrett,' said Linton, when he had handed everyone his portion of the prize. 'Come in useful as an ornament for your mantelpiece at home.'

But Theodore never troubled to exhibit his share of the spoil in that way. And he still wants a banjo.

I

Aubrey Mickley's meditations, as he travelled to Wrykyn to begin his career as a member of a public school, would have revealed, if investigated, a certain amount of confusion. A public school was something altogether outside his ken. He had never, though he was within a month of his fifteenth birthday, been even to a private school, his education to date having been entrusted to a series of governesses, merging imperceptibly into a series of tutors. The last but one of the latter series, in conversation with a friend shortly after the expiration of his term of office, had delivered judgement on his late charge in the following words:

'Of all the little beasts, of all the little hounds I ever met, that Mickley kid is the worst. Not that it's altogether his fault. It's his fool of a mother. If he's sent to a public school quick, there's just a chance that he may get turned into something almost human. But it's got to be done at once, before she spoils him past repair.'

Which sentiments, by a roundabout route, had reached the ears of Mrs Mickley's brother, George; and brother George, who occasionally stayed a week or so with his sister and was a man of observation, came to the conclusion that this exactly summed up his own views on his nephew. The result was an interview, tearful on the part of Mrs Mickley, purple-faced on that of brother George. Mrs Mickley said George was unjust to Aubrey. George replied that that was only because words could not do justice to him. Mrs Mickley mentioned that George was forgetting that Aubrey was his only nephew, the only child of his only sister. George said it was precisely because he remembered that that he was taking steps; for he was tired of being the only uncle of a booby, a milksop – George's vocabulary was a little behind the times – a sneak, a greedy little pig, and a snob. The meeting had then broken up in confusion; but letters had been exchanged, like desultory artillery fire after a battle, and finally the progressive element in the family had carried its point; and Aubrey found himself in the corner of a first-class carriage on his way to Wrykyn and the unknown.

In the main the musings were gloomy. He had not asked to be sent to school. He had sulked for two days when the news was broken to him. He disliked the idea of school. At home you knew where you were. There was an inexhaustible supply of tutors in the world. If you didn't like one, you complained to your mother, and he was sent back to the shop. Then, in the few days which were bound to elapse before another could be sent on approval, you had a bit of a holiday to yourself. He doubted very much whether this excellent system obtained at a public school.

Then there was the question of food. Rumours had reached him of a certain Spartan element in the public-school cuisine. At home he had always had more than enough of anything he had cared to ask for. A hinted preference for *charlotte russe* had meant that there would be *charlotte russe*, not that there might be. He doubted whether at Wrykyn there even might be.

Take it for all in all, this idea of going to school did not appeal to him.

Two things buoyed him up. First, the home authorities had pledged themselves to keep him adequately supplied with hampers – Uncle George, who had put his foot down on the altogether excessive sum which his sister wished to bestow as pocket-money, had been unable to prevent this – and a regular flow of hampers does much to ameliorate the greyest existence. Secondly, Jack Pearse was at Wrykyn, and in West's house, too, the house at which he himself had been entered.

He hoped for much from Jack Pearse, not on the strength of long acquaintanceship, for they had never met, but owing to the latter's somewhat unusual relations with his, Aubrey's, Uncle George.

There is no doubt that, on several counts, Aubrey's Uncle George deserves our sympathy, consideration and respect. In the first place, he disliked and despised Aubrey. That in itself prejudices one in his favour. In the second place, he had exploited Jack Pearse.

Without his help, Jack would probably have followed in his father's footsteps and become a gamekeeper on Uncle George's estate in Shropshire. There is nothing vivid and revolutionary in the conditions of life in those parts, and the odds on a Shropshire gamekeeper's son becoming in the fullness of time a Shropshire gamekeeper are large. The world is far away, and the noise of it seldom reaches the quiet meadows by the banks of the Severn, unsettling the minds of budding gamekeepers and turning their thoughts to larger things. But for the fact that by a mere accident Uncle George had been struck by Jack's infantile intelligence and had decided to develop it, Jack might never have got further south than Wolverhampton. As it was, he had reached

Wrykyn, and was flourishing there with great success. He was now seventeen, high up in the Engineering Sixth, a useful bowler and one of the best and most energetic forwards the school had had for half a dozen seasons.

It was on this man of mettle that Aubrey was relying to introduce him to Wrykyn as he should be introduced. To others he might be unknown, but Jack Pearse would reverence him. By degrees, as the train raced on towards his destination, Jack Pearse had taken on in his eyes an attitude of humble devotion which would have been almost excessive in an old family retainer in melodrama.

Meanwhile, at West's, the object of his meditations was also thinking of him, though hardly as humbly or devotionally as he should have done. Jack Pearse, who had received instructions from Uncle George before leaving, had taken an early train to school in order to see Fry, the head of West's, as soon as possible. He was now having tea with him in his study. Fry was a large, stout, placid individual, with a broad, good-natured face. Everybody liked him, but his best friend would not have denied that he was quite incompetent to be head of a house. Fortunately for the peace of mind of Mr West, his post was practically a sinecure, for the house had never been in a better state. Houses pass through phases, and West's, six years ago one of the worst in the school, was running along now on oiled wheels.

'There's a kid called Mickley coming here this term,' said Pearse. 'I know his uncle. Do you mind if he fags for me?'

'I don't mind anything,' said Fry placidly and with truth. 'What sort of a kid is he?'

'I've never met him,' said Pearse guardedly. Uncle George had spoken his mind with freedom on the subject of Aubrey, but it would be rough luck to prejudice Fry against him from the start. 'His uncle's an awfully good sort. The best sort I've ever met. An absolute ripper!'

'Pity it isn't the uncle instead of the kid that's coming here. By the way, did you know that Stanworth was coming to West's this term? He's up in Baxter's old study now. Shall I ask him down here?'

'Stanworth! Great Scott, that blighter!'

'Oh, I don't mind Stanworth,' said Fry comfortably. 'He's not a bad sort.'

'I can't stand the man.'

'He'll be a lot of help at cricket,' argued Fry.

This was true. Whatever his other defects, there was no doubt that next term Stanworth would be the best bat in the school. He was one of those tall, languid youths who seem to take to batting naturally. Batting was his one form of athletic expression. He did not play football, and even on the cricket-field rarely ran except between the wickets. He was one of Nature's points, born to stand in an attitude of limp grace and watch cover or third-man sprinting in pursuit of an agile ball. As to his other qualities, he was old for his years, brilliantly clever at Classics, and what theatrical advertisements call a 'good dresser'. In addition to being in the first eleven, he was a school prefect.

'He's an amusing chap, Stanworth,' continued Fry. 'He was making me laugh just now about a Frenchman he saw at the Casino at Nice. His people have taken a villa at Nice for a bit; that's why he's coming here. This Frenchman chap was gambling at the tables, and thought he had put five francs on something, whereas really it was on something else, or something like that. I can't quite remember how it went. Anyhow, I know he thought he'd won when he'd really lost. But you get him to tell it you. You'll laugh.'

'I'll save it up for a rainy day.' said Pearse, without enthusiasm. 'It sounds screamingly funny. I can't make out what you see in the man. He makes me sick.'

'Oh, I don't know,' said Fry.

II

Aubrey's first impressions of Wrykyn need not be recounted, especially as, at the end of the first quarter of an hour, they were one and all engulfed, swamped, avalanched and tidal-waved by the cataclysmal information that he would have to fag – and fag, at that, for Jack Pearse. Just as a man might feel who, arrayed in his best, and walking rapidly along Piccadilly on his way to lunch with a duke, should cannon into a lamppost, so did Aubrey feel at the first shock of the news.

Pearse found him in the matron's room, being treated with a certain motherly familiarity, perhaps, but still quite tolerably respectfully, and slapped the information into him like a charge of round-shot.

'Are you Mickley?' he said. 'My name's Pearse. I know your uncle.' ('Know your uncle!' Great feudal system!) 'You'll be fagging for me this term.'

'Fagging?' said Aubrey. The word conveyed nothing to him.

And it was at this point, when Pearse began to explain the precise nature and meaning of the word 'fagging', that the avalanche-cum-tidal-wave started on its course.

To Pearse his dumb stupefaction seemed merely the decent

shyness of a new boy, strange to his surroundings. He approved of it. It seemed to him that Uncle George must have been wrong in his diagnosis. This kid was not the terror his uncle had imagined him.

'It's all right,' he said. 'It isn't anything to spoil your sleep. And, anyhow, you haven't got to start at once. You don't have to fag here your first week. Whose dormitory are you in?'

'Stanworth's,' said the matron, replying, *vice* Aubrey, incapacitated. 'The one that was Baxter's, last term. He will be a house prefect, of course, being a school prefect.'

'Isn't there any room in mine?' asked Pearse.

Aubrey found speech.

'I prefer Stanworth's,' he said haughtily. He did not know what exactly Stanworth's might be, but it was imperative that this person be put in his place.

On the whole, Aubrey did not find his first week at Wrykyn unpleasant. It was a Wrykyn tradition that things should be made as easy as possible for a new boy until he might be expected to have grown accustomed to the place; and in West's house in particular there was very little to grumble at. The food suffered by comparison with his mother's generous menus, but it was eatable, there was plenty of it, and the school shop was very handy. Work was a nuisance, but apparently inevitable, and he resigned himself to it.

He liked being in Stanworth's dormitory. Stanworth struck him as an excellent sort of fellow. He was the only member of the house who seemed really to enjoy listening to his, Aubrey's, conversation. Twice in the first week Aubrey took tea with him in his study. His view of the matter was that he and Stanworth were kindred souls. Stanworth's, as confided to his friend Benger, a day-boy, differed slightly from this.

'West's is a pretty slow sort of hole,' he said, 'but at any rate I've found one genuine freak in it. Do you know a new kid named Mickley, a little fat brute who looks as if he was bursting out of his clothes? This is apparently the first time he's been to any sort of school, and his views on things in general are worth hearing. I can sit and listen to him by the hour.'

Life only began to show itself as not all joy, jollity and song when the first week came to an end and his period of servitude commenced. In the rush of events he had almost forgotten what was hanging over him, and the shock when young Gooch, who fagged for Fry, came to him, as he was chatting with Stanworth in his study, with the information that Pearse was waiting for him to get his tea ready, was almost as great as that which he had received on his first evening when the nature of fagging had been explained to him in the matron's room.

He looked helplessly at Stanworth.

'Don't you want to?' said Stanworth. 'You'd better write him a note. Put it nicely. Say that you have a previous engagement, and add that you will be delighted if he will drop in and join us here.'

It struck Aubrey as an excellent idea, all but the last part.

'But I don't want him here,' he said.

'No? Well, just say you've got a previous engagement.'

Jack Pearse's feelings, when Aubrey's civil but rather distant note was brought to him, were mixed. The bearer was Hopwood, Stanworth's fag and, making his deductions from this fact, he suspected the hand of Stanworth in the matter. Even Aubrey would not have been such a fool, after a week's experience of school and its ways, as to write the note, unless he had gathered, from someone who might be supposed to know, that it would be all right. He was furious with Stanworth. He did not suppose that his fellow prefect had deliberately urged Aubrey to serious revolt. He imagined, correctly, that he had done it merely to amuse himself, and he objected strongly to Stanworth amusing himself at his expense. If any of the other house prefects had done it, he would have laughed; but he disliked Stanworth, and a joke is the last thing one wants to share with a person one dislikes.

His distaste for Stanworth had grown with closer acquaintance. As a day-boy, the other had come but seldom into immediate contact with him; but fellow house prefects cross one another's paths frequently. He would have found it difficult to say exactly why he objected to Stanworth. To himself he put it vaguely that the other's 'side' annoyed him. But he knew that it was more than that. What was really the trouble, though he could not analyse it, was that Stanworth was an individual in a community, an alien, an unassimilated unit. In other words, though he wore a West's tie, he was at heart still a day-boy. He did not belong to West's. Jack, who had been a member of the house for nearly five years, was filled with the house spirit. West's mattered a great deal to him. It did not matter in the least to Stanworth.

He thought the thing over as he prepared tea for himself. He must keep his head. To lose his temper would constitute an unmistakable score to Stanworth.

Having finished tea, and judging that his fag-to-be had probably finished his, he went upstairs to the other study. Aubrey was still there. He looked replete and contented.

'Hullo, Pearse,' said Stanworth. 'Pity you didn't come earlier. We've finished.'

'I've had tea, thanks,' said Pearse. 'Come along to my study, Mickley, for a minute, will you?'

Aubrey looked at Stanworth for guidance, but Stanworth merely beamed.

'Sorry you have to be going, Mickley,' he said. 'Look in any time you like.'

'What do you want?' said Aubrey, when he and Jack Pearse were outside.

'Just a chat,' said Pearse. 'I'm seeing nothing of you.'

He led the way to the study. The remains of his solitary tea were on the table.

'You might just wash those up first,' he said. 'There's a tin basin over in the corner. You can fill it in the bathroom. Buck along!'

Aubrey hesitated. He was on the point of refusing, but the absence of Stanworth robbed him of the necessary courage.

He compromised.

'I don't see why I've got to,' he said.

'Got to!' said Pearse. 'Don't say that. It ought to be a pleasure. Charge along. You know where the bathroom is.'

Aubrey felt out of his depth. It was all wrong that he should be compelled to do menial work like this for a social inferior, but it didn't seem possible to get out of it. Jack Pearse was quite quiet and pleasant, but there was something in his manner that suggested possibilities. He picked up the basin and went out.

'You mustn't let Stanworth rot you,' said Pearse, as the water splashed over the plates.

The idea that Stanworth could treat him with anything but sympathetic respect offended Aubrey. He grunted.

'You must look out for that,' continued Jack. 'Fellows will, if you give them a chance. A safe rule for you is to do just what

I tell you. If I tell you do a thing and somebody else tells you not to, you go ahead and do it, and refer him to me.'

'I don't see why—'

'You don't have to. Yours is not to reason why, yours but to do – or die.'

He picked up a swagger-stick, toyed with it for a moment, and laid it down. A thrill of dismay shot through Aubrey. He had not realised this factor in the situation. He addressed himself to his work with a thoughtful energy.

'Finished?' said Pearse. 'That's right. You can pop off now. I shall want tea tomorrow after school – for two. Fry's coming. Don't forget.'

III

By the end of the third week of term Jack Pearse was feeling discouraged. Things were going against him. That Aubrey now looked on fagging as another of the unavoidable evils of public-school life, and went through with it without further attempt at resistance, mattered little, for in every other respect he was unchanged; and the problem of how his improvement was to be effected worried Pearse.

If it had not been for Uncle George, he would have dismissed it from his mind, for there was nothing in the least attractive in the prospect of being a combination of nurse and policeman to a small boy. But he knew that Uncle George felt very strongly on the subject of Aubrey, and the older he grew and the more clearly he saw the possibilities which his backer had opened to him by sending him to Wrykyn, the deeper became his sense of obligation. The only possible way in which he could repay him at present was by reforming Aubrey; and he certainly had not made much progress in that direction.

There seemed so little that he could do. He had so small a control over his charge's movements. If Aubrey, when not fagging, had spent his time, like other juniors, in the junior day-room, his mind would have been easy. The atmosphere of a junior day-room in a public school is essentially bracing, and characters like Aubrey's seldom fail to derive benefit from it. But Aubrey avoided the junior day-room. As far as Pearse could see, he appeared to have the free run of Stanworth's study. At any rate, he was nearly always to be found there of an afternoon.

It irritated Jack, this incessant intrusion of Stanworth into his affairs. He objected to him. Stanworth refused to be assimilated into the house. His friends were all day-boys. He held day-boy tea-parties nearly every afternoon. To Pearse, with his boarder outlook on life, he seemed to cheapen the house. Your genuine boarder resents strangers in his house almost as keenly as the Constantinople dog used to resent strange dogs in his street. It was maddening to meet grinning day-boys wandering about the house as if they had bought it. He had no objection to day-boys in their proper place, but that place was not the interior of West's. And Stanworth's friends were such wasters, too, the louts!

Nevertheless, it was a bad move to assail Aubrey on the subject. He regretted it directly he had done it; but he was feeling particularly irritated that afternoon. To begin with, a degraded weed in a day-boy's cap had charged into his study while he was changing after football and, having grinned all across his beastly face, had retired with the statement that he had 'thought this was Stanworth's'. That had upset him. And when, on the top of it, Aubrey had given, as an excuse for being late, that he had been up in Stanworth's study, where the clock was wrong, he spoke his mind.

'Why the dickens are you always up there?' he growled. 'Why can't you stay in the junior day-room like other kids?'

And more to the same effect.

Aubrey listened in silence, and duly handed it all on to Stanworth.

Stanworth was not likely to miss such a chance. It was, as the Americans say, pie to him. On the following afternoon he knocked at Pearse's door. 'Oh, please, Pearse,' he said timidly, 'may Mickley come to my study this evening?'

Pearse glared.

'Would you mind very much? I thought I'd better come and ask you.'

'In other words,' said Jack, hot about the ears, 'I suppose you mean that I'd better mind my own business?'

'I shouldn't have put it in that way,' said Stanworth smoothly. 'But still, as you *have* suggested it—'

'Oh, all right,' said Jack. 'I know it's a score to you; you needn't go on. But if you can't see what rotten bad form it is for a prefect always having a kid fooling about in his study—'

'What's the objection? This kid's a freak. He amuses me!'

'The objection is,' snapped Jack, 'that he's already got side enough for ten, and if you encourage him he will probably in time get almost as bad as you. Goodbye! Run along to your beastly day-boys.'

Which outburst, however satisfying to the feelings, did not, as he saw perfectly clearly, advance him in the slightest degree towards the accomplishment of his object. With the difference that he and Stanworth, instead of exchanging an occasional word when they met, now maintained a frigid silence, the situation was unaltered.

* * *

It was the easy-going Fry who first revealed to him an un-suspected joint in Stanworth's armour. Fry, plainly with some-thing on his mind, settled himself in one of Pearse's deck-chairs one evening when West's, with the exception of the prefects, were over at the Great Hall, doing prep, and talked jerkily for a while of house football prospects.

'I say,' he said at last, 'what ought I to do, do you think, in a case like this?'

'Like what?'

'Well, it's this way. I was up in Stanworth's study just now, and he's got one of those what-d'you-call-it things. *You* know.'

Lucid as this statement was, Pearse asked for further par-ticulars.

'One of those gambling things,' said Fry. 'A sort of board with holes and numbers, and you roll a ball.'

'Roulette?'

'No; it's not roulette. It's a different sort of game. Stanworth got it at Nice. It's a sort of small model of the game they play at the Casino there. You roll an indiarubber ball, and it falls into one of the holes.'

'Well?'

'Well, I mean, what ought I to do? Of course, he's got no right to have a thing like that in the house. West would be frightfully sick. There'd be an awful row.'

'Does he use it?'

'That's what I can't make out. You know what Stanworth is. He puts you off. I asked him that, and he said that nobody in the house except me had ever seen it. That sounds all right, don't you think?'

'Probably he plays with that day-boy crew he's always having in. I don't see that you can do anything.'

'I don't either. It isn't as if he played with chaps in the house.'

'If he does, you can jump on him.'

Fry looked doubtful.

'I don't know – even then. You see, he's a school prefect, and all that. It's beastly awkward. Still, I suppose it'll be all right.'

He wandered out of the study; and Pearse, who was in the middle of a Latin Prose, dismissed the thing from his mind. He disliked thinking of Stanworth.

He had completely forgotten the conversation, when, about a week later, having a note to send across to the School House, and having failed to find Aubrey in the junior day-room, he went in search of him to Stanworth's study. He was rather pleased at having a legitimate excuse for routing him out from that secure retreat.

He was wearing carpet slippers, and his feet made no noise. He knocked sharply, and went in.

He had never been inside this study since it had become Stanworth's, and he was surprised at the luxury of it. He had always known that Stanworth had a good deal of money, but he was not prepared for the display of wealth that met his eye.

He did not look at the ornaments long, however. He found the occupants of the room more interesting. There were four of them – Stanworth himself, two day-boys (whom he only knew by sight), and Aubrey. They were gathered round a small table in the middle of the room, and on the table was a curious apparatus that puzzled him for a moment, and then sent his mind back like a flash to his conversation with Fry. It consisted of a polished, cuplike piece of wood, in the bottom of which was a circle of holes, each with a number opposite it, and a strip of green baize, divided into numbered sections. There was money lying about this green baize, a half-crown, a shilling, and some coppers. A small red ball was bumping slowly round the circle of holes.

His entry effectually diverted attention from the game. All four players faced sharply round.

Stanworth was the first to recover himself.

'And what can we do for our Mr Pearse?' he said.

'What's all this?' demanded Pearse.

Stanworth smiled, the supercilious smile that was the cause of a good deal of his unpopularity.

'Do you remember a little talk we had the other day on the subject of minding one's own business?' he said.

'This is my business!'

'How do you make that out?'

'Because you've lugged this kid Mickley into it. I promised his people that I'd keep an eye on him in this place, and I'm not going to have him rooked by the first bounder that's cad enough to take his money off him!'

Stanworth rolled the ball gently to and fro with his forefinger.

'And what do you propose to do about it?' he said.

The question brought Jack up with a jerk. What *did* he propose to do about it? It suddenly occurred to him that he did not know.

'Going to tell West?'

No; he was not going to tell West. Etiquette is rigid at school, and a house prefect has to have a contempt for it before he reports a matter to the Housemaster on his own account. Etiquette demanded that he should consider his part done when he had told Fry. And he could see Fry handling the situation. There would be an unofficial protest to Stanworth, a lazy 'I-say-old-chap-you-know', and Fry would doze off again, thankful that the business was over. To Pearse, in his militant state of mind, this did not seem the ideal method.

'Or are you going to give me a good, hard knock?'

Jack's eyes gleamed joyfully. An idea had come to him.

'The first thing I'm going to do is to ask your two moth-eaten friends to toddle!' he said. 'This is purely a house affair. We don't want outsiders mixed up in it.'

He looked from one day-boy to the other and back again, and opened the door. For a moment they hesitated, but not longer. The fact presented itself to their minds that while Stanworth was a school prefect, and, as such, sacrosanct, and not to be smitten by inferiors, they were nothing of the kind. They had no intention of brawling with Pearse. As he had very sensibly put it, it was a house affair. They were not needed. They would withdraw.

They withdrew.

Jack closed the door gently behind them.

'Now!' he said.

There was a serviceable walking-stick in the corner, one of those sticks with a heavy knob for a handle. He picked it up, and gave it a half swing. His eye moved about the room till it rested on a bulbous china vase. He raised the stick, and brought it down with a crash.

Stanworth sprang forward, with a howl of wrath and dismay.

'Get back!' said Jack. 'You're in the way!'

'What the deuce do you think you're playing at?'

Jack raised the stick again.

'Indoor hockey,' he said. 'Society's latest craze. Some people,' he continued thoughtfully, 'think it's bad luck to break a looking-glass. I wonder!'

There was a second crash, louder than the first.

Stanworth had seized his wrist, and was trying to wrench the stick from his hand. Jack's left came into play, and Stanworth fell back against the table.

Jack looked at him reproachfully.

'I told you you were in the way,' he said, smashing a photograph-glass.

'I'm a school prefect!' cried Stanworth. 'I'll have you up before a prefects' meeting!'

'Do!' Another vase burst into a shower of china. 'And tell 'em all the facts. It'll keep them merry and bright. The Easter term's always pretty dull.'

Two minutes later Jack looked round him with satisfaction.

'That'll do for the present,' he said. 'Thanks for the loan of the stick. Mickley, come down to my study. I want a short talk with you. No; better take this note over to the School House first. There's no answer. Come to my study when you get back.'

The distance between West's and the School House was not large, but Aubrey managed to put in a good deal of hard thinking while covering it. There had been a remarkable upheaval in his mind. Primitive things had been happening, and he was readjusting his views. A sudden humility competed for first place among his emotions, with an equally sudden respect for Jack Pearse. For the first time he realised that he was in a world where antecedents, however aristocratic, are as nothing beside present performances; where muscles were more than coronets, and a simple swagger-stick than Norman blood.

He entered Jack's study, walking mincingly, like Agag.

'Come in!' said Jack. 'Now, then, what about it? This is where you make your big decision, my blue-eyed boy. We have here a handy swagger-stick. Shall it be ten of the premier quality with this, or will you listen to a small scheme I have mapped out?

This is the scheme: that you stop behaving like a young blighter, and settle down to be a credit to the house and yourself. You'd be a pretty decent weight even without the fat, and there's no reason, if you work hard, why you shouldn't play in the house second scrum in the house matches at the end of the term. It'll mean sweating. You'll have to learn the game, and you'll have to train. Well, which is it to be?'

He switched the swagger-stick meditatively in the air.

'I believe they shove whalebone, or something, in these things,' he said pensively. 'Awfully supple they are!'

Towards the middle of March – Uncle George had forbidden her to do it earlier – Mrs Mickley paid her first visit to the school, and bore Aubrey off to tea in the town.

'My poor darling,' she said sympathetically, 'you look positively starved! Never mind, the holidays will soon be here. Now, shall we begin with muffins, my pet? And then you would like some of those nice cream cakes in the win—'

A look slightly wistful, but in the main of horror and repulsion, spread itself over Aubrey's face.

'I think I'd like some of those oatmeal biscuits,' he said austerely.

'Oatmeal biscuits!'

'Or a rusk or two. I'm in training. I'm playing for the house second against Seymour's on Saturday. And Jack Pearse says if we buck up like we did against Day's last week, we shall simply knock the stuffing out of them!'

ELSEWHERE

St Asterisk's

In looking over the notes I have made from time to time of the cases unravelled by the peculiar methods of my friend, Mr Burdock Rose, I find mention of what I have called 'The Disappearance of Mr Buxton-Smythe'. It is a curious case. This Buxton-Smythe was a schoolmaster – but I will begin at the beginning.

It was in our old Grocer Square days, before my marriage. We had finished breakfast and were sitting smoking by the window.

'Look at that man there, Wotsing,' said my friend, suddenly.

'Where? Which one?' I replied. 'I see so many men. Do you mean the elderly sergeant of marines, who retired, as far as I can judge from a hasty glance, in the summer of eighty-six, or the stockbroker, who seems to me unable to make up his mind whether to invest in Eries or South Africans, and who, I am sorry to say, sat up last night past his usual hour drinking black coffee while trying to decide on the best course, or—'

At this point Rose interrupted. I had noticed lately that my success in studying his methods had not been altogether to his taste. His disapproval had been especially marked during the last week, notably on the occasion when the King of Fiji had called to consult him, and I had solved the case from my armchair before he could speak, thereby losing him a handsome fee.

'Wotsing,' he said, quietly.

'Rose?'

'In a household of two I am inclined to think that one detective is ample, a pair excessive.' I apologised. After all, he had the prior claim in the matter of deductions.

'The man I mean,' said he, 'is the schoolmaster in the frock-coat.'

A year before I should have exclaimed 'My *dear* Rose! How—?' but now I merely endorsed his opinion.

'I see the man you mean. He is a Fifth-form master, I should be inclined to say.'

'Sixth,' said Rose, sharply.

'Well, the point will not be long in doubt. I deduced from his movements that he was coming here. That, if I mistake not, is his knock.'

That my surmise was correct was proved a moment later by the landlady, who ushered in a tall, good-looking man in a frock-coat with the curt but lucid observation, 'Mr Theophilus Wright'.

'Sit down, Mr Wright,' said Rose, genially. 'That basket-chair will be your fancy, I think. I trust you left your form in good health?'

'Very good, thank you. But how—?'

'Tut, tut, my dear sir, these are trifles. Wotsing, how did I know that Mr Wright was a schoolmaster?'

'Why,' I said, with a laugh, 'when we see a man with a—'

'Yes, yes,' interrupted Rose, quickly, 'that was how it was done, of course. You are a Sixth-form master, Mr Wright, I think?'

'No, Mr Rose; I take the Fifth.'

When Rose asked me at this point why I smiled, I said that I was thinking of something.

'It was, however, about the Sixth-form master that I came to consult you. My school, Mr Rose, is St Asterisk's.'

'Wotsing,' said Rose, without moving from his position (closed eyes and touching fingertips), 'look up St Asterisk's in my scrapbook.'

I replied that as Rose was himself able to reach the book without rising whereas I should be obliged to get up and come round the table, the best and wisest course would be for him to get it himself. He did so.

The information concerning St Asterisk's was wedged in between a statement (extracted from 'Useful Bits') to the effect that Mr Joseph Chamberlain never eats mushrooms, and a letter to the *Daily Telegraph* on the question 'Are Hairpins Hygienic?'

'Ha!' said Rose, 'H'm! St Asterisk's, I see, is the school which lost a Sixth-form master in 1884.'

'Quite so; that brings me to my point. Our present Sixth-form master, Mr Buxton-Smythe, has also disappeared.'

'How old was he?'

'About twenty-four. He had just come down from Oxford.'

'Young for a Sixth-form master, I imagine.'

'Very much so; but a fine scholar.'

'Ah! What colour was his hair?'

'Brown.'

'Ah, yes, quite so, quite so. So I had expected. Well, let me hear the particulars.'

'They may be given very shortly,' said our visitor. 'Buxton-Smythe was seen to enter his form room at two o'clock last Tuesday. He was never seen to come out.'

'What do the form say on the subject?'

'Nothing, except that they do not know where he is. Their manner, I may add, seems to me suspicious.'

I could see from Rose's eyes that the case interested him.

'Proceed,' he said.

'The Headmaster is, of course, prostrated with grief. He fainted on hearing the news, and is now on a sofa in the library gradually recovering. The junior school masters are feeding him with gruel from a spoon. Somebody advised me, as senior surviving master, to ask you to look into the case.'

'I shall be very happy to do so. Wotsing, can you leave your practice for a couple of days?'

'My what? – Oh yes, I remember. Why, my dear Rose, I have no practice now. I found I had no time to spare from observing your methods. I will accompany you with pleasure. To St Asterisk's?'

'Precisely. To St Asterisk's. By the way, Mr Wright, was the first disappearance at the school ever cleared up?'

'Well, no,' admitted our visitor, with some reluctance, 'not absolutely. The name of that master was Wotherspoon. I believe it is almost certain that the boys of his house murdered him and concealed the body. You see he was in the habit of reciting extracts from Shakespeare to them on Saturday nights, and attendance was compulsory. Well, he disappeared one day, and a month afterwards some workmen came upon a mouldering skeleton. You see the inference?'

'Perfectly. I suppose there was nothing of that sort in this case?'

'Oh, no. Poor Buxton-Smythe was a most inoffensive man.'

'Very good. Well, Mr Wright, this appears to be a very pretty little problem. I always shut the windows and doors and smoke a pound of shag over cases of this sort. Wotsing generally goes out to see a friend of his about a canary. Perhaps you would care to join him? Then good morning. Expect me at St Asterisk's tomorrow at one.'

* * *

'It is a case that presents many attractive points, Wotsing,' said Rose, as we left the form room on the following day. 'Did you observe anything just now? Have you formed any theory?'

I replied that I never formed theories. I found that they were fatal, for one involuntarily attempted to twist facts to suit theories instead of theories to suit facts.

'Very sensible,' said he. 'By the way, Wotsing, didn't I make a remark very like that to you once?'

'Did you? I don't remember. Very possibly,' I replied, off-handedly.

'Of course,' he continued, after a pause, 'one thing is obvious. Mr Theophilus Wright has made away with Buxton-Smythe. The question is, how?'

'My dear Rose!'

'My dear Wotsing, it is surely perfectly plain. Do you ask for motive? Ambition. The chance of getting the vacant place. Clues? Millions of them. To begin with—'

'One moment, Rose. You remember that Sixth-form boy I attended this morning?'

'Yes.'

'He was suffering from indigestion. He had eaten something that had disagreed with him. Now, Sixth-form boys do not eat sweets or green apples or buns or anything else of that sort. A chance question put me on the right track, and by dint of severe examination, aided by remorse and indigestion, I extracted the truth. *He had eaten a considerable portion of the late Buxton-Smythe raw!* No,' I went on, seeing his look of amazement, 'I am not romancing. I have his written confession in my pocket. He told me the whole story. Buxton-Smythe appears to have been a per-fectly harmless man, but with one flaw in his character. He set essays. Now, there are many ways of setting essays. Buxton-Smythe's was the worst. His subjects ran in series of six. The facts in connection with his death are briefly as follows: On the first Monday of term he gave out as his subject 'David'. This suited the form very well, for they knew nothing of the flaw in their master's character, which, as I said, made him set series of six. They showed up excellent essays on David. David's character was the next subject. The form were not so pleased at this, but there was, so far, little inclination to take justice into their own hands. 'David's character and its influence upon his people' on the third week altered this frame of mind for the worse. There were ominous growls and whispers. Anybody might have been expected to notice this, but Buxton-Smythe was either incredibly dense or outrageously rash. Of course, he was an enthusiast, which may explain it. But the fact remains that on the fourth Monday, whether from innocence or sheer bravado, he announced, as the week's essay subject, 'David's character, and its influence upon himself'. Upon this portion of the proceedings my informant does not dwell. He merely states baldly that the form rose as one man from their seats, tore him to pieces, and ate him. You remember, when we were examining the form room, that I directed your attention to a shirt-stud and a spot of blood on the floor by the master's desk, but you said it was only red ink, and that you had dropped the stud yourself. As a matter of fact, they were Buxton-Smythe's. The local coroner sat on them before they went to Woking, and brought in what I considered to be a very sensible verdict of suicide. He said that a master who could act as Buxton-Smythe had done had, to all intents and purposes, committed suicide. He added a rider to the effect that the form had behaved in a most conscientious and praiseworthy manner.

I am sorry to interfere with any little deduction you may have made, Rose, but those are the true facts.'

Rose said nothing. I think he was a little disappointed.

He did not speak again until we had reached our lodgings and were retiring for the night. Then he put his head in at my door.

'Wotsing,' he said, 'I suppose I shall see very little of you when you're married?'

'Not quite as much as you do now, Rose, I fear.'

He was silent for a moment. Then a soft smile lit up his sharp features.

'I'm glad you're going to be married, Wotsing,' said he, pensively.

I

We sprang into the night-mail. It was in the old Grocer Square days, when springing into night-mails came all in the day's work to us.

We had the carriage to ourselves. A glance had shown Rose that the guard of the train had at one period of his life been a cannibal, and, thinking it a pity to conceal the fact, he had mentioned it to him casually, at the same time expressing a desire for an empty carriage. The guard was kindness itself. He bundled the two bishops, an elderly professor, and three prize fighters out of a compartment in record time, and motioned us to be seated.

The train sped on its way.

'A curious case, Wotsing,' said Rose, at last.

'Which is that?' I asked.

'This St Asterisk's murder.'

'Buxton-Smythe, do you mean? I – I mean we solved that long ago.'

'No, no,' said Rose, irritably. Somehow the mention of that case always irritates him. 'This is a different thing altogether. Wotsing' – he broke off suddenly – 'why did you shave in cold water this morning?'

'I didn't. Why did you drink only one lemon squash when you went out this afternoon?'

'My dear Wotsing – how—?'

'Tut, tut. I cannot explain these little things, Rose. What is this about St Asterisk's?'

Rose drew from his pocket a newspaper cutting.

'I will not read this to you,' he said, 'the style is really too painful. Not that there is not some excuse for the reporter in the present case. He was suffering from earache when he wrote, and, from his curious partiality for quotations from Juvenal, I should judge that he had only recently recovered from an attack of gout. The gist of what he says is this. Smith, the school porter at St Asterisk's, going his rounds last Friday morning, discovered – to his horror – that a ghastly crime had been committed in the Sixth-form room. The victim was an infinitive. It had been split, probably, Smith asserts, by some blunt weapon such as a bad pen. The body was on a scrap of paper, and several drops of ink on the paper, together with a general crumpled appearance, showed that the victim had not succumbed without a struggle. Smith, with an intelligence which some of these Scotland Yard bunglers would do well to imitate, left everything exactly as he had found it.'

'Anyone suspected?' I asked.

'I was coming to that. One of the form, Vanderpoop by name, under whose desk the corpse was discovered, has already been arrested.'

'Did he make any statement?'

'Well, he hit the policeman under the jaw, if that could be called making a statement. He is now in the local police station awaiting trial. Popular opinion is, I should say, strongly against him.'

'That I should think is in itself almost enough to clear him. Popular opinion is always wrong.'

'Well, well, we shall see,' said Rose. 'At any rate the problem is one that presents many attractive features.'

'And,' I interrupted, 'it has saved me from a black reaction.'

Rose glared at me. He had been meaning to say that himself.

II

'Well, here we are again,' said I, as we stepped into the form room on the following day. 'This form room, Rose, has been the scene of some exciting episodes. Where is the corpse?'

Smith, the porter, produced it, and left the room. Instantly Rose dropped on all fours, whipped out a microscope, and, in short, commenced his usual operations. I made my investigations more quietly.

At last Rose got up.

'Wotsing,' he said, 'the case is plain. Vanderpoop did it.'

'Did you see the local paper this morning, Rose?'

'No.'

'Ah. If you had, you would have read that Vanderpoop has been released without a stain on his character.'

'Fools, fools! Oh, these Scotland Yard—'

'But he proved an alibi, a most convincing alibi. The murder must have been committed some time on Thursday. That, I think, is plain. Vanderpoop was in the Infirmary on Wednesday and Thursday. But, Rose—'

'Well?'

'I have discovered the real man.'

Rose gasped with astonishment.

'And he is—?'

'The Headmaster, sir,' said Smith, suddenly opening the door.

'Good morning, sir,' I said as he entered. 'Pray take a chair. Ah, but there are no chairs. Take a desk.'

He sat down on the window-sill, a curiously mournful figure. A day before he had been stout. Now he was thin.

'I got your note, Dr Wotsing,' he said, in a low voice. 'But who is this?' He pointed to Rose, who was still on all fours.

'That,' I replied, 'is my friend Mr Burdock Rose. You can speak as freely before him as you would before me. Indeed, strictly speaking, he is supposed to be bossing this show on his own account. But proceed, sir, I beg.'

'I got your note,' repeated the Headmaster. 'How you found out all you have found out, I do not know.'

'My system. Perfectly simple. Yes, you were saying—?'

'You are right in every detail, Dr Wotsing. I and no other, split that infinitive. Pity the sorrows of a poor old man.' He looked as if he were about to collapse.

'If you are thinking of fainting,' I said, 'I will do my best to revive you with ink. There is no water. But, take the advice of a medical man, sir, and don't.' He did not.

'You might explain,' I said.

'I will,' said he. 'Born of rich but honest parents, Dr Wotsing, I was sent at an early age to a public school.'

'Excuse my interrupting,' I said, courteously, 'but if you could cut it fairly short I should be very much obliged. I have a train to catch. Condense your ideas.'

'Very well. Public school. Latin. Greek. Greek. Latin. No English. English no good. University. Latin. Greek. Greek. Latin. English no good. So here I am. You take me?'

'I understand you to say that your English education was neglected in favour of Latin and Greek. Am I right?'

'Absolutely on the bull's eye.'

'Sir,' I said, 'I acquit you of all blame. You are more sinned against than sinning. Run away and reform.'

He ran away, and, I hope, reformed.

'I really am glad you are going to be married, Wotsing,' said Rose to me on the way back to town. 'When is it to be?'

'In another month.'

And the first thing he did on getting out of the train was to buy a calendar. He keeps it in his desk, and every day he erases a date, and smiles.

St Austin's

How long the feud between Welch and his Housemaster Merevale had been going on is uncertain. Probably it had started from a remark that Merevale made about Welch after the final house match of the previous summer, when, owing principally to his mismanagement of the bowling – he was captain of Merevale's – Perkins's had won by a wicket. Merevale was a quick-tempered man with a rather rich vein of sarcasm in him, and his comment on Welch's performance was pungent and personal. He delivered it as the latter was coming up the pavilion steps after the match. The pavilion was, as was usual on the final house-match day, packed with lookers-on, all of whom heard the remark, and the majority of whom laughed audibly. Nobody could be expected actually to enjoy this sort of thing, but anybody else but Welch would have forgotten the incident next day. Welch, however, was one of those people who, though they look as if they were morally pachydermatous, really feel everything. He hated being laughed at. The result was that he nursed his grievance against Merevale until it became a sort of second nature to him to be at daggers drawn. That was the flaw in Welch's character, a character in other ways distinctly up to the average. He was inclined to sulk in these sorts of emergencies.

It was now nearing the end of the Easter term, and the air was thick with sports and rumours of sports. Welch was a fine runner. The mile was his distance, though, like most milers, he also dabbled in the half. He had the easy springy stride which marks the runner with a future as distinguished from the runner who does great things at school but nothing afterwards.

The interest of a school in its sports is generally rather in the prospective times than in the actual struggle for first place. It usually happens that one runner is first favourite, while the rest enter principally for the look of the thing and the chance of second prize. It was so with the mile. Given anything but the worst of bad luck, a sprained ankle or a fall, for instance, Welch could not help winning it. It only remained to see whether he would do a record. The record for the mile at St Austin's was an exceptionally good one – four forty-four and a fifth. Mitchell-Jones, afterwards president of the O.U.A.C., and winner of many and various desirable trophies on the track, was responsible for it. He had done it in his last year at school, ten years before, and nobody had come near it since. A respectable four fifty-eight or nine was the average time. Last year Drake of Dacre's house, with Thomson of Merevale's a foot behind, had covered the distance, amidst tremendous enthusiasm, in four minutes and forty-eight seconds. It was generally felt that this had reached the high-water mark. Then rumours began to be spread abroad about Welch's form. Two of the junior school had timed him surreptitiously before breakfast one morning, and he had done his mile in four forty-seven without turning a hair. In ordinary football clothes, too, not running clothes at all! The school allowed the usual discount necessary in dealing with junior-school statements, and resolved to keep its eye on Welch. He ran a mile three times a week, always before breakfast. On the third day after the two juniors had made their report, several seniors, sportsmen in whose eyes sport ranked before sleep, got up early with reliable watches, and strolled about until Welch appeared. A little group formed at the scratch to see him off, several enthusiasts pacing him for the last lap. Three stop-watches of unimpeachable reputation agreed on four forty-five as the time. As there was still a week before the sports it seemed almost certain that he would be able to rub off the last remaining second of Mitchell-Jones's time, and so hand his name down to eternal fame as the holder of the St Austin's mile record. The school was excited. Welch went to bed early on the night before the sports. He felt he owed it to the school to take no risks. For the past week Elliman's had flowed like water, pastry had been regarded with an aversion that amounted to loathing, and Mere-vale had even gone to the length of allowing him toast instead of bread, a great concession. Welch thought this a very graceful act on Merevale's part. He fell asleep that night wondering vaguely if he had not better make advances in the matter of the feud, and place matters once more on a peace footing.

He had been asleep four hours or more when he woke with a start. Somebody had entered his cubicle, and was shaking him by the shoulder. A hastily-formed impression that this was the advance guard of another dormitory making a midnight raid was dispelled by the rasping sound of a match on its box. Then it flared suddenly, and when his eyes had become accustomed to the light he saw that it was Merevale. Merevale, in pyjamas and a Balliol blazer, with a look on his face so ghastly that it woke Welch far more effectively than the shaking had done.

'Welch,' whispered Mr Merevale, as the match gave a dying flicker.

'Yes, sir.'

'Get some clothes on. Get your running clothes on. Don't make a noise. I don't want the rest of the dormitory to wake. Then come to my study. And be quick. Don't make a noise.'

He stole silently out again. Welch heard him open the door which separated his private house from the boys' half. Then he began to dress in a dazed way, wondering all the time what was going to happen. It must be something important, or Merevale would hardly have dragged him out of bed like this at one o'clock. He had looked pretty bad, thought Welch. Why? And why running clothes? And why – a hundred things. Well, he would soon know.

He was not sorry to be out of the room and in the passage. There is always something very unpleasant and eerie in the sound of other people breathing heavily in the dark when one is awake oneself. Queer little moans and grunts and sighs were uttered from time to time as he groped for his running things and put them on. It was very cold, too. Altogether a most unpleasant situation. Why, why, why, he asked himself again.

Suddenly somebody began to talk in his sleep. The sound acted on Welch like an electric shock. He was surprised to find how near he had been to falling asleep again. He was quite awake now, and he made his way stealthily to Mr Merevale's study.

Merevale was waiting there for him. There was a candle burning on the table. It cast an indistinct light, and made the House-master's face look worse than ever.

'Welch,' said he, 'listen to me. Sit down. Now, in the first place, are you quite awake?'

This was exactly the question Welch had been asking of himself. Could he be awake?

'Yes, sir,' he said.

'Quite awake? Then listen to me. Welch, I am going to ask

you to do rather a big thing. Do you know where Doctor Adamson lives?'

Adamson was the doctor who ministered to St Austin's when it was sick or when it thought it was. He lived in the village, and from St Austin's to the village is just a mile by road. The road is well laid, and as nearly level as a road can be.

'Yes, sir,' said Welch. He began to understand dimly.

'You could find the house in the dark? Good. Then listen. I want you to run your very hardest to Adamson's and give him this note. Tell him to come at once. It's important. Very important.'

Welch's face became one large mark of interrogation. Mr Merevale explained.

'Marjorie is very ill. Diphtheria, we think.'

Welch was on his feet in a moment at that. Marjorie was Merevale's ten-year-old daughter. The house worshipped her to a man, and with reason, for the Mere Kid, as she was called, was a patriot and sportswoman to her small fingertips, and wore out vast supplies of gloves annually in applauding the doings of her house in the cricket and football fields.

'Your bicycle, sir?' he said.

'Punctured yesterday. Not another in the house.' Welch was silent.

'Can you do it in time? In another quarter of an hour it may be too late.'

Welch did what every other member of the house would have done. He held out his hand for the note.

'It's just twenty-five past,' said Merevale, as he let him out of the front door. 'Can you get there by half past?'

'Easily, sir,' said Welch, and started.

Doctor Adamson was returning from a night visit to a patient, when just as he reached the door of his house, he pulled up in blank astonishment. Down the road to the left, from the direction of St Austin's, a white figure was running at an extraordinary pace. The doctor's professional ear recognised the heavy breathing of a fine trained runner who has all but run himself out. For a moment he was profoundly puzzled.

'Training! At this time of night! Can't be. By Jove, he's making for my house. Must be something wrong.'

'Here,' he shouted, 'this way. I am Doctor Adamson, if you are after me.'

Welch wheeled round in the direction of the voice, and staggered up to the dog-cart. 'Note,' he gasped, 'Merevale'. He was terribly tired in spite of his training. 'Time?' he gasped.

The doctor whipped out his watch.

'The exact time is eighteen seconds to the half-hour. Half past one practically. Now, let's see what it's all about.'

He frowned as he read Merevale's letter. 'Diphtheria. H'm. Thinks it's diphtheria. Can't be anything else by the symptoms. Jump up, young man. We must hurry.'

But Welch could not move. He lay by the side of the road and panted. The doctor was a powerful man. He sprang down, and lifted him in his arms. It took him two minutes to carry him into the house and place him on a sofa. Then he returned to the dog-cart. He gathered up the reins again and turned the horse's head towards St Austin's.

Merevale was standing at the front door.

'That you, doctor?' he said. 'Thank God you were in. Come on quickly, man. She's worse.'

'How about the horse?' asked the doctor. 'He won't improve the flower beds if he gets on to them.'

'Never mind the flower beds. Let the beast roll in them if he wants to. This way.'

Doctor Adamson rose from his inspection of the patient, and turned to Merevale with a smile. 'I think it will be all right,' he said, 'I am in time by exactly five minutes.'

'I must be going back to my other patient now,' said the doctor an hour afterwards.

'Your other patient?'

'The runner.'

'Oh, Welch.'

'Welch is his name, is it? I used to know some Welches in Somersetshire. Wonder if it is the same family. I suppose you realise what you owe to him?'

'Yes, by Jove,' said Mr Merevale. 'If you will give me a lift, doctor, I'll come back with you now and see him.'

Welch did not break the record on sports day, as he was too knocked up to run at all, and the race went to Roberts, of Dacre's house, in the very mediocre time of five one. But he has the satisfaction of knowing that in his run that night he must have been a clear second inside Mitchell-Jones's historic time, making all allowances. The occasion is also kept green in his memory by a silver cup, the exact double of the school mile cup, which Merevale presented to him as a memento of the occasion.

Welch did better times after he left school, but, as he very justly observes, that was the best mile he ever did, or was ever likely to do.

And Merevale is of much the same opinion.

Life at St Austin's was rendered somewhat hollow and burdensome for Pillingshot by the fact that he fagged for Scott. Not that Scott was the Beetle-Browed Bully in any way. Far from it. He showed a kindly interest in Pillingshot's welfare, and sometimes even did his Latin verses for him. But the noblest natures have flaws, and Scott's was no exception. He was by way of being a humorist, and Pillingshot, with his rather serious outlook on life, was puzzled and inconvenienced by this.

It was through this defect in Scott's character that Pillingshot first became a detective.

He was toasting muffins at the study fire one evening, while Scott, seated on two chairs and five cushions, read *Sherlock Holmes*, when the Prefect laid down his book and fixed him with an earnest eye.

'Do you know, Pillingshot,' he said, 'you've got a bright, intelligent face. I shouldn't wonder if you weren't rather clever. Why do you hide your light under a bushel?'

Pillingshot grunted.

'We must find some way of advertising you. Why don't you go in for a Junior Scholarship?'

'Too old,' said Pillingshot with satisfaction.

'Senior, then?'

'Too young.'

'I believe by sitting up all night and swotting—'

'Here, I say!' said Pillingshot, alarmed.

'You've got no enterprise,' said Scott sadly. 'What are those? Muffins? Well, well, I suppose I had better try and peck a bit.'

He ate four in rapid succession, and resumed his scrutiny of Pillingshot's countenance.

'The great thing,' he said, 'is to find out your special line. Till then we are working in the dark. Perhaps it's music? Singing? Sing me a bar or two.'

Pillingshot wriggled uncomfortably.

'Left your music at home?' said Scott. 'Never mind, then. Perhaps it's all for the best. What are those? Still muffins? Hand me another. After all, one must keep one's strength up. You can have one if you like.'

Pillingshot's face brightened. He became more affable. He chatted.

'There's rather a row on downstairs,' he said. 'In the junior day-room.'

'There always is,' said Scott. 'If it grows too loud, I shall get in amongst them with a swagger-stick. I attribute half my success at bringing off late-cuts to the practice I have had in the junior day-room. It keeps the wrist supple.'

'I don't mean that sort of row. It's about Evans.'

'What about Evans?'

'He's lost a sovereign.'

'Silly young ass.'

Pillingshot furtively helped himself to another muffin.

'He thinks someone's taken it,' he said.

'What! Stolen it?'

Pillingshot nodded.

'What makes him think that?'

'He doesn't see how else it could have gone.'

'Oh, I don't— By Jove!'

Scott sat up with some excitement.

'I've got it,' he said. 'I knew we should hit on it sooner or later. Here's a field for your genius. You shall be a detective. Pillingshot, I hand this case over to you. I employ you.'

Pillingshot gaped.

'I feel certain that's your line. I've often noticed you walking over to school, looking exactly like a bloodhound. Get to work. As a start you'd better fetch Evans up here and question him.'

'But, look here—'

'Buck up, man, buck up. Don't you know that every moment is precious?'

Evans, a small stout youth, was not disposed to be reticent. The gist of his rambling statement was as follows. Rich uncle. Impecunious nephew. Visit of former to latter. Handsome tip, one sovereign. Impecunious nephew pouches sovereign, and it vanishes.

'And I call it beastly rot,' concluded Evans volubly. 'And if I could find the cad who's pinched it, I'd jolly well—'

'Less of it,' said Scott. 'Now, then, Pillingshot, I'll begin this thing, just to start you off. What makes you think the quid has been stolen, Evans?'

'Because I jolly well know it has.'

'What you jolly well know isn't evidence. We must thresh this thing out. To begin with, where did you last see it?'

'When I put it in my pocket.'

'Good. Make a note of that, Pillingshot. Where's your notebook? Not got one? Here you are then. You can tear out the first few pages, the ones I've written on. Ready? Carry on, Evans. When?'

'When what?'

'When did you put it in your pocket?'

'Yesterday afternoon.'

'What time?'

'About five.'

'Same pair of bags you're wearing now?'

'No, my cricket bags. I was playing at the nets when my uncle came.'

'Ah! Cricket bags? Put it down, Pillingshot. That's a clue. Work on it. Where are they?'

'They've gone to the wash.'

'About time, too. I noticed them. How do you know the quid didn't go to the wash as well?'

'I turned both the pockets inside out.'

'Any hole in the pocket?'

'No.'

'Well, when did you take off the bags? Did you sleep in them?'

'I wore 'em till bed-time, and then shoved them on a chair by the side of the bed. It wasn't till next morning that I remembered the quid was in them—'

'But it wasn't,' objected Scott.

'I thought it was. It ought to have been.'

'He thought it was. That's a clue, young Pillingshot. Work on it. Well?'

'Well, when I went to take the quid out of my cricket bags, it wasn't there.'

'What time was that?'

'Half past seven this morning.'

'What time did you go to bed?'

'Ten.'

'Then the theft occurred between the hours of ten and seven-thirty. Mind you, I'm giving you a jolly good leg-up, young Pillingshot. But as it's your first case I don't mind. That'll be all from you, Evans. Pop off.'

Evans disappeared. Scott turned to the detective.

'Well, young Pillingshot,' he said, 'what do you make of it?'

'I don't know.'

'What steps do you propose to take?'

'I don't know.'

'You're a lot of use, aren't you? As a start, you'd better examine the scene of the robbery, I should say.'

Pillingshot reluctantly left the room.

'Well?' said Scott, when he returned. 'Any clues?'

'No.'

'You thoroughly examined the scene of the robbery?'

'I looked under the bed.'

'*Under* the bed? What's the good of that? Did you go over every inch of the strip of carpet leading to the chair with a magnifying-glass?'

'Hadn't got a magnifying-glass.'

'Then you'd better buck up and get one, if you're going to be a detective. Do you think Sherlock Holmes ever moved a step without his? Not much. Well, anyhow. Did you find any foot-prints or tobacco-ash?'

'There was a jolly lot of dust about.'

'Did you preserve a sample?'

'No.'

'My word, you've a lot to learn. Now, weighing the evidence does anything strike you?'

'No.'

'You're a bright sort of sleuth-hound, aren't you! It seems to me I'm doing all the work on this case. I'll have to give you another leg-up. Considering the time when the quid disappeared, I should say that somebody in the dormitory must have collared it. How many fellows are there in Evans's dormitory?'

'I don't know.'

'Cut along and find out.'

The detective reluctantly trudged off once more.

'Well?' said Scott, on his return.

'Seven,' said Pillingshot. 'Counting Evans.'

'We needn't count Evans. If he's ass enough to steal his own quids, he deserves to lose them. Who are the other six?'

'There's Trent. He's a prefect.'

'The Napoleon of Crime. Watch his every move. Yes?'

'Simms.'

'A dangerous man. Sinister to the core.'

'And Green, Berkeley, Hanson, and Daubeny.'

'Every one of them well known to the police. Why, the place is a perfect Thieves' Kitchen. Look here, we must act swiftly, young Pillingshot. This is a black business. We'll take them in alphabetical order. Run and fetch Berkeley.'

Berkeley, interrupted in a game of Halma, came unwillingly.

'Now then, Pillingshot, put your questions,' said Scott. 'This is a black business, Berkeley. Young Evans has lost a sovereign—'

'If you think I've taken his beastly quid—!' said Berkeley warmly.

'Make a note that, on being questioned, the man Berkeley exhibited suspicious emotion. Go on. Jam it down.'

Pillingshot reluctantly entered the statement under Berkeley's indignant gaze.

'Now then, carry on.'

'You know, it's all rot,' protested Pillingshot. 'I never said Berkeley had anything to do with it.'

'Never mind. Ask him what his movements were on the night of the – what was yesterday? – on the night of the sixteenth of July.'

Pillingshot put the question nervously.

'I was in bed, of course, you silly ass.'

'Were you asleep?' enquired Scott.

'Of course I was.'

'Then how do you know what you were doing? Pillingshot, make a note of the fact that the man Berkeley's statement was confused and contradictory. It's a clue. Work on it. Who's next? Daubeny. Berkeley, send Daubeny up here.'

'All right, Pillingshot, you wait,' was Berkeley's exit speech.

Daubeny, when examined, exhibited the same suspicious emotion that Berkeley had shown; and Hanson, Simms, and Green behaved in a precisely similar manner.

'This,' said Scott, 'somewhat complicates the case. We must have further clues. You'd better pop off now, Pillingshot. I've got a Latin Prose to do. Bring me reports of your progress daily, and don't overlook the importance of trifles. Why, in *Silver Blaze* it was a burnt match that first put Holmes on the scent.'

Entering the junior day-room with some apprehension, the sleuth-hound found an excited gathering of suspects waiting to interview him.

One sentiment animated the meeting. Each of the five wanted to know what Pillingshot meant by it.

'What's the row?' queried interested spectators, rallying round.

'That cad Pillingshot's been accusing us of bagging Evans's quid.'

'What's Scott got to do with it?' enquired one of the spectators.

Pillingshot explained his position.

'All the same,' said Daubeny, 'you needn't have dragged us into it.'

'I couldn't help it. He made me.'

'Awful ass, Scott,' admitted Green.

Pillingshot welcomed this sign that the focus of popular indignation was being shifted.

'Shoving himself into other people's business,' grumbled Pillingshot.

'Trying to be funny,' Berkeley summed up.

'Rotten at cricket, too.'

'Can't play a yorker for nuts.'

'See him drop that sitter on Saturday?'

So that was all right. As far as the junior day-room was concerned, Pillingshot felt himself vindicated.

But his employer was less easily satisfied. Pillingshot had hoped that by the next day he would have forgotten the subject. But, when he went into the study to get tea ready, up it came again.

'Any clues yet, Pillingshot?'

Pillingshot had to admit that there were none.

'Hullo, this won't do. You must bustle about. You must get your nose to the trail. Have you cross-examined Trent yet? No? Well, there you are, then. Nip off and do it now.'

'But, I say, Scott! He's a prefect!'

'In the dictionary of crime,' said Scott sententiously, 'there is no such word as prefect. All are alike. Go and take down Trent's statement.'

To tax the prefect with having stolen a sovereign was a task at which Pillingshot's imagination boggled. He went to Trent's study in a sort of dream.

A hoarse roar answered his feeble tap. There was no doubt about Trent being in. Inspection revealed the fact that the prefect was working and evidently ill-attuned to conversation. He wore a haggard look and his eye, as it caught that of the collector of statements, was dangerous.

'Well?' said Trent, scowling murderously.

Pillingshot's legs felt perfectly boneless.

'*Well?*' said Trent.

Pillingshot yammered.

'*Well?*'

The roar shook the window, and Pillingshot's presence of mind deserted him altogether.

'Have you bagged a sovereign?' he asked.

There was an awful silence, during which the detective, his limbs suddenly becoming active again, banged the door, and shot off down the passage.

He re-entered Scott's study at the double.

'Well?' said Scott. 'What did he say?'

'Nothing.'

'Get out your note-book, and put down, under the heading 'Trent': 'Suspicious silence'. A very bad lot, Trent. Keep him under constant espionage. It's a clue. Work on it.'

Pillingshot made a note of the silence, but later on, when he and the prefect met in the dormitory, felt inclined to erase it. For silence was the last epithet one would have applied to Trent on that occasion. As he crawled painfully into bed Pillingshot became more than ever convinced that the path of the amateur detective was a thorny one.

This conviction deepened next day.

Scott's help was possibly well meant, but it was certainly inconvenient. His theories were of the brilliant, dashing order, and Pillingshot could never be certain who and in what rank of life the next suspect would be. He spent that afternoon shadowing the Greaser (the combination of boot-boy and butler who did the odd jobs about the School House), and in the evening seemed likely to be about to move in the very highest circles. This was when Scott remarked in a dreamy voice, 'You know, I'm told the Old Man has been spending a good lot of money lately...'

To which the burden of Pillingshot's reply was that he would do anything in reason, but he was blowed if he was going to cross-examine the Headmaster.

'It seems to me,' said Scott sadly, 'that you don't *want* to find that sovereign. Don't you like Evans, or what is it?'

It was on the following morning, after breakfast, that the close observer might have noticed a change in the detective's demeanour. He no longer looked as if he were weighed down by a secret sorrow. His manner was even jaunty.

Scott noticed it.

'What's up?' he enquired. 'Got a clue?'

Pillingshot nodded.

'What is it? Let's have a look.'

'Sh – h – h!' said Pillingshot mysteriously.

Scott's interest was aroused. When his fag was making tea in the afternoon, he questioned him again.

'Out with it,' he said. 'What's the point of all this silent mystery business?'

'Sherlock Holmes never gave anything away.'

'Out with it.'

'Walls have ears,' said Pillingshot.

'So have you,' replied Scott crisply, 'and I'll smite them in half a second.'

Pillingshot sighed resignedly, and produced an envelope. From this he poured some dried mud.

'Here, steady on with my table-cloth,' said Scott. 'What's this?'

'Mud.'

'What about it?'

'Where do you think it came from?'

'How should I know? Road, I suppose.'

Pillingshot smiled faintly.

'Eighteen different kinds of mud about here,' he said patronisingly. 'This is flower-bed mud from the house front-garden.'

'Well? What about it?'

'Sh – h – h!' said Pillingshot, and glided out of the room.

'Well?' asked Scott next day. 'Clues pouring in all right?'

'Rather.'

'What? Got another?'

Pillingshot walked silently to the door and flung it open. He looked up and down the passage. Then he closed the door and returned to the table, where he took from his waistcoat-pocket a used match.

Scott turned it over enquiringly.

'What's the idea of this?'

'A clue,' said Pillingshot. 'See anything queer about it? See that rummy brown stain on it?'

'Yes.'

'Blood!' snorted Pillingshot.

'What's the good of blood? There's been no murder.'

Pillingshot looked serious.

'I never thought of that.'

'You must think of everything. The worst mistake a detective can make is to get switched off on to another track while he's working on a case. This match is a clue to something else. You can't work on it.'

'I suppose not,' said Pillingshot.

'Don't be discouraged. You're doing fine.'

'I know,' said Pillingshot. 'I shall find that quid all right.'

'Nothing like sticking to it.'

Pillingshot shuffled, then rose to a point of order.

'I've been reading those Sherlock Holmes stories,' he said, 'and Sherlock Holmes always got a fee if he brought a thing off. I think I ought to, too.'

'Mercenary young brute.'

'It has been a beastly sweat.'

'Done you good. Supplied you with a serious interest in life. Well, I expect Evans will give you something – a jewelled snuff-box or something – if you pull the thing off.'

'*I* don't.'

'Well, he'll buy you a tea or something.'

'He won't. He's not going to break the quid. He's saving up for a camera.'

'Well, what are you going to do about it?'

Pillingshot kicked the leg of the table.

'*You* put me on to the case,' he said casually.

'What! If you think I'm going to squander—'

'I think you ought to let me off fagging for the rest of the term.'

Scott reflected.

'There's something in that. All right.'

'Thanks.'

'Don't mention it. You haven't found the quid yet.'

'I know where it is.'

'Where?'

'Ah!'

'Fool,' said Scott.

After breakfast next day Scott was seated in his study when Pillingshot entered.

'Here you are,' said Pillingshot.

He unclasped his right hand and exhibited a sovereign. Scott inspected it.

'Is this the one?' he said.

'Yes,' said Pillingshot.

'How do you know?'

'It *is*. I've sifted all the evidence.'

'Who had bagged it?'

'I don't want to mention names.'

'Oh, all right. As he didn't spend any of it, it doesn't much matter. Not that it's much catch having a thief roaming at large about the house. Anyhow, what put you on to him? How did you get on the track? You're a jolly smart kid, young Pillingshot. How did you work it?'

'I have my methods,' said Pillingshot with dignity.

'Buck up. I shall have to be going over to school in a second.'

'I hardly like to tell you.'

'Tell me! Dash it all, I put you on to the case. I'm your employer.'

'You won't touch me up if I tell you?'

'I will if you don't.'

'But not if I do?'

'No.'

'And how about the fee?'

'That's all right. Go on.'

'All right then. Well, I thought the whole thing over, and I couldn't make anything out of it at first, because it didn't seem likely that Trent or any of the other fellows in the dormitory had taken it, and then suddenly something Evans told me the day before yesterday made it all clear.'

'What was that?'

'He said that the matron had just given him back his quid, which one of the housemaids had found on the floor by his bed. It had dropped out of his pocket that first night.'

Scott eyed him fixedly. Pillingshot coyly evaded his gaze.

'That was it, was it?' said Scott.

Pillingshot nodded.

'It was a clue,' he said. 'I worked on it.'

I

Scott, of the School House, had an active mind. He disliked monotony in his life. He had to be kept merry and bright; and he seemed to look on the rest of the community more as a collection of entertainers than anything else.

Consequently it was not long before Pillingshot, revelling in the unaccustomed leisure which his successful quest of Evans's sovereign had won for him, found himself once more set to work. It is true that Scott had promised to let him off fagging for the rest of the term; but, then, Scott's ideas of what constituted fagging differed substantially from those held by Pillingshot. Only a week after the sovereign incident, for example, Scott had invited his ex-fag to tea. The tea was all right when it was ready; but it was Pillingshot who got it ready, Scott's new fag having apparently been given an afternoon off for some reason. It was Pillingshot who toasted the muffins, boiled the water, cut the bread, spread the butter, mixed the tea, and poured out. It was Scott who lay in a deck-chair with his feet on the window-sill and remarked that after all these picnic meals weren't half bad fun, and that one didn't really need a fag at all, because one could do the work just as well one's self. It was Scott, too, who, after the meal, asked Pillingshot to take a note for him over to Merevale's house, and on his way back, to look in at Gubby's in the High

Street and order a fresh tin of mixed biscuits. It is true that Scott made these requests as one boyhood's friend to another in a Dick-old-man-stand-by-me manner; but that did not alter the fact that Merevale's was a quarter of a mile from the School House, and Gubby's in the High Street a little over a mile from Merevale's. This sort of thing might not be fagging, but it was an excellent imitation of it.

As a result, Pillingshot had avoided Scott. He was not harsh with him in his mind. He still liked him. But he kept at a distance. It was not till Scott's fag arrived in the junior day-room with a message that Scott would like to see him that he had any dealings with him at all.

'Oh, dash,' said Pillingshot, who was busily engaged on a peculiarly futile bit of fretsawing, and resented being interrupted.

'What does he want?'

'I don't know. He just said ask you to come up.'

Despite his previous experience, Pillingshot could not help being a little gratified. It was not every junior who was 'asked to come up' by first-eleven men. Scott might have his faults, yes, but this chumminess was certainly complimentary.

'Oh, all right,' he said.

He found Scott in his deck-chair, reading a magazine.

'Hullo, young Pillingshot,' said Scott. 'Sit down. I want to have a talk with you. Did you write this story?'

'What?'

'There's a story in this magazine by a chap named Pillingshot. Not a bad story. I thought it must be you.'

'No,' said Pillingshot.

Scott turned the pages.

'Listen to this. "'Ah, Percy,' she said sadly, 'but where now shall I find rest?' He held out his hands. 'Here, Muriel, here in my heart.'" Surely that's you, young Pillingshot? No? I made certain it was. It seemed just your style. Some relation, anyhow?'

'Not that I know of. I never heard of him. May be a cousin or something.'

'Must be. The Pillingshot family simply drips with literary talent. Directly I saw you, I knew that you could write.'

'I've never done any.'

'Never mind. It's all there. I'm going to give you your chance. I'm going to start a paper, young Pillingshot, and you shall edit it.'

'What!'

'Do you know why people start papers? To fill obvious voids. You hunt about till you find an obvious void, and then you start your paper. I've been keeping my eyes open lately, and, as far as I can see, there's no paper in existence that devotes itself solely to attacking Henry's. So I'm going to start one.

'I would have started it sooner,' continued Scott. 'If ever there was an obvious void, this is it. But I couldn't find the right editor. I had to have someone who was not only crammed to the brim with brain, but who wouldn't mind taking a risk or two in the good cause. The Editor of *The Rapier* – that's what I'm going to call it – must combine the courage of the lion with the wisdom of the what-d'you-call-it. That's why I thought of you. You see, it's not only that Henry's will probably try to lynch you. There's Rudd, too. He's pretty certain to cut up rough.'

There was truth in this. Rudd, the head of the School House, was a serious-minded individual, who preferred peace to pictur-esqueness in his surroundings. He objected to the feud with Henry's, and had been known to smite the bellicose of his house hip and thigh for assaulting Henryites. And when Rudd smote, he smote as if he meant it, not as one playfully tapping. He was a man of muscle, in the gym six and secretary of football.

'I say!' said Pillingshot, alarmed.

'I knew you'd like the idea,' said Scott. 'Sit down at that table, and we'll hammer out a few rough ideas for number one.'

'But, I say, Scott, how about Rudd?'

'Oh, never mind Rudd. The chances are he won't see the paper. He lives in a world of his own, above all that kind of thing.'

'Yes, but—'

'Buck along, old chap,' said Scott. 'You'll find paper and pens there. Don't upset the ink. Ready? Now, to start off with, we shall want a well-written character-sketch of somebody in Henry's. Let's see. Greyson. Yes, he'll do to begin with. I'll dictate you a few things to say about Greyson.'

It was a remarkable phenomenon, the ease with which Scott could get people to do things for him. Pillingshot was as wax in his hands. He sat down at the table, and took up the pen.

II

The first number of *The Rapier* certainly made a sensation. The idea of an unofficial newspaper was not new at St Austin's. For some terms a publication entitled *The Glow-Worm* had been appearing, edited, though only a select few knew it, by Charteris, of Merevale's. But *The Rapier* differed in many respects from *The Glow-Worm*. In the first place it was presented free, not sold. Secondly, it was many degrees more scurrilous. *The Glow-Worm* was bright, but it was not militant. It simply aimed at being a readable version of the dull *Austinian*, the official organ of the school. It chronicled school events in a snappy way, but it never libelled anyone. *The Rapier* never did anything else. The fact that Henry's house was not popular in the school, for one of those mysterious reasons which make houses unpopular, helped to increase the favourable warmth of the new paper's reception. In the eleven o'clock interval on the day of publication, nearly everyone in and around the school shop had his jellygraphed copy. Henry's raved, to a man. And Pillingshot, overhearing Greyson's comments on the character-sketch, for the first time found his fears blended with a certain complacency. It was no small thing to be associated with such an epoch-making event, whatever the risks.

Scott's prediction that Rudd would not see the new paper was not borne out by the facts. The head of the house may have lived in a world of his own, above the common things of life, but when two-hundred-odd people round you are discussing a thing, it is not easy to avoid it. On the afternoon of the day of publication, Rudd entered Scott's study, a copy of *The Rapier* in his hand.

'I say, Scott,' he said. 'Seen this?'

Rudd was a solid, grave youth, who always looked a little mournful. The look of care on his face now was more marked than ever.

'What's that?' said Scott. '*The Rapier*? I did glance at it. It seemed to me to supply a long-felt want. Fill an obvious void, if you know what I mean.'

'I don't like it.'

'Don't like it? That's wrong with it?'

Rudd sat down.

'Of course it's been got up by somebody in this house,' he said.

'What makes you think that?'

'Well, you know we've got this row on with Henry's?'

'Row? Henry's?' Scott's face cleared. 'Of course, yes,' he said, 'I remember. I did hear something about some row.'

'This'll make it worse.'

'Not a bit of it,' said Scott. 'By showing Henry's exhibits how they appear to the casual outside observer, the paper will lead them to reform. Once they have reformed, we shall have no objection to them. The row will cease automatically.'

'That's all very well—' began Rudd.

'I should think it was.'

'All the same, this thing will have to be stopped.'

'Stopped!'

'Yes. It's causing no end of disturbance already. I've stopped two fights already between our kids and Henry's.'

'Why, weren't we winning?' queried Scott, interested.

'So I mean to find out who is running this rotten paper and stop it.'

Scott sat up.

'I know the man for you,' he said. 'Mind you, I don't agree with you about this business. I think it serves a useful end. Still, you're a good chap, and I'd like to do you a turn. So I'll put Pillingshot on to the case.'

'Who's Pillingshot?'

'Gracious, don't you know Pillingshot? The Human Bloodhound. Better known as the Boy Detective of Hanging Gulch. I'll send for him.'

Pillingshot, torn once again from his fretwork, appeared reluctantly. He wore a somewhat battered air. One of his eyes was closed.

'Hullo, young Pillingshot,' said Scott. 'What have you been playing at?'

'Some of those Henry's louts—'

'There you are,' said Rudd, pointing the moral. 'I told you so, Scott. Was it about this newspaper?' he said to Pillingshot.

Pillingshot nodded.

'That's just why I sent for you, Pillingshot,' said Scott. 'This is a black business. Like your eye. By the way, do you know Rudd? You may speak as freely before him as you would before me. Now—'

Rudd interrupted.

'It's nothing to rot about,' he said. 'It's a jolly serious business.'

'Who's rotting?' said Scott. 'You mustn't judge Pillingshot by appearances. He's chock full of the finest inductive reasoning. I'm going to put this case into your hands, Pillingshot. Who's running *The Rapier*? That's what you've got to find out. That's all. Run away and look for clues.'

'I wish you wouldn't fool about so, Scott,' said Rudd seriously, when the door had closed. 'I don't want the kids in the house to feel it's all no end of a rag, this *Rapier* business.'

'My dear chap, I'm not fooling about. Honestly, there's not another fellow in the house more likely to be able to spot our man than Pillingshot. You can't go hunting about to find him. It wouldn't do. Whereas a kid like Pillingshot, being in the thick of things and having no position to keep up, can find out all sorts of things.'

'There's something in that,' admitted Rudd.

'Of course there is. You leave the case to Pillingshot. He'll see you through.'

Rudd retired. Two minutes later Pillingshot's fretsawing was once more interrupted by a summons to his employer's presence.

'Come along, young Pillingshot,' said Scott, settling himself comfortably in his chair. 'This is no time for slacking. We must work. We must perspire. Having disarmed any suspicions which Rudd may have had, we can now get on to the business again. Sit down and let's start roughing out number two.'

'But, I say—'

'There's the pen,' said Scott, reaching out for another cushion, 'just by your hand. If you want more paper, there's some in the drawer.'

III

How long *The Rapier* would have flourished if it had been allowed an uninterrupted run is uncertain. Probably not very long, for Scott's was the sort of mind which soon gets bored with a thing, especially if a counter-attraction presents itself.

In Scott's case the counter-attraction was football. He was an established cricketer, a veteran of two years' standing in the first eleven, but at football he had yet to rise above third-fifteen colours. This season, however, there seemed an excellent chance of his securing one of the numerous vacancies in the first. All the forwards of the previous year, except Rudd, had left, and only four remained of last season's second-fifteen pack; so that Scott, who had ranked in the first three of the third, practised daily with the elect, and hoped for the best. He had played for the first fifteen in the two matches, and, as both had been won with some ease, there seemed no reason why he should not be given a place in the first school match, against Daleby.

It is probable, therefore, that *The Rapier* might have lost its powers of attraction for him after a while.

As a matter of fact, however, he was not given the opportunity of getting tired of it. With the appearance of its third number, fate abruptly stopped it.

The second number, while not creating the same sensation as the first, had been well received by the school, the character-sketch – this of Hammond, of Henry's – being admitted to be particularly happy. Everybody, outside Henry's, seemed anxious for the appearance of number three; and Scott, pleased with this public demand, proceeded to work his staff overtime in order to produce the next number during the same week. It was finished by tea-time on the Thursday.

Now, it so happened that Pillingshot was looking forward to an easy evening's work during preparation that Thursday. The form of which he was an ornament was doing Livy on the following day; and Pillingshot never prepared Livy. All great men have their peculiarities. Lord Roberts dislikes cats. Doctor Johnson used to tap every post he passed in the street. Pillingshot never prepared Livy.

Consequently, to lift an advance copy of the third number from the pile on the table was with him the work of a moment. He had all the affection for *The Rapier* in its jellygraphed form that other authors have for proof-sheets. To read a novel during preparation was too risky; but no master would suspect the slim *Rapier* of being unconnected with school work.

He took the thing into prep, therefore, and spent a very pleasant half-hour over it. Scott had certainly excelled himself. Pillingshot grinned expansively as he read.

It was these grins that undid him, and, in the end, caused the bright little journal to expire just as it had thoroughly gripped its public. Almost immediately opposite him, at the next table, sat Beale, one of the junior members of Henry's house – the very junior member, in fact, who had so maltreated the young journalist's eye on the appearance of *The Rapier*'s first number. Beale was in Pillingshot's form, and shared that youth's prejudice against preparing Livy. Having omitted to provide himself with any form of light literature, he was compelled, after playing paper-cricket till he wearied of the sport, to fill in the time by looking about the room and observing and brooding upon his neighbours.

After a few moments, his gaze, circling like a hawk, descended upon Pillingshot. This was due partly to the fact of the latter's position – he could look at him without turning in his seat – but principally to the fact that Pillingshot, to judge by his face, was evidently on to a good thing. Whatever his defects as a member of the social cosmos, Pillingshot seemed to Beale in one respect deserving of envy: he was not bored. For the space of thirty-five minutes, Beale gazed tensely at Pillingshot.

At the end of that period came the three minutes' interval which divided the two halves of evening preparation. During the interval, it was the custom of the workers to stroll about the room, chatting with friends and acquaintances till the voice of the master from the dais – preparation took place in the Great Hall – recalled them to their seats. Pillingshot was a confirmed stroller. He was always the first to leave his seat and the last to return to it.

On the present occasion, the signal to relax having been given, he sped to the further end of the hall, where he fell into earnest talk with a group of School House juniors. This was Beale's opportunity. He had seen Pillingshot slip whatever it was that he had been reading under the sheet of blotting-paper. He darted round his table, and, unobserved, commandeered the thing.

It was not immediately that he realised the full value of his capture. In his hurried flight, he had not had time to examine it. He had merely seen that it was not, as he had fancied, a half-penny comic weekly. Not till the interval was over did he attempt a perusal.

When he did, his first feeling was one of keen disappointment. After all this trouble it was only that rotten rag, *The*

Rapier. Then, suddenly, a certain unfamiliarity in the reading matter struck him. He had read the second number of the paper with unwilling thoroughness; and this was all different. Then he saw in the top right-hand corner the words 'Number Three'; and realised for the first time the magnitude of his discovery. Ever since the new paper had started, the brains of Henry's had been exercised as to the identity of the man behind it. The evidence supported the theory that somebody in the School House was running it, but beyond that point, the investigators had not gone.

But now, argued Beale, a hot scent had been struck. If Pillingshot was in a position to get hold of advance copies of the journal, then he must also be in a position to give information as to the journal's source. He did not suspect Pillingshot, for whose mental powers he entertained a vast contempt, of being the author; but he was certain that he must know who the author was.

After school on the following afternoon, Rudd called on Scott. Scott was not altogether unprepared for the visit. It followed naturally on the one paid him the previous night by Pillingshot. He had surmised that Rudd, on reflection, would suspect his hand in this matter.

He welcomed the head of the house warmly. 'Come in, Rudd,' he said. 'How well you were running at the footer-practice just now. Like a mustang.'

Rudd sat down, turning a deaf ear to this flattery.

'I say, Scott.'

'Well?'

'I want to have a word with you.'

'Say on. This study is open for having words in, at about this hour.'

'It's about this *Rapier* thing.'

'A bright little sheet. I read it regularly.'

'Do you write it? That's more to the point.'

'Write it! What on earth makes you think that?'

Rudd's manner became portentous.

'I'll tell you what makes me think it. That kid Pillingshot was found reading an advance number of the thing in prep last night. A kid in Henry's collared the paper—'

'So Henry's is a hot-bed of theft, too, is it?' sighed Scott. 'Well, well, I must make a note of that for the next number.'

Rudd jumped at the admission.

'So it *is* you?' he cried.

'I see no reason to hide the fact. I'm proud of it. I'm the only public-spirited man in the school, bar young Pillingshot, of course. For years the slackness of public opinion has allowed Henry's to flourish unchecked in our midst. But I have altered all that. No, no,' he went on deprecatingly, as Rudd started to speak. 'I want no thanks. I have only tried to do my duty.'

Rudd got up.

'You may have meant well,' he said. 'I don't say the thing wasn't funny. But I'm jolly glad it's stopped.'

Scott's eyebrows rose.

'Stopped?' he said. 'I don't understand. You don't imagine it has stopped, do you?'

'What!' cried Rudd, pausing on his way to the door, 'surely you aren't going on with it?'

'My dear chap, it's just turned the corner. You novices don't understand these things. We of the old Fleet Street gang, brought up from our youth in the newspaper business, take them more seriously. Do you realise what it means to found a paper – the expense, the months of brain-fag, the worry?' He reached behind him, and produced the jellygraph machine. 'Look at our expensive plant. You can't expect us to abandon that simply to humour some casual whim of yours. It isn't reasonable.'

Rudd was silent for a moment. He seemed to be thinking. When he spoke, his manner was rather ominously quiet.

'You mean that?' he said.

'Rather. Of course, I'd like to oblige you—'

'Keeps you pretty busy, this sort of thing, I suppose?'

'The brain-work is practically incessant.'

Rudd nodded.

'I thought so. It must be.'

He paused.

'When does the next number come out?'

'Tomorrow. It's all ready now.'

'Too late to shove in a short notice?'

'Won't it stand over for Number Four?'

'No. It's topical.'

'What's it about?'

Rudd went to the table, and scribbled a few words on a sheet of paper.

'I'll read it to you. "Owing to the pressure of his journalistic work J. G. Scott will be unable to play for the first fifteen against Daleby." Could you put that in?'

There was a long silence.

Rudd spoke.

'It's official,' he said. 'I was talking to Stopford this morning' – Stopford was captain of football at St Austin's – 'and he's going to give up the captaincy so as to be able to put in more work. He's trying for a schol. at Cambridge, you know, at the end of the term. So I'm captain now. You'll see it on the notice-board tomorrow. I thought I'd let you know in advance.'

'Thanks,' said Scott, meditatively. 'Thanks.'

Rudd moved to the door.

'Well, so long,' he said.

'Half a minute,' said Scott. 'On second thoughts I'm not sure that the sedentary life of the journalist is quite in my line. After all, footer's much healthier, isn't it? Sit down and have some tea. We ought to lick Daleby this year, don't you think?'

Locksley

It was the hottest day on record. The day on which the cele-brated American engine-driver was obliged to sit inside his furnace in order to keep cool must have been warm; but it could not have been warmer than this. The thermometer had been going up steadily for hours. It had been high at the end of morn-ing school. During the dinner-hour it had risen. Lying under the trees you could see a sort of dancing haze over the cricket-field, as if the earth were smoking. And now at three o'clock it was worse than ever.

The Upper Fifth struggled painfully across the cloisters, keep-ing as much as possible in what little shade was thrown by the pillars. They were due at M. Gautier's room at the top of the middle block for their French lesson. From under the trees at the other side of the cricket-field came the raucous voice of the school sergeant, who was engaged in putting a junior form through its drill. Somehow the sound seemed to intensify the heat.

In the middle block it was cool. But the Upper Fifth had got so warm by the time they reached it, that they barely noticed the difference. They lurched into M. Gautier's room and sank languidly into their places, where they sat, looking as if all they wanted was to be left alone. Surely the man wasn't going to be brute enough to try and do any work that afternoon? Given absolute peace and full permission to doze, they might, they felt, just manage to scrape through till four o'clock. Otherwise they could not answer for the consequences.

But the French master, a brown, dried-up little man, who looked as if he had spent a lifetime in the tropics, was sternly determined to waste no time.

'Dictée!' he said crisply.

The form looked stupefied. Not *dictation* with the thermometer at a hundred and eighty or thereabouts, in the shade! It was an outrage. He must be joking. He couldn't expect a chap to write on a day like that. They took up their pens in disgust. Ten minutes' dictation reduced the Upper Fifth to pulp. The leisurely translation of Erckmann-Chatrian's *L'Invasion*, which followed, came as a boon and a blessing, except to the unfortunates who had to stand up and translate. The rest of the form leaned back comfortably in their seats, and composed themselves for slumber.

Jackson, who sat next to the open door, was better off than the others. All the windows of the form room were open, and he got the benefit of the cooling breezes thus created. But even with this advantage it was sufficiently baking. The voice of the sergeant sounded faintly from without, but now it not only made the air seem warmer, but suggested somehow how cool it must be under those trees, or better still, in the pond.

One of the features of Locksley School grounds was the pond. It was an idyllic spot, and the thought of it was maddening on an afternoon like this. This pond stood in the middle of a thick clump of trees at the pavilion end of the cricket-field. Its waters, though not deep – about four feet in the middle – were clear as crystal, owing to the fact that a stream ran through it to the river which divided the school from the town.

It would be very pleasant, thought Jackson, to be in the pond. Locksley, as a rule, bathed in the river; but somehow even the river's attractions paled at this moment before those of the pond.

To put a finishing touch on the thing, his next-door neighbour asked him at this point if he was coming to the river after school.

Jackson's mind was made up. At all costs he must go and have a bathe in the pond immediately. If he were expelled for it on his return he must, nevertheless, go. His position next to the door favoured the scheme. All that it was necessary to do was to seize his opportunity.

He confided his intention to his neighbour, who, appropriately, threw cold water on it.

'You'll be an ass if you do,' was his criticism.

'Well, I'm going to,' said Jackson. 'I'm simply boiled. If I don't get cool soon I shall have a fit or something. I wish you'd shunt up more to the end of the form directly I've gone. Ten to one Gautier won't spot that there's anyone away.'

'All right. But I shouldn't advise you to.'

Jackson made no reply. His eyes were on the master.

His opportunity soon came. M. Gautier put Firmin on to translate. Firmin sat at the opposite end of the room so that the master turned his back on Jackson. It speedily became evident that M. Gautier would not have much attention to spare for the rest of the form. All his available stock must be lavished on Firmin, who was making perhaps as complete a hash of *L'Invasion* as mortal had ever done. M. Gautier's moustache bristled with horror. His manner and speech began to resemble those of a tragedian in his 'big scene'.

'Ah, no, no, my boy! No, no!'

Firmin looked up from his book in mild astonishment, as if he could hardly believe that he was wrong. Then, with the air of one who is always anxious to comply with even the most unreasonable request, he gave out another rendering of the sentence. M. Gautier writhed, dashed a hand across his brow, and spun round in his direction again.

Simultaneously Jackson shot silently out of the door, and began to creep downstairs. On the first landing he waited to see if there was going to be any hue and cry. If M. Gautier had discovered his absence, it would not be too late to return and smooth things over with some excuse.

'Ah, no, no, Fir-r-min, my boy! No, no!' from the class-room.

Jackson concluded that all was well. He continued his descent.

It was very pleasant out of doors, pleasanter perhaps because the pleasure was a stolen one. There was a world of difference between the look of the grounds now and their appearance twenty-five minutes ago. The thought of the pond lent a beauty even to the gravel.

From the middle block to the pond was a distance of about two hundred yards across very open country. He must look to it that no one saw him making for the pond. He wished he had had to approach it from the opposite side; for behind the pond, some dozen yards from the edge of the clump in which it stood, there began a deep belt of shrubbery, which ran all the way to the end of the grounds. It was separated from the high road by a wooden fence of moderate height.

This shrubbery, trackless to the uninitiated, had no secrets for Jackson. When a fag he had ranged through it from end to end with a delightful sense of secrecy and Robin Hood-cum-Fenimore-Cooper's-Indian daredevilry; and, though he had not entered it since time had brought discretion and a place in the eleven, he was confident that he still knew it through and through.

But, since this ideal approach was out of the question, he must risk the open way. After all, everybody was in school, so that there was no one to see him. The sergeant and his junior drillers had moved, in the execution of some intricate and probably brilliant manœuvre, to the football ground at the other side of the shrubbery. He could hear the sergeant urging them on to glory or death in a voice that sounded faint and metallic, as of one speaking in a gramophone.

He made his dash. All went well. He arrived at the clump streaming but jubilant, and stood panting by the edge of the pond. How cool the water looked, and how clear. He remembered reading somewhere, or being told by someone, that it was very bad for you to go into the water in a state of perspiration. You ought to cool down first. Or was it that, if you were in a state of perspiration, it was very bad for you to cool down before going to the water? He could not remember. Both seemed probable. By way of settling the matter he flung himself out of his clothes, and slid into the pond.

Jackson had had some comfortable dips in his time. He could remember occasions when the river had been remarkably pleasant. The first bathe in Cove Reservoir, too, after the arrival of the school corps at Aldershot Camp – that had had its points. But for absolute and solid luxury this stolen wallow in the pond beat everything he had ever dreamed of. The only drawback was that, being stolen, it was not a bath which it would be advisable to prolong beyond a certain time. The longer he stayed away, the more likely was M. Gautier to notice his absence.

He tore himself reluctantly from the water and began to dress. Having no towel, he did not stop to dry himself, and it was fortunate for him that he did not.

He had reached a sort of half-way stage in his toilet – that is to say, the lower half of him was clothed, but he had still to don his shirt and coat – when he noticed with horror that somebody was coming towards the clump, and that person was Mr Knight, the master of the Lower Fifth.

Each form on the classical side at Locksley spent the last hour of afternoon school on two days in the week with its French master, and the regular master of the form was consequently off duty. The French days of the Upper and Lower Fifth coincided. The master of the Upper Fifth had taken himself off at three o'clock to the masters' garden at the back of the junior block. Mr Knight had done the same, but at half past three had suddenly been seized with the notion of trying the pond clump as a resting-place. It seemed to him that it would be so much cooler than the masters' garden. So he gathered up his novel and deck-chair and sallied forth.

For a moment Jackson was paralysed. The danger was so near, Mr Knight being only a few yards from the clump when he saw him, that it seemed hopeless to try and escape. Then he recollected the shrubbery, and determined to make a dash for safety. At the same time, it flashed across his mind that Mr Knight was short-sighted – at least, he wore spectacles. Possibly he might not recognise him, for he would only get a back view, and once on board the lugger, once in the shrubbery, and the situation was saved.

The result of these reflections was that the master, on entering the near side of the clump, was astonished to catch sight of a figure flitting rapidly away from the other side. The figure was clad as to its nether limbs in the grey flannels which nearly all the school wore during the hot weather. It was the upper half that struck Mr Knight as peculiar. A canvas shirt enveloped the head and beneath this he caught a glimpse of bare back. Over his arm the runner carried a blue flannel coat. Even as Mr Knight looked, the figure disappeared into the shrubbery.

'Extraordinary!' said Mr Knight to himself. 'Most extraordinary!'

He trotted round the pond and out of the clump. The excitement of the chase, instinct in the mildest of human beings, banished from his mind his desire for a comfortable seat in a cool spot. He went out into the sunshine, and hurried to the edge of the shrubbery.

Here he paused.

It was a little difficult to know what was the best thing to do next. He did not feel equal to probing the shrubbery in search of the fugitive. It was very thick, and he was disposed to think that there were insects in it, 'things with wings what stings'. Wasps even. No. The course to pursue here was to parley with the boy. He was certain on reflection that it was a boy, though he had not recognised him. Yes, a parley was the thing.

But how to begin was the question. No manual of polite conversation ever dealt with the problem. 'What to say to semi-naked strangers hidden in shrubberies.' He resolved to try a happy blend of command and statement of fact. 'Come out directly,' he cried. 'I can see you!'

'Liar!' murmured Jackson happily, wriggling into his shirt behind a bush.

'Come out, boy!'

Jackson, clothed now and in his right mind, did not hear the observation. He was half-way towards the fence, threading his way through the bushes with the ease of old acquaintanceship. At the fence he stopped, and peered round a bush to see how Mr Knight was faring. That gentleman had his back turned, and seemed to be still engaged in addressing the shrubbery. Jackson was over the fence and in the road in a couple of seconds.

It was a long way round by the road, but he re-entered the middle block in safety just as the quarter-to struck from the clock-tower. He trotted upstairs to M. Gautier's room, and there he received his second shock of the afternoon. The door was shut.

There are moments when the gamest man feels that there is nothing left to do but to throw up the sponge, Fate being too strong for him. That was how Jackson felt when he looked at the door which shut him out from the class-room. Anxious as he had been three-quarters of an hour before to get out, he was still more anxious now to get in.

I hope I have made it more or less clear that Jackson was a youth of some little resource. He proved himself so in this crisis.

He knocked at the door and opened it. M. Gautier glared at him from the desk. He did not seem to have enjoyed the last three-quarters of an hour. Firmin's translation on a hot afternoon was enough to drive any man distracted, especially an excitable man like the French master.

'Please, sir,' said Jackson humbly, 'may I come in now?'

M. Gautier continued to glare, as if he were trying without much success to recall the earlier portion of the lesson. When had he sent Jackson out of the room and why? His mind was a blank upon the matter.

'I will be very quiet, sir,' urged Jackson.

Royce, his next-door neighbour, caught on to the points of the idea with rapidity.

'Please, sir,' he said, 'it was really my fault. I think it would be only fair if you allowed Jackson to come in and sent me out instead.'

He rose as he spoke. M. Gautier looked bewildered. Then a solution of the problem occurred to him. The hot weather, brain-fag, and so on. He must have sent Jackson out of the room, and forgotten all about it; but it would never do to show that he had forgotten.

'Yes, come in, my boy; come in,' he said. Jackson came in.

'Really,' said Mr Knight for the third time that night, over a quiet pipe with Mr Ferguson in the latter's study, 'it was the most extraordinary thing. The boy went into the shrubbery. Of that I am positive. But I am equally positive that he never came out. It was an amazing thing, quite amazing. I waited and watched for nearly an hour, and I am certain that he did not come out.'

'Then,' said Mr Ferguson earnestly, 'he must be there still. Probably he was attacked with heat apoplexy and fell in his tracks. All you have to do is to see who has not returned to his house tonight, and the missing boy is your friend. You had better begin to make the round of the houses now.'

But Mr Knight did not move. His chair was comfortable, and his zeal for detective work decidedly abated.

'Nevertheless,' he said, 'it was a most extraordinary thing, most. And I am certain he did not come out of the shrubbery.'

Jackson was rather anxious for the next few days. He knew that Mr Knight was still puzzled about the 'extraordinary' sight he had seen by the pool, and Jackson feared that he might mention it in the presence of M. Gautier.

Had he done so, it was quite likely that M. Gautier would have brought his mind to bear upon a certain member of the Upper Fifth he was instructing that afternoon, who had timidly requested to be allowed to rejoin the class.

Fortunately for Jackson, M. Gautier was of a somewhat

reticent and timid disposition in the presence of his colleagues. Seldom did he converse with them. And it is certain that he would never have confessed – not even in his most talkative moments – that the heat had dealt him a scurvy trick. M. Gautier was particularly proud of his memory. Had he done so it is extremely probable that Mr Knight would have solved his problem. And having done so would, doubtless, have preferred to let the mystery remain a mystery.

Mr Knight was a sensitive little person and disliked very much having trouble with the boys, consequently he decided to let the matter drop and fortunately for Jackson, at any rate, the whole affair died a natural death.

Of all the useless and irritating things in this world, lines are probably the most useless and the most irritating. In fact, I only know of two people who ever got any good out of them. Dunstable, of Day's, was one, Linton, of Seymour's, the other. For a portion of one winter term they flourished on lines. The more there were set, the better they liked it. They would have been disappointed if masters had given up the habit of doling them out.

Dunstable was a youth of ideas. He saw far more possibilities in the routine of life at Locksley than did the majority of his contemporaries, and every now and then he made use of these possibilities in a way that caused a considerable sensation in the school.

In the ordinary way of school work, however, he was not particularly brilliant, and suffered in consequence. His chief foe was his form-master, Mr Langridge. The feud between them had begun on Dunstable's arrival in the form two terms before, and had continued ever since. The balance of points lay with the master. The staff has ways of scoring which the school has not. This story really begins with the last day but one of the summer term. It happened that Dunstable's people were going to make their annual migration to Scotland on that day, and the Head-master, approached on the subject both by letter and in person, saw no reason why – the examinations being over – Dunstable should not leave Locksley a day before the end of term.

He called Dunstable to his study one night after preparation.

'Your father has written to me, Dunstable,' he said, 'to ask that you may be allowed to go home on Wednesday instead of Thursday. I think that, under the special circumstances, there will be no objection to this. You had better see that the matron packs your boxes.'

'Yes, sir,' said Dunstable. 'Good business,' he added to himself, as he left the room.

When he got back to his own den, he began to ponder over the matter, to see if something could not be made out of it. That was Dunstable's way. He never let anything drop until he had made certain that he had exhausted all its possibilities.

Just before he went to bed he had evolved a neat little scheme for scoring off Mr Langridge. The knowledge of his plans was confined to himself and the Headmaster. His dorm-master would imagine that he was going to stay on till the last day of term. Therefore, if he misbehaved himself in form, Mr Langridge would set him lines in blissful ignorance of the fact that he would not be there next day to show them up. At the beginning of the following term, moreover, he would not be in Mr Langridge's form, for he was certain of his move up.

He acted accordingly.

He spent the earlier part of Wednesday morning in breaches of the peace. Mr Langridge, instead of pulling him up, put him on to translate; Dunstable went on to translate. As he had not prepared the lesson and was not an adept at construing unseen, his performance was poor.

After a minute and a half, the form-master wearied.

'Have you looked at this, Dunstable?' he asked.

There was a time-honoured answer to this question.

'Yes, sir,' he said.

Public-school ethics do not demand that you should reply truthfully to the spirit of a question. The letter of it is all that requires attention. Dunstable had *looked* at the lesson. He was looking at it then. Masters should practise exactness of speech. A certain form at Harrow were in the habit of walking across a copy of a Latin author before morning school. They could then say with truth that they 'had been over it'. This is not an isolated case.

'Go on,' said Mr Langridge.

Dunstable smiled as he did so.

Mr Langridge was annoyed.

'What are you laughing at? What do you mean by it? Stand up. You will write out the lesson in Latin and English, and show it up to me by four this afternoon. I know what you are thinking. You imagine that because this is the end of the term you can do as you please, but you will find yourself mistaken. Mind – by four o'clock.'

At four o'clock Dunstable was enjoying an excellent tea in Green Street, Park Lane, and telling his mother that he had had a most enjoyable term, marred by no unpleasantness whatever. His holidays were sweetened by the thought of Mr Langridge's baffled wrath on discovering the true inwardness of the recent episode.

When he returned to Locksley at the beginning of the winter term, he was at once made aware that the episode was not to be considered closed. On the first evening, Mr Day, his House-master, sent for him.

'Well, Dunstable,' he said, 'where is that imposition?'

Dunstable affected ignorance.

'Please, sir, you set me no imposition.'

'No, Dunstable, no.' Mr Day peered at him gravely through his spectacles. '*I* set you no imposition; but Mr Langridge did.'

Dunstable imitated that eminent tactician, Br'er Rabbit. He 'lay low and said nuffin'.

'Surely,' continued Mr Day, in tones of mild reproach, 'you did not think that you could take Mr Langridge in?'

Dunstable rather thought he *had* taken Mr Langridge in; but he made no reply.

'Well,' said Mr Day. 'I must set you some punishment. I shall give the butler instructions to hand you a note from me at three o'clock tomorrow.' (The next day was a half-holiday.) 'In that note you will find indicated what I wish you to write out.'

Why this comic-opera secret-society business, Dunstable wondered. Then it dawned upon him. Mr Day wished to break up his half-holiday thoroughly.

That afternoon Dunstable retired in disgust to his study to brood over his wrongs; to him entered Charles, his friend, one C. J. Linton, to wit, of Seymour's, a very hearty sportsman.

'Good,' said Linton. 'Didn't think I should find you in. Thought you might have gone off somewhere as it's such a ripping day. Tell you what we'll do. Scull a mile or two up the river and have tea somewhere.'

'I should like to awfully,' said Dunstable, 'but I'm afraid I can't.'

And he explained Mr Day's ingenious scheme for preventing him from straying that afternoon.

'Rot, isn't it,' he said.

'Beastly. Wouldn't have thought old Day had it in him. But I'll tell you what,' he said. 'Do the impot now, and then you'll be able to start at three sharp, and we shall get in a good time on the river. Day always sets the same thing. I've known scores of chaps get impots from him, and they all had to do the Greek numerals. He's mad on the Greek numerals. Never does anything else. You'll be as safe as anything if you do them. Buck up, I'll help.'

They accordingly sat down there and then. By three o'clock an imposing array of sheets of foolscap covered with badly-written Greek lay on the study table.

'That ought to be enough,' said Linton, laying down his pen. 'He can't set you more than we've done, I should think.'

'Rummy how alike our writing looks,' said Dunstable, collecting the sheets and examining them. 'You can hardly tell which is which even when you know. Well, there goes three. My watch is slow, as it always is. I'll go and get that note.'

Two minutes later he returned, full of abusive references to Mr Day. The crafty pedagogue appeared to have foreseen Dunstable's attempt to circumvent him by doing the Greek numerals on the chance of his setting them. The imposition he had set in his note was ten pages of irregular verbs, and they were to be shown up in his study before five o'clock. Linton's programme for the afternoon was out of the question now. But he loyally gave up any other plans which he might have formed in order to help Dunstable with his irregular verbs. Dunstable was too disgusted with fate to be properly grateful.

'And the worst of it is,' he said, as they adjourned for tea at half past four, having deposited the verbs on Mr Day's table, 'that all those numerals will be wasted now.'

'I should keep them, though,' said Linton. 'They may come in useful. You never know.'

* * *

Towards the end of the second week of term Fate, by way of compensation, allowed Dunstable a distinct stroke of luck. Mr Forman, the master of his new form, set him a hundred lines of Virgil, and told him to show them up next day. To Dunstable's delight, the next day passed without mention of them; and when the day after that went by, and still nothing was said, he came to the conclusion that Mr Forman had forgotten all about them.

Which was indeed the case. Mr Forman was engaged in editing a new edition of the *Bacchae*, and was apt to be absent-minded in consequence. So Dunstable, with a glad smile, hove the lines into a cupboard in his study to keep company with the Greek numerals which he had done for Mr Day, and went out to play fives with Linton.

Linton, curiously enough, had also had a stroke of luck in a rather similar way. He told Dunstable about it as they strolled back to the houses after their game.

'Bit of luck this afternoon,' he said. 'You remember Appleby setting me a hundred and fifty the day before yesterday? Well, I showed them up today, and he looked through them and chucked them into the waste-paper basket under his desk. I thought at the time I hadn't seen him muck them up at all with his pencil, which is his usual game, so after he had gone at the end of school I nipped to the basket and fished them out. They were as good as new, so I saved them up in case I get any more.'

Dunstable hastened to tell of his own good fortune. Linton was impressed by the coincidence.

'I tell you what,' he said, 'we score either way. Because if we never get any more lines—'

Dunstable laughed.

'Yes, I know,' Linton went on, 'we're bound to. But even supposing we don't, what we've got in stock needn't be wasted.'

'I don't see that,' said Dunstable. 'Going to have 'em bound in cloth and published? Or were you thinking of framing them?'

'Why, don't you see? Sell them, of course. There are dozens of chaps in the school who would be glad of a few hundred lines cheap.'

'It wouldn't work. They'd be spotted.'

'Rot. It's been done before, and nobody said anything. A chap in Seymour's who left last Easter sold all his stock lines by auction on the last day of term. They were Virgil mostly and Greek numerals. They sold like hot cakes. There were about five hundred of them altogether. And I happen to know that every word of them has been given up and passed all right.'

'Well, I shall keep mine,' said Dunstable. 'I am sure to want all the lines in stock that I can get. I used to think Langridge was fairly bad in the way of impots, but Forman takes the biscuit easily. It seems to be a sort of hobby of his. You can't stop him.'

But it was not until the middle of preparation that the great idea flashed upon Dunstable's mind.

It was the simplicity of the thing that took his breath away. That and its possibilities. This was the idea. Why not start a Lines Trust in the school? An agency for supplying lines at moderate rates to all who desired them? There did not seem to be a single flaw in the scheme. He and Linton between them could turn out enough material in a week to give the Trust a good working capital. And as for the risk of detection when customers came to show up the goods supplied to them, that was very slight. As has been pointed out before, there was practically one handwriting common to the whole school when it came to writing lines. It resembled the movements of a fly that had fallen into an ink-pot, and subsequently taken a little brisk exercise on a sheet of foolscap by way of restoring the circulation. Then, again, the attitude of the master to whom the lines were shown was not likely to be critical. So that everything seemed in favour of Dunstable's scheme.

Linton, to whom he confided it, was inclined to scoff at first, but when he had had the beauties of the idea explained to him at length, became an enthusiastic supporter of the scheme.

'But,' he objected, 'it'll take up all our time. Is it worth it? We can't spend every afternoon sweating away at impots for other people.'

'It's all right,' said Dunstable, 'I've though of that. We shall need to pitch in pretty hard for about a week or ten days. That will give us a good big stock, and after that if we turn out a hundred each every day it will be all right. A hundred's not much fag if you spread them over a day.'

Linton admitted that this was sound, and the Locksley Lines Supplying Trust, Ltd., set to work in earnest.

It must not be supposed that the agency left a great deal to chance. The writing of lines in advance may seem a very speculative business; but both Dunstable and Linton had had a wide experience of Locksley masters, and the methods of the same when roused, and they were thus enabled to reduce the element of chance to a minimum. They knew, for example, that Mr Day's favourite imposition was the Greek numerals, and that in nine cases out of ten that would be what the youth who had dealings with him would need to ask for from the Lines Trust. Mr Appleby, on the other hand, invariably set Virgil. The oldest inhabitant had never known him to depart from this custom. For the French masters extracts from the works of Victor Hugo would probably pass muster.

A week from the date of the above conversation, everyone in the school, with the exception of the prefects and the Sixth form, found in his desk on arriving at his form room a printed slip of paper. (Spiking, the stationer in the High Street, had printed it.) It was nothing less than the prospectus of the new Trust. It set forth in glowing terms the advantages offered by the agency. Dunstable had written it – he had a certain amount of skill with his pen – and Linton had suggested subtle and captivating additions. The whole presented rather a striking appearance.

The document was headed with the name of the Trust in large letters. Under this came a number of 'scare headlines' such as:

SEE WHAT YOU SAVE!

NO MORE WORRY!

PEACE, PERFECT PEACE!

Why Do Lines When We Do Them For You?

Then came the real prospectus:

The Locksley Lines Supplying Trust, Ltd. has been instituted to meet the growing demand for lines and other impositions. While there are masters at our public schools there will always be lines. At Locksley the crop of masters has always flourished – and still flourishes – very rankly, and the demand for lines has greatly taxed the powers of those to whom has been assigned the task of supplying them.

It is for the purpose of affording relief to these that the Lines Trust has been formed. It is proposed that all orders for lines shall be supplied out of our vast stock. Our charges are moderate, and vary between threepence and sixpence per hundred lines. The higher charge is made for Greek impositions, which, for obvious reasons, entail a greater degree of labour on our large and efficient staff of writers.

All orders, which will be promptly executed, should be forwarded to Mr P. A. Dunstable, 6 College Grounds, Locksley, or to Mr C. J. Linton, 10 College Grounds, Locksley. *Payment must be enclosed with order, or the latter will not be executed.* Under no conditions will notes of hand or cheques be accepted as legal tender. There is no trust about us except the name.

Come in your thousands. We have lines for all. If the Trust's stock of lines were to be placed end to end it would reach part of the way to London. You pay the threepence. We do the rest.

Then a blank space, after which came a few 'unsolicited testimonials':

'Lower Fifth' writes: 'I was set two hundred lines of Virgil on Saturday last at one o'clock. Having laid in a supply from your agency I was enabled to show them up at five minutes past one. The master who gave me the commission was unable to restrain his admiration at the rapidity and neatness of my work. You may make what use of this you please.'

'Dexter's House' writes: 'Please send me one hundred (100) lines from *Aeneid*, Book Two. Mr Dexter was so delighted with the last I showed him that he has asked me to do some more.'

'Enthusiast' writes: 'Thank you for your Greek numerals. Day took them without blinking. So beautifully were they executed that I can hardly believe even now that I did not write them myself.'

There could be no doubt about the popularity of the Trust. It caught on instantly.

Nothing else was discussed in the form rooms at the quarter to eleven interval, and in the houses after lunch it was the sole topic of conversation. Dunstable and Linton were bombarded with questions and witticisms of the near personal sort. To the latter they replied with directness, to the former evasively.

'What's it all *about*?' someone would ask, fluttering the leaflet before Dunstable's unmoved face.

'You should read it carefully,' Dunstable would reply. 'It's all there.'

'But what are you playing at?'

'We tried to make it clear to the meanest intelligence. Sorry you can't understand it.'

While at the same time Linton, in his form room, would be explaining to excited enquirers that he was sorry, but it was impossible to reply to their query as to who was running the Trust. He was not at liberty to reveal business secrets. Suffice it that there the lines were, waiting to be bought, and he was there to sell them. So that if anybody cared to lay in a stock, large or small, according to taste, would he kindly walk up and deposit the necessary coin?

But here the public showed an unaccountable disinclination to deal. It was gratifying to have acquaintances coming up and saying admiringly: 'You *are* an *ass*, you know,' as if they were paying the highest of compliments – as, indeed, they probably imagined that they were. All this was magnificent, but it was not business. Dunstable and Linton felt that the whole attitude of the public towards the new enterprise was wrong. Locksley seemed to regard the Trust as a huge joke, and its prospectus as a literary *jeu d'esprit*.

In fact, it looked very much as if – from a purely commercial point of view – the great Lines Supplying Trust was going to be what is known in theatrical circles as a frost.

For two whole days the public refused to bite, and Dunstable and Linton, turning over the stacks of lines in their studies, thought gloomily that this world is no place for original enterprise.

Then things began to move.

It was quite an accident that started them. Jackson, of Dexter's, was tea-ing with Linton, and, as was his habit, was giving him a condensed history of his life since he last saw him. In the course of this he touched on a small encounter with M. Gaudinois which had occurred that afternoon.

'So I got two pages of *Quatre-vingt-treize* to write,' he concluded, 'for doing practically nothing.'

All Jackson's impositions, according to him, were given him for doing practically nothing. Now and then he got them for doing literally nothing – when he ought to have been doing form-work.

'Done 'em?' asked Linton.

'Not yet; no,' replied Jackson. 'More tea, please.'

'What you want to do, then,' said Linton, 'is to apply to the Locksley Lines Supplying Trust. That's what you must do.'

'You needn't rot a chap on a painful subject,' protested Jackson.

'I wasn't rotting,' said Linton. 'Why don't you apply to the Lines Trust?'

'Then do you mean to say that there really is such a thing?' Jackson said incredulously. 'Why I thought it was all a rag.'

'I know you did. It's the rotten sort of thing you would think. Rag, by Jove! Look at this. Now do you understand that this is a genuine concern?'

He got up and went to the cupboard which filled the space between the stove and the bookshelf. From this resting-place he extracted a great pile of manuscript and dumped it down on the table with a bang which caused a good deal of Jackson's tea to spring from its native cup on to its owner's trousers.

'When you've finished,' protested Jackson, mopping himself with a handkerchief that had seen better days.

'Sorry. But look at these. What did you say your impot was? Oh, I remember. Here you are. Two pages of *Quatre-vingt-treize*. I don't know which two pages, but I suppose any will do.'

Jackson was amazed.

'Great Scott! what a wad of stuff! When did you do it all?'

'Oh, at odd times. Dunstable's got just as much over at Day's. So you see the Trust is a jolly big show. Here are your two pages.

That looks just like your scrawl, doesn't it? These would be four-pence in the ordinary way, but you can have 'em for nothing this time.'

'Oh, I say,' said Jackson gratefully, 'that's awfully good of you.'

After that the Locksley Lines Supplying Trust, Ltd. went ahead with a rush. The brilliant success which attended its first specimen – M. Gaudinois took Jackson's imposition without a murmur – promoted confidence in the public, and they rushed to buy. Orders poured in from all the houses, and by the middle of the term the organisers of the scheme were able to divide a substantial sum.

'How are you getting on round your way?' asked Linton of Dunstable at the end of the sixth week of term.

'Ripping. Selling like hot cakes.'

'So are mine,' said Linton. 'I've almost come to the end of my stock. I ought to have written some more, but I've been a bit slack lately.'

'Yes, buck up. We must keep a lot in hand.'

'I say, did you hear that about Merrett in our house?' asked Linton.

'What about him?'

'Why, he tried to start a rival show. Wrote a prospectus and everything. But it didn't catch on a bit. The only chap who bought any of his lines was young Shoeblossom. He wanted a couple of hundred for Appleby. Appleby was on to them like bricks. Spotted Shoeblossom hadn't written them, and asked who had. He wouldn't say, so he got them doubled. Everyone in the house is jolly sick with Merrett. They think he ought to have owned up.'

'Did that smash up Merrett's show? Is he going to turn out any more?'

'Rather not. Who'd buy 'em?'

It would have been better for the Lines Supplying Trust if Merrett had not received this crushing blow and had been allowed to carry on a rival business on legitimate lines. Locksley was conservative in its habits, and would probably have continued to support the old firm.

As it was, the baffled Merrett, a youth of vindictive nature, brooded over his defeat, and presently hit upon a scheme whereby things might be levelled up.

One afternoon, shortly before lock-up, Dunstable was surprised by the advent of Linton to his study in a bruised and dishevelled condition. One of his expressive eyes was closed and blackened. He also wore what is known in ring circles as a thick ear.

'What on earth's up?' enquired Dunstable, amazed at these phenomena. 'Have you been scrapping?'

'Yes – Merrett – I won. What are you up to – writing lines? You may as well save yourself the trouble. They won't be any good.'

Dunstable stared.

'The Trust's bust,' said Linton.

He never wasted words in moments of emotion.

'What!'

'"Bust" was what I said. That beast Merrett gave the show away.'

'What did he do? Surely he didn't tell a master?'

'Well, he did the next thing to it. He hauled out that prospectus, and started reading it in form. I watched him do it. He kept it under the desk and made a foul row, laughing over it. Appleby couldn't help spotting him. Of course, he told him to bring him what he was reading. Up went Merrett with the prospectus.'

'Was Appleby sick?'

'I don't believe he was, really. At least, he laughed when he read the thing. But he hauled me up after school and gave me a long jaw, and made me take all the lines I'd got to his house. He burnt them. I had it out with Merrett just now. He swears he didn't mean to get the thing spotted, but I knew he did.'

'Where did you scrag him?'

'In the dormitory. He chucked it after the third round.'

There was a knock at the door.

'Come in,' shouted Dunstable.

Buxton appeared, a member of Appleby's house.

'Oh, Dunstable, Appleby wants to see you.'

'All right,' said Dunstable wearily.

Mr Appleby was in facetious mood. He chaffed Dunstable genially about his prospectus, and admitted that it had amused him. Dunstable smiled without enjoyment. It was a good thing, perhaps, that Mr Appleby saw the humorous rather than the lawless side of the Trust; but all the quips in the world could not save the institution from ruin.

Presently Mr Appleby's manner changed. 'I am a funny dog, I know,' he seemed to say; 'but duty is duty, and must be done.'

'How many lines have you at your house, Dunstable?' he asked.

'About eight hundred, sir.'

'Then you had better write me eight hundred lines, and show them up to me in this room at – shall we say at ten minutes to five? It is now a quarter to, so that you will have plenty of time.'

Dunstable went, and returned five minutes later, bearing an armful of manuscript.

'I don't think I shall need to count them,' said Mr Appleby. 'Kindly take them in batches of ten sheets, and tear them in half, Dunstable.'

'Yes, sir.'

The last sheet fluttered in two sections into the surfeited waste-paper basket.

'It's an awful waste, sir,' said Dunstable regretfully.

Mr Appleby beamed.

'We must, however,' he said, 'always endeavour to look on the bright side, Dunstable. The writing of these eight hundred lines will have given you a fine grip of the rhythm of Virgil, the splendid prose of Victor Hugo, and the unstudied majesty of the Greek numerals. Good-night, Dunstable.'

'Good-night, sir,' said the President of the Locksley Lines Supplying Trust, Ltd.

Dunstable had his reasons for wishing to obtain Mr Montagu Watson's autograph, but admiration for that gentleman's novels was not one of them.

It was nothing to him that critics considered Mr Watson one of the most remarkable figures in English literature since Scott. If you had told him of this, he would merely have wondered in his coarse, material way how much Mr Watson gave the critics for saying so. To the reviewer of the *Weekly Booklover* the great man's latest effort, *The Soul of Anthony Carrington* (Popgood and Grooly: 6s.) seemed 'a work that speaks eloquently in every line of a genius that time cannot wither nor custom stale'. To Dunstable, who got it out of the school library, where it had been placed at the request of a literary prefect, and read the first eleven pages, it seemed rot, and he said as much to the librarian on returning it.

Yet he was very anxious to get the novelist's autograph. The fact was that Mr Day, his Housemaster, a man whose private life was in other ways unstained by vicious habits, collected autographs. Also Mr Day had behaved in a square manner towards Dunstable on several occasions in the past, and Dunstable, always ready to punish bad behaviour in a master, was equally anxious to reward and foster any good trait which he might exhibit.

On the occasion of the announcement that Mr Watson had taken the big white house near Chesterton, a couple of miles from the school, Mr Day had expressed in Dunstable's hearing a wish that he could add that celebrity's signature to his collection. Dunstable had instantly determined to play the part of a benevolent Providence. He would get the autograph and present it to the Housemaster, as who should say, 'see what comes of being good'. It would be pleasant to observe the innocent joy of the recipient, his child-like triumph, and his amazement at the donor's ingenuity in securing the treasure. A touching scene – well worth the trouble involved in the quest.

And there would be trouble. For Mr Montagu Watson was notoriously a foe to the autograph-hunter. His curt, type-written replies (signed by a secretary) had damped the ardour of scores of brave men and – more or less – fair women. A genuine Montagu Watson was a prize in the autograph market.

Dunstable was a man of action. When Mark, the boot-boy at Day's, carried his burden of letters to the post that evening there nestled among them one addressed to M. Watson, Esq., The White House, Chesterton. Looking at it casually, few of his friends would have recognised Dunstable's handwriting. For it had seemed good to that man of guile to adopt for the occasion the role of a backward youth of twelve years old. He thought tender years might touch Mr Watson's heart.

This was the letter:

Dear Sir – I am only a little boy, but I think your books ripping. I often wonder how you think of it all. Will you please send me your ortograf? I like your books very much. I have named my white rabit Montagu after you. I punched Jones II in the eye today becos he didn't like your books. I have spent the only penny I have on the stampe for this letter which I might have spent on tuck. I want to be like Maltby in 'The Soul of Anthony Carrington' when I grow up.

Your sincere reader,

P. A. DUNSTABLE

It was a little unfortunate, perhaps, that he selected Maltby as his ideal character. That gentleman was considered by critics a masterly portrait of the cynical roué. But it was the only name he remembered.

'Hot stuff!' said Dunstable to himself, as he closed the envelope.

'Little beast!' said Mr Watson to himself as he opened it. It arrived by the morning post, and he never felt really himself till after breakfast.

'Here, Morrison,' he said to his secretary, later in the morning: just answer this, will you? The usual thing – thanks and most deeply grateful, y'know.'

Next day the following was included in Dunstable's correspondence:

Mr Montagu Watson presents his compliments to Mr P. A. Dunstable, and begs to thank him for all the kind things he says about his work in his letter of the 18th inst., for which he is deeply grateful.

'Foiled!' said Dunstable, and went off to Seymour's to see his friend Linton.

'Got any notepaper?' he asked.

'Heaps,' said Linton. 'Why? Want some?'

'Then get out a piece. I want to dictate a letter.'

Linton stared.

'What's up? Hurt your hand?'

Dunstable explained.

'Day collects autographs, you know, and he wants Montagu Watson's badly. Pining away, and all that sort of thing. Won't smile until he gets it. I had a shot at it yesterday, and got this.'

Linton inspected the document.

'So I can't send up another myself, you see.'

'Why worry?'

'Oh, I'd like to put Day one up. He's not been bad this term. Come on.'

'All right. Let her rip.'

Dunstable let her rip.

Dear Sir – I cannot refrain from writing to tell you what an inestimable comfort your novels have been to me during years of sore tribulation and distress—

'Look here,' interrupted Linton with decision at this point. 'If you think I'm going to shove my name at the end of this rot, you're making the mistake of a lifetime.'

'Of course not. You're a widow who has lost two sons in South Africa. We'll think of a good name afterwards. Ready?

'Ever since my darling Charles Herbert and Percy Lionel were taken from me in that dreadful war, I have turned for consolation to the pages of "The Soul of Anthony Carrington" and—'

'What, another?' asked Linton.

'There's one called "Pancakes".'

'Sure? Sounds rummy.'

'That's all right. You have to get a queer title nowadays if you want to sell a book.'

'Go on, then. Jam it down.'

'—and "Pancakes". I hate to bother you, but if you could send me your autograph I should be more grateful than words can say. Yours admiringly.'

'What's a good name? How would Dorothy Maynard do?'

'You want something more aristocratic. What price Hilda Foulke-Ponsonby?'

Dunstable made no objection, and Linton signed the letter with a flourish.

They installed Mrs Foulke-Ponsonby at Spiking's in the High Street. It was not a very likely address for a lady whose blood was presumably of the bluest, but they could think of none except that obliging stationer who would take in letters for them.

There was a letter for Mrs Foulke-Ponsonby next day. Whatever his other defects as a correspondent, Mr Watson was at least prompt with his responses.

Mr Montagu Watson presented his compliments, and was deeply grateful for all the kind things Mrs Foulke-Ponsonby had said about his work in her letter of the 19th inst. He was, however, afraid that he scarcely deserved them. Her opportunities of deriving consolation from 'The Soul of Anthony Carrington' had been limited by the fact that that book had only been published ten days before: while, as for 'Pancakes', to which she had referred in such flattering terms, he feared that another author must have the credit of any refreshment her bereaved spirit might have extracted from that volume, for he had written no work of such a name. His own 'Pan Wakes' would, he hoped, administer an equal quantity of balm.

Mr Secretary Morrison had slept badly on the night before he wrote this letter, and had expended some venom upon its composition.

'Sold again!' said Dunstable.

'You'd better chuck it now. It's no good,' said Linton.

'I'll have another shot. Then I'll try and think of something else.'

Two days later Mr Morrison replied to Mr Edgar Habbesham-Morley, of 3a Green Street, Park Lane, to the effect that

Mr Montagu Watson was deeply grateful for all the kind things, etc. – 3a, Green Street was Dunstable's home address.

At this juncture the Watson-Dunstable correspondence ceases, and the relations become more personal.

On the afternoon of the twenty-third of the month, Mr Watson, taking a meditative stroll through the wood which formed part of his property, was infuriated by the sight of a boy.

He was not a man who was fond of boys even in their proper place, and the sight of one in the middle of his wood, prancing lightly about among the nesting pheasants, stirred his never too placid mind to its depths.

He shouted.

The apparition paused.

'Here! Hi! you boy!'

'Sir?' said the stripling, with a winning smile, lifting his cap with the air of a D'Orsay.

'What business have you in my wood?'

'Not business,' corrected the visitor, 'pleasure.'

'Come here!' shrilled the novelist.

The stranger receded coyly.

Mr Watson advanced at the double.

His quarry dodged behind a tree.

For five minutes the great man devoted his powerful mind solely to the task of catching his visitor.

The latter, however, proved as elusive as the point of a half formed epigram, and at the end of the five minutes he was no longer within sight.

Mr Watson went off and addressed his keeper in terms which made that worthy envious for a week.

'It's eddication,' he said subsequently to a friend at the Cowslip Inn. 'You and me couldn't talk like that. It wants eddication.'

For the next few days the keeper's existence was enlivened by visits from what appeared to be a most enthusiastic bird's-nester. By no other theory could he account for it. Only a boy with a collection to support would run such risks.

To the keeper's mind the human boy up to the age of twenty or so had no object in life except to collect eggs. After twenty, of course, he took to poaching. This was a boy of about seventeen.

On the fifth day he caught him, and conducted him into the presence of Mr Montagu Watson.

Mr Watson was brief and to the point. He recognised his visitor as the boy for whose benefit he had made himself stiff for two days.

The keeper added further damaging facts.

'Bin here every day, he 'as, sir, for the last week. Well, I says to myself, supposition is he'll come once too often. He'll come once too often, I says. And then, I says, I'll cotch him. And I cotched him.'

The keeper's narrative style had something of the classic simplicity of Julius Caesar's.

Mr Watson bit his pen.

'What you boys come for I can't understand,' he said irritably. 'You're from the school, of course?'

'Yes,' said the captive.

'Well, I shall report you to your Housemaster. What is your name?'

'Dunstable.'

'Your house?'

'Day's.'

'Very good. That is all.'

Dunstable retired.

His next appearance in public life was in Mr Day's study.

Mr Day had sent for him after preparation. He held a letter in his hand, and he looked annoyed.

'Come in, Dunstable. I have just received a letter complaining of you. It seems that you have been trespassing.'

'Yes, sir.'

'I am surprised, Dunstable, that a sensible boy like you should have done such a foolish thing. It seems so objectless. You know how greatly the Headmaster dislikes any sort of friction between the school and the neighbours, and yet you deliberately trespass in Mr Watson's wood.'

'I'm very sorry, sir.'

'I have had a most indignant letter from him – you may see what he says. You do not deny it?'

Dunstable ran his eye over the straggling, untidy sentences.

'No, sir. It's quite true.'

'In that case I shall have to punish you severely. You will write me out the Greek numerals ten times, and show them up to me on Tuesday.'

'Yes, sir.'

'That will do.'

At the door Dunstable paused.

'Well, Dunstable?' said Mr Day.

'Er – I'm glad you've got his autograph after all, sir,' he said.

Then he closed the door.

As he was going to bed that night, Dunstable met the House-master on the stairs.

'Dunstable,' said Mr Day.

'Yes, sir.'

'On second thoughts, it would be better if, instead of the Greek numerals ten times, you wrote me the first ode of the first book of Horace. The numerals would be a little long, perhaps.'

Oh, woman, woman!

As somebody once said. I forget who.

Woman, always noted for serpentine snakiness, is perhaps more snakily serpentine at the age when her hair is wavering on the point of going up, and her skirts hesitating on the brink of going down than at any other moment in her career. It is then most of all that she will bear watching. Take, for example, Scott's sister. Which brings me to my story.

Charteris first made the acquaintance of Scott's sister when Scott asked him home to spend the last week of the Easter holidays with him. They were in different houses at Locksley, Scott being a member of the School House, while Charteris was in Merevale's; but as they were both in the first eleven they saw a good deal of one another. In addition, Charteris frequently put in an evening in the winter and Easter terms at those teas which Scott gave in his study, where the guests did all the work, and the host the greater part of the feeding. So that it came as no surprise when be received the invitation.

He hesitated about accepting it. He was a wary youth, and knew that scores of school friendships have died an untimely death owing to one of the pair spending part of the holidays at the other's home. Something nearly always happens to disturb the harmony. Most people are different in the home circle, and the alteration is generally for the worse. However, things being a little dull at home with illness in the house, and Scott's letter mentioning that there was a big lawn with a cricket net, where they could get into form for next term, he decided to risk it.

The shades of night were beginning to fall when the train brought Charteris to his destination.

Looking up and down the platform he could see no signs of his host. Former instances of his casualness, for which quality Scott was notorious, floated across his mind. It would be just like him to forget that his guest was to arrive that day.

The platform gradually emptied of the few passengers who had alighted. He walked out of the station, hoping to find a cab which would convey him to Scott's house.

'I say,' said a voice, as he paused outside and looked round about him.

Through the gathering dusk he could see the dim outline of a dog-cart.

'Hullo,' he said.

'Are you Charteris?'

'Somebody's been telling you,' said he in an aggrieved voice. His spirits had risen with a bound at the prospect of getting to his destination at last.

'Jump in, then. I thought you couldn't have come. I was just going to drive off.'

'Don't talk of it,' said Charteris.

'Billy couldn't come to meet you. He had to get the net down. You mustn't leave it up all night. The gardener's boy is a perfect idiot and always gets it tangled up. So he sent me. Have this rug. Is the box all right? Then gee up, Peter. Good-night, Mr Brown.'

'Good-night, miss,' said the station-master affably. Charteris examined her out of the corner of his eyes. As far as he could see through the darkness she was pretty. Her hair was in the transition stage between mane and bun. It hung over her shoulders, but it was tied round with a ribbon. He had got thus far with his inspection when she broke the silence.

'I hope you'll like our wicket,' she said. 'It's slow, as there's a good deal of moss on the lawn, but it plays pretty true. Billy smashed a bedroom window yesterday.'

'He would,' said Charteris. The School House man was the biggest hitter at Locksley.

'What do you think of Billy as a bat?' asked the lady turning to face him.

'He can hit,' said Charteris.

'But his defence isn't any good at all, is it? And he's nervous before he gets started, and a man who goes in for a forcing game oughtn't to be that, ought he?'

'I didn't know he was nervous. He's not got that reputation at school. I should have thought that if there was one chap who went in without caring a bit about the bowling, it was Scott.'

It surprised him in a vague sort of way that a girl should have such a firm and sensible grasp on the important problems of life. He had taken his sister to Lord's one summer to watch the Gentlemen v. Players match, and she had asked him if the sight screens were there to keep the wind off the players. He had not felt really well since.

'Oh, no,' said the girl. 'He's as jumpy as a cat. He's often told me that it all depends on the first ball. If he can hit that, he's all right. If he doesn't he's nervous till he gets out or slogs a four. You remember his seventy-one against the MCC last year. He managed to get Trott round past mid-on for three the first ball.

After that he was as right as anything. Against Haileybury, too, when he made fifty-four. He didn't see his first ball at all. He simply slogged blindly, and got it by a fluke, and sent it clean into the pavilion.'

'Did you see those games?' enquired Charteris, amazed.

'No. Oh, how I wish I had. But I make Billy promise faithfully when he goes back to school that he'll write me a full account of every match. And he does it, too, though those are about the only letters he does write. He hates writing letters. But he's awfully good about mine. I love cricket. Billy says I'm not half a bad bat. Here we are.'

The dog-cart swung into a long drive, at the end of which a few lighted windows broke the blackness. A dog barked inside the house as they drove up, and rushed out as the door opened and Scott's drawl made itself heard.

'That you, Charteris?'

'It looks like me, doesn't it?' said Charteris, jumping down.

'How many times has Molly spilt you on the way here?' enquired Scott.

'I drove jolly well,' protested his sister with indignation. 'Didn't I?'

'Ripping,' said Charteris.

'It's very decent of you to hush it up,' said Scott. 'Come along in and brush some of the mud off.'

Charteris woke abruptly on the following morning at twenty-three minutes and eight seconds past seven. What woke him was a cricket ball. It hummed through the open window, crashed against the opposite wall – an inch lower and an engraving of 'The Fallowfield Hunt' would have needed extensive alterations and repairs – and, after circling round the room, came to a standstill under the chest of drawers. Charteris hopped out of bed and retrieved it.

'I say,' said a penetrating voice from the regions of the drive.

Charteris put on a blazer and looked out. Scott's sister was standing below. She held a bat in her hand. In the offing lurked a shirt-sleeved youth whom he took to be the gardener's boy. He was grinning sheepishly. Across the lawn stood the net and wickets.

'Hullo, are you awake?' enquired Molly.

'More or less,' said Charteris.

'Did you see a ball come in just now?'

'I thought I noticed something of the sort. Is this it?'

She dropped the bat, and caught the descending ball neatly. Charteris looked on with approval.

'I'm sorry if it disturbed you,' said Miss Scott.

'Not at all,' said Charteris. 'Jolly good way of calling people in the morning. You ought to take out a patent. Did you hit it?'

'Yes.'

'Rather a pull,' said Charteris judicially.

'I know – I can't help pulling. It runs in the family. Billy will do it, too. Are you coming out?'

'Ten minutes,' said Charteris. 'Shall I do some bowling for you?'

The lady expressed surprise.

'Can you bowl?' she said.

'Trumble isn't in it,' replied Charteris. 'It's an education to watch my off-break.'

'They never put you on in first matches.'

'That,' said Charteris, 'is because they don't know a good thing when they see one.'

'All right, then. Don't be long.'

'Well,' said Molly half an hour later, as the gong sounded for breakfast and they walked round to the door, 'I think your bowling's jolly good, and I don't know why they don't give you a chance for the first. Still, you couldn't get Billy out, I don't think.'

'Billy!' said Charteris. 'As a matter of fact, Billy is a gift to me. He can't stand up against my stuff. When he sees my slow hanging ball coming he generally chucks down his bat, hides his face in his hands, and bursts into tears.'

'I'll tell him that.'

'I shouldn't,' said Charteris. 'Don't rub it into the poor chap. We all have these skeletons in our cupboards.'

Molly regarded him seriously.

'Do you know,' she said, 'I believe you're very conceited?'

'I've been told so,' replied Charteris complacently, 'by some of the best judges.'

The dining-room was empty when they arrived. The Scott family was limited to Molly, her brother, and Mrs Scott, who was a semi-invalid and generally breakfasted in bed. Colonel Scott had been dead some years.

Molly made the tea in a business-like manner, and Charteris was half-way through his second cup when his host strolled in. Scott had been known to come down in time for the beginning of breakfast, but he did not spoil a good thing by doing it too often.

'Slacker,' said Charteris, 'we've been up and out for an hour.'

'What do you think of the wicket?'

'Very good. Miss Scott—'

'You can call me Molly if you like,' interrupted that lady, biting a section out of a healthy slab of bread and butter.

'Thanks,' said Charteris. 'Molly has got that stroke of yours to the on. She pretty nearly knocked a corner off the house with it once.'

'Molly is always imitating her elders and betters,' replied her brother. 'At a picnic last summer—'

'Billy, stop! You're not to.'

'Now, I can't do the dashing host, and make the home bright and lively,' said Scott complainingly, 'if you go interrupting my best stories. Molly went to a picnic – grown-up affair – last summer. Wanted to be taken for about ten years older than she is.'

'Be quiet, Billy.'

The story became jerky from this point, for the heroine was holding the narrator by the shoulders from behind, and doing her best to shake him.

'So,' continued Scott, 'she turned up the collar of her jacket, and shoved – shoved her hair underneath it. See? Looked as if it was up instead of down her back. Palled up with another girl. Other girl began talking about dances and things. "Oh," said Molly. "I haven't been out a great deal lately." After a bit it got so hot that Molly had to take off her jacket, and down came the hair. "Why," said the other girl, "you're only a child after all!"'

And Scott, who had been present at the massacre, howled with brotherly laughter at the recollection.

Molly looked across at Charteris with flaming cheeks. Charteris's face was grave and composed. This, he felt, was not the place to exhibit a sense of humour.

'I don't see the joke,' said Charteris. 'I think the other girl was a beast.'

Charteris found a note on his dressing-table when he went to his room that night.

It was a model of epistolary terseness. 'Thanks awfully for not laughing,' it ran.

Charteris went back to Locksley at the end of the Easter holidays fit both in body and mind. In the first card match, against the local regiment, he compiled a faultless eighty-six. The wretched Scott, coming to the crease second wicket down outwardly confident but inwardly palpitating, had his usual wild swing at his first ball, and was yorked.

A long letter from Molly arrived in the course of the next week. Apparently Scott sent her details of all the matches, not only of those in which he himself had figured to advantage. One sentence in the letter amused Charteris. 'I'm sorry I called you conceited about your bowling. I asked Billy after you had gone, and he said he was more afraid of you till he got set than of anyone else in the school.' This was news to Charteris. Like many people who bat well he had always treated his bowling as a huge joke. He bowled for the house first change, but then Merevale's were not strong in that department. Batting was their speciality. It had never occurred to him that anyone could really be afraid of his strange deliveries. And Scott of all people, who invariably hit him off after three overs! It was good news, however, for the School House was Merevale's chief rival in the house matches, and Scott was the School House star performer. If there was a chance of his being too much for Scott, then Merevale's should win the cup.

The house matches at Locksley were played on the knocking-out system. And this year a great stroke of luck befell Merevale's. The only other house with any pretensions to the cup, Dacre's, drew the School House for their first match. The School House won, Scott making a hundred and two in an hour. And it was now evident that the cup lay between Merevale's and the School House. These two easily disposed of their opponents and qualified for the final.

There was much discussion in the school on the merits of the two teams. The general impression was that Merevale's would fail for want of bowling. Scott, it was thought, ought to have a day out against the inferior bowling of Merevale's. If he got out early, anything might happen, for Merevale's had the strongest batting side in the school.

Then it was that Charteris went to Venables, the captain of Merevale's, on the evening before the match.

'Look here, Venables,' he said. 'I'll start by saying I'm not ragging, or you might have your doubts. I want you to put me on tomorrow when Scott comes in. Whoever's bowling, take him off, and give me an over. I shall only want one. If I can't get him in that, I shan't get him at all.'

'Have you developed a new ball?' enquired Venables. It was Charteris's habit to announce every other day that he had developed a new ball. He was always burlesquing his bowling.

'Don't rag,' said Charteris earnestly. 'I'm quite serious. I mean it. I happen to know that Scott's in a funk for his first over, and that my rotten stuff worries him till he gets set. You might give me a shot. It can't do any harm.'

'You really aren't pulling my leg?'

'I swear I'm not. Of course, it's a million to one that I shan't get him out, but it's quite true that he doesn't like my bowling.'

'I don't wonder,' said Venables. 'It's uncanny stuff. All right.'

'Thanks,' said Charteris.

We now come to that portion of the story which more particularly illustrates the truth of the profound remarks, with which it began, on the serpentine snakiness of woman. Coming down to breakfast on the day of the match, Charteris saw a letter by the side of his plate. It was from Molly.

Their correspondence had become, since her first letter, quite voluminous. Writing to Molly was like talking to a sympathetic listener. No detail of a match or of school gossip was too small to interest her; and when, as he had been doing frequently that term, he made a fifty or even a century, there was no need for him to slur modestly over the feat; he was expected to describe it vividly from beginning to end.

The bulk of the letter was not unusual. It was in the postscript that, like most feminine letter-writers, she had embodied her most important words. Charteris re-read them several times before the colossal awfulness of them dawned upon him.

This was the postscript:

'Now I want you to do me a favour. I wish you would. Poor old Billy is quite cut up about his luck this season. You know how badly he has done in matches. That century against Dacre's is the only really good thing he's done at all. *Can't* you give him an easy ball when the School House play you? I don't mean to hit, but just so that he doesn't get out. He told me that he hated your bowling, and he *is* so nervous in his first over. Do! It *is* such hard lines on him making ducks, and I'm awfully fond of him. So you will, won't you? P.P.S. – If you do, you shall have that photograph you wanted. The proofs have just come back, and they are *very* good. I like the one best where I've got my hair sort of done up.'

Charteris did not join the usual after-breakfast gathering of house prefects in Venables' study that morning. He sat in his own den, and pondered. At a quarter to nine he might have been overheard to murmur a remark.

'And that,' he murmured, 'is the girl I thought really understood the finer points of cricket!'

It is a pity that the Problem Story has ceased to be fashionable. I should have preferred this narrative to have ended at the above point. As it is, I must add two quotations – one from the school magazine, the other from a letter from Miss Molly Scott to Charteris. *Place aux dames.* Here is the extract from the letter:

'I am sending the photograph. I hope you will like it.'

And here is the quotation from the magazine:

'W. L. Scott, b Charteris 0; c Welch, b Charteris 2.'

Beckford

I

It was while playing cricket that I saw Blenkinsop – for the first time for seven years. I was on tour with the Weary Willies (that eminent club!), and a combination of circumstances had brought us to a village in Somersetshire which you will not find on the map. Our captain, a mere child in the art of tossing – which requires long and constant practice before a man can become really proficient at it – called 'Heads' when it was perfectly obvious that the coin was going to come down tails, and, the wicket being good, our opponents selfishly elected to take first knock.

One of the first pair was Blenkinsop. I did not recognise him at first, but when he shaped to face my first ball – I was on at one end – his identity became certain. No two human beings in this vale of sorrow could stand like that. Blenkinsop's batting attitude had once been the joy of his peers at Beckford, and the despair of the professional who looked after the junior cricket. He had much of the easy *abandon* of a cat in a strange garret – right leg well away from the bat, to facilitate flight towards the umpire in the event of a speedy yorker on the toes, left knee bent, body curved in a graceful arc over the handle of the bat. It was Blenkinsop all the way.

For old times' sake I sent him down a long hop to leg. Any

ordinary person would have put it joyfully out of the county. Blenkinsop was no ordinary person. He steered it very gently away for a single, and trotted up to my end.

'Hullo, Blenkinsop,' I said.

'Hul*lo*!'

The progress of the game was interrupted for a few minutes, while he shook hands.

'Fancy seeing you!' he said; 'Great Scott, why, it's years since we met. Nearly ten. By Jove. I am glad to see you. Come round to my place after the match. I'm curate here, you know, and getting on splendidly.'

The batsman at the other end, who had been standing for some time in batting attitude, patiently waiting for the next ball, now gave the thing up, sat down with a resigned expression, and began to talk to the wicket-keeper. Mid-on lay down and apparently went to sleep, and short slip retired to the pavilion for one more gin and ginger beer. These phenomena had not the slightest effect on Blenkinsop.

'What are you doing now?' he continued. 'Have you seen any old Beckfordians lately? Do you remember—?'

Here mid-off asked the umpire to wake him if necessary and lay down like his colleague on the leg-side. The voice of the Weary Willies' captain, a slightly irascible person, made itself heard from the deep field, full of recriminations and enquiries. I thought I had better go on bowling, and did so. The next ball took a wicket, a fact which the batsman attributed audibly to the awful suspense in which he had been kept for the last five minutes, and I had leisure for some more Blenkinsopic conversation.

It was at this point that he asked me if I remembered his benefit.

'Do you remember Perkyn that night?' he said.

I did. Blenkinsop's benefit stands out in my mind as the cheeriest memory of my school career. And there were some stirring episodes in that career. The affair of Mr Stoker and the dog (which is 'another story') had caused me no little enjoyment. The episode of Tudway and the superannuated apple (I must tell you about that some time) had been not unamusing. But Blenkinsop's benefit, in my humble opinion, defied competition.

The juniors of Jephson's house were always rather a clannish lot. In my time we formed quite a close corporation. We walked together, and brewed together. We were most of us in the same form. I think now that they ought to have paid the master who took that form something extra, for his lot was certainly not cast in a pleasant place. There was Benson, for instance, a perfect prince of raggers, whose methods baffled detection, and Nicholas, second only to Benson. Perkyn, too, and Inge, and, indeed, all of us – we were all full of spirits.

Of this corporation Blenkinsop was a distinguished member. He had not the brilliance of a Benson, or the fertility of invention in the matter of excuses which characterised Inge, but he did his best, and showed clearly that he meant well. And there was no doubt that he was very popular with the rest of us.

It was with consternation, therefore, that we received the news one afternoon that at the end of term he was to leave us.

It appeared that Blenkinsop was to go for a couple of years to France, then to Germany for another year. Finally, if he survived this sentence, he would go up to Oxford, and become a clergyman. The idea of Blenkinsop as a clergyman had a marked effect on the company.

'But, look here, man,' said Benson, 'you can't leave. It's rot. Why, who's to umpire in the junior house match next term if you go? We shall probably have to have Jephson!'

This was an awful thought. The sustained success of Jephson's house junior team was largely due – and we recognised it – to the really magnificent umpiring of Blenkinsop.

Blenkinsop's was one of those beautifully emotional natures which cannot turn a deaf ear to an appeal for lbw in the mouth of a friend. Alas! such natures are rare indeed, and Jephson's was distinctly not one of them. There was once an umpire who claimed proudly that he never forgot which side he was umpiring for. Jephson was the exact antithesis of that conscientious sportsman.

'Besides,' said Inge, 'you're so young. What's the good of leaving when you're not fifteen yet? Why, if you stopped on, you might get your first.'

The idea of Blenkinsop figuring in the first eleven – unless they smuggled him in as an umpire – had the good effect of restoring the company to cheerfulness, and the conversation turned to less gloomy topics.

It was some days after this that I received a note in school. The bottom part of it had been freshly smeared with ink for the convenience of the reader, but I was up to this conventional pleasantry, and handled the letter with caution. It was short, and ran as follows:

Dear Sir – Your presence is earnestly requested at a meeting of the Blenkinsop Benefit Society this evening at six sharp over the Gym.

> We are, dear Sir,
> Yours, &c.,
> JAMES BENSON
> (Hon. Sec. B.B.Soc.)

P.S. – Don't tell Blenkinsop about it as we want to keep it dark. Answer, R.S.V.P., if you please.

I replied that I would be there, and of the style and nature of the Blenkinsop Benefit Society I was soon made aware.

All our set, with the exception of Blenkinsop, had assembled at the gymnasium. Benson addressed the meeting.

'You see,' he said, 'it's awful rot about old Blenk leaving, and all that sort of thing, so I thought we might do something to testify – er – that is to er—'

'To testify to our esteem?' I suggested. 'That's the idea,' said Benson, gratefully, '— testify to our esteem.'

Nicholas wanted to know what was the exact meaning of the expression. 'Why, give him a send-off, of course, you idiot,' said Benson.

'Then why don't you say so?'

'I think,' continued Benson, ignoring the interruption, 'we ought to have a regular bust-up in his honour. We'll put that to the vote. That this meeting approves of the proposal to give Blenkinsop a send-off. Ayes to the right, noes to the left.'

Everybody stood still, and Benson announced that the motion had been carried nem. con.

'Well, the next thing,' he went on, 'is the tin. How are we going to manage about that?'

'Hang it all,' Inge protested, 'you surely aren't going to give him a set of silver tea-things, or anything of that sort?'

'No, what I was thinking of was a dormitory supper!'

Unrestrained applause on the part of the audience.

'But we aren't all in Blenk's dorm,' said Smith.

'Doesn't matter. You can buck out of your dorm when the prefect's asleep. Admission on presentation of a visiting-card.'

'That sounds all right. What time is the thing coming off?'

'We'd better have it the last Saturday of term. That's a fortnight from tomorrow.'

'No, I mean what *time*?'

'Oh, about five o'clock I should think. That'll be early enough.'

'Oh yes, rather.'

'It will be a scene of unrestrained revelry,' observed Benson, prophetically – a remark which elicited another objection, this time from Inge.

'How about Norris?' he asked.

Norris was the prefect who presided with an uncomfortably firm hand over the destinies of Blenkinsop's dormitory.

'I thought of that,' he said, 'ages ago. Norris's people have just taken a house near Horton for the holidays, and he has got leave to spend the last weekend of term there. I was standing close by when he asked the Old Man.

'But they may shove someone else in instead of him,' said Inge.

'They won't. Or even if they do, it'll only be Mainwaring, or somebody like that, who won't mind what we get up to so long as we don't make too much row about it. And, I say, there's one thing we must remember. We must lie awfully low for the next fortnight, at any rate, in the dorm. The less we rag the less likely it is that anybody will be put into the dorm when Norris is away. If they think that we can get on all right by ourselves, they'll let us. See?'

We saw.

'That's all right, then. Now, about the money again. How much can we raise?'

Money, as they say on 'Change, was rather tight. Towards the end of term one's purse is never very heavy. There are so many things that one must buy; those luxuries, as somebody says, which are so much more necessary than necessities – buns at the quarter to eleven interval, potted meat for tea, and so on. However, in cash and promises of cash we managed to scrape together about six shillings, which Benson, who in addition to acting as secretary had modestly assumed the treasurership of the society, thought might almost be enough. And it was resolved that every member should write home and attempt, by specially representing himself on the verge of starvation, and compiling an excursus on the type of food we got at Jephson's as a rule, to extract money from the parental coffers. This, said Benson, might or might not come off. If it did, we should have a Simple Beano (I quote his own classic expression). If not – well, we should have to get along as best we could with what we had already. A true philosopher, Benson.

Then somebody – Lucas, that was the man – made a brilliant suggestion.

'Look here,' he said, 'if Norris is going to be away two nights, why not have two busts instead of one? Have the supper on the second night, and something in the assault-at-arms line on the first. We might get up a boxing comp, or something.'

Here Lucas, a passionate devotee of the Ring, shaped at an imaginary opponent, and delivered the left hook at the jaw with what would, in all probability, have been immense precision.

'Ripping,' said Benson. 'That's what we'll do. Only we mustn't have anything that'll make too much row. Well, that's all, I think. We might draw up some programmes in the meantime, and don't you chaps forget to write to your people. Say grub will do if they can't send money. Only money preferred, of course.'

'Of *course*,' we echoed as one man, and the meeting broke up.

II

The next fortnight was dull. Very dull. Benson insisted on the members of the society lying low, with a strictness worthy of Norris. The consequence was that we behaved in form, and gave up stump cricket in the junior day-room, and in many other ways deprived ourselves of much (more or less) innocent pleasure. The only one of us who declined to alter his mode of life was Blenkinsop. He could not understand it at all, and Benson refused to allow us to explain. He said it would be much better to spring the great news suddenly on the favoured youth than to let him know beforehand what honours the future had in store for him. So Blenkinsop continued to be disorderly in a lonely, dazed sort of way, and complained bitterly at intervals that the glory had departed from Jephson's junior day-room.

'I say,' he said to me one morning, 'what on earth is the matter with you chaps? Why didn't any of you back me up in maths this morning?'

'Oh, I don't know,' I said, 'one doesn't always feel in form for ragging, somehow.' A revolutionary sentiment, which made Blenkinsop open his eyes and wonder what the world was coming to.

Meanwhile the preparations for the festivities went on apace. Inge managed to extract five shillings from an uncle, and an aunt of mine sent me one and six. After adding these and other subscriptions to the fund, Benson was able to announce officially that not only would there be enough for a Simple Beano, but it would also be possible to offer prizes in the preliminary assault-at-arms on the first night. Enthusiasm ran high at the news.

About a week before the date of the performance, the programmes were circulated. I still have one in my possession, very dirty and dog-eared, but still readable. It would be trespassing on the kindness of the reader to quote it in *extenso*. Suffice it to say that nearly every branch of sport was represented, from boxing to ping-pong, and that an elaborate menu of the banquet was embodied in it. This last was a distinct work of art, and a credit to Benson's imaginative talents. It concluded with apt quotations from the works of Mr W. S. Gilbert, a particular protégé of Benson's, such as:

'Gentlemen, will you allow us to offer you a magnificent banquet?'

'Cut the satisfying sandwich, broach the exhilarating Marsala, and let us rejoice today if we never rejoice again.'

'Tell me, major, are you fond of toffee?'

'Today he is not well.'

There were a good many more.

The spot event, so to speak, of the banquet would, according to the programme, be a case of pineapples – none of your tinned imitations, but real! Perkyn's brother from the West Indies was sending them over. Perkyn had just received a letter from him, informing him that the case would arrive next week. Keen anxiety was felt as to whether it would come in time. The moment had now arrived when all should be revealed to Blenkinsop. Benson did it in a touching speech, in which he dwelt so long and fondly on the departing one's sterling qualities, now as a ragger, now as an umpire, that that youth almost broke down. And when Benson reminded us how, against Leicester's last year, he had given their two best men out lbw and caught at the wicket in the first over, and so won us the match in the most handsome style, there was not a dry eye in the house.

'It's awfully good of you chaps,' observed Blenkinsop, on being called on to reply, 'and I tell you what.'

'What?' we asked.

'They're having a house sing-song on Saturday evening, and as our dorm's the largest, they're going to hold it there. If we have luck they may leave the piano in the room till the next morning, and if anybody can play, we might have a bit of a rag.'

Roars of applause, during which Nicholas owned up to being able to play some waltz tunes. This news plunged the meeting into a tremendous state of enthusiasm. Everybody liked waltz tunes, a few knew how to dance, and all were very certain that they were going to dance, whether they knew how to or not. It was agreed that the assault-at-arms, which would be over by – say – half past six, should conclude with a grand concert. Could Nicholas play anything else? Rather. All sorts of things. Inge knew a comic song or two. I could play the bones. It was evident that the proceedings would not fall flat for lack of musical talent. The only thing was – would the piano be left? While we were still in doubt on this important point the case of pineapples arrived. It was a good large case. We decided not to open it 'till the night'.

The day came. The concert went off splendidly. We were always more or less in form at these sing-songs, and on this occasion I suppose we made as much noise as any dozen juniors of our weight and age in the kingdom could have done. It was an idiosyncrasy of ours to make noise. We were of opinion that everyone who wished to leave the world a brighter and happier place for his presence in it should adopt some speciality, and make himself a thorough master of it. Our speciality was noise. Benson's prohibition of ragging was felt not to apply to an end of term dormitory concert. To prevent us enjoying ourselves at that would have been to have struck a deadly blow at the inalienable rights of the citizen. Such a blow we were determined to prevent, and Benson, seeing the force of our arguments, was wise enough to allow us to take our own way. We took it.

And the piano was left after all. Jephson and the prefects did think of moving it, but they decided not to.

It was about seven the next morning before proceedings re-commenced. At that hour I awoke, with a hastily-formed impression that I was drowning, to find Nicholas, with every appearance of keen enjoyment, squeezing water into my mouth from a large and evidently very full sponge.

'Buck up,' he said, encouragingly, 'we're two hours late as it is.'

'Why, what's the time?'

'Seven. And we ought to have begun at five. Come and help me get these chaps up.'

I seized my sponge, plunged it into the jug, and in less than two minutes the dormitory was awake.

Once begun, affairs marched rapidly. We cleared a space by moving the beds back along the walls, and opened the entertainment with a little football under Association rules. I am happy to say that I led my side to victory in a style that would have done credit to a captain of England. Three times in the first moiety did I put the sponge-bag under the chest of drawers, and twice after half-time did it hurtle from my toe and crash against the door. I have seldom played a finer game. We won by five goals to one, and the one was a fluke.

Lucas got the boxing, and the ping-pong – played on the floor with a tennis-ball and hairbrushes, a cricket-bag acting as a net – fell to Blenkinsop, a popular victory. In fact, everything went splendidly, until at seven-fifty, the purely athletic portion of the entertainment being over, we began on the music. That was fatal. Chapel at Beckford is at eight on Sunday mornings, and such were the ensnaring qualities of Nicholas's playing – with the soft pedal down to minimise the volume of sound – that the bell rang while we were still at it, as if we had had the whole of the day before us. We stopped, and stared at one another blankly.

'I didn't know it was half so late,' said Inge.

Benson rose to the occasion as usual.

'Well,' he said, 'there's one thing pretty certain, we can't get to chapel in time. We're bound to be too late to get in. So I votes we don't try to. We can't get into any worse row than we're in at present. Forge ahead with the music, Nick.'

He turned to Inge with a brilliant smile.

'My dance, I think,' he said.

A couple of seconds later the ball was in progress once more. As I have had occasion to remark before, a true philosopher, Benson.

III

'Lines,' said Inge, as we left Jephson's presence after a painful interview some two hours later, 'are the beastliest nuisance ever invented. And they don't do you any good, either. They only spoil your handwriting, and then you get more lines because they say they can't read your work.'

Jephson, always the soul of generosity, had given us three hundred lines apiece for our morning's manœuvres. If we so much as breathed during the remainder of the term, he had hinted, he should make a point of enlisting the crude but effective aid of the flagellum.

I think we would all have preferred such a course on this occasion. Jephson's canes – the brown one particularly – stung like adders, but he rarely gave you more than six, and though a touching-up is undoubtedly painful while it lasts (and a little longer, perhaps), it is soon over. Whereas with lines – but the subject is too melancholy.

Inge had come particularly badly out of the business. The rest of us had received our sentence with quiet resignation. Inge, on the other hand, had perceived a chance of scoring off the Bench. 'Please, sir,' he asked, 'can I do mine out of Homer?'

'I shall be disappointed if you do not, Inge,' replied Jephson, politely. 'With the accents, of course.' 'Accents!' thought Inge, 'what's the man driving at?' Then in a flash he saw his hideous mistake. He had meant to say Horace, not Homer. Horace, sensible man, foreseeing that in some future century lines would be invented, turned out a certain quantity of his work in verses with about half a dozen syllables in them, a boon to the line writer. Homer, on the other hand, not only wrote in Greek, but wrote the longest possible lines he could. Three hundred lines of Homer are equivalent to about double the number of Virgil, the man one usually goes to for lines.

'I meant Horace, sir,' said Inge, hastily.

Jephson waved aside the suggestion.

'Homer will do equally well, Inge,' he said, and the interview terminated.

Benson took a more cheerful view of things. This may have been due to his dauntless spirit, or possibly the reflection that he had in his desk some eight hundred lines, written in odd moments and stocked against such a day as this, may have comforted him. He looked on the bright side.

'After all,' he said, 'we haven't got it nearly as hot as I thought we should have done. And there's no doubt that we're giving Blenk a ripping good send-off.'

There we admitted that he was right.

'All the same,' he continued, 'perhaps under the circumstances we ought to run as few risks as possible till the end of term. If we're late for chapel again there'll be no end of a row. So I think, instead of having the supper at five tomorrow morning, we'd better have it at twelve tonight. Jephson will have finished his rounds by then, and there won't be any danger if we don't make a row. What do you chaps say?'

We were unanimously of the opinion that the sooner we got at the provisions the better. Our mouths had been watering for days.

So at the eerie hour mentioned, when churchyards yawn and graves give up their dead, we yawned and gave ourselves up to the pleasures of the palate.

Banquets are always pleasant things, says an authority, consisting as they do mostly of eating and drinking; but the specially nice thing about a banquet is that it comes when something's over, and tomorrow seems a long way off, and there's nothing more to worry about. Gazing upon the varied refreshments, we forgot the lines of today, and had no thought for what might happen when the remnants of the feast were discovered littering the floor on the morrow.

Benson had certainly laid out the Blenkinsop Benefit Society funds well in his capacity of treasurer. Without going into full details, I may touch lightly upon such items as sardines and chocolate éclairs, buns and potted turkey, consumed in the order given.

The *pièce de résistance* was the case of pineapples. It was a thrilling moment when Benson, with the rapt air of a high priest at some mystic ceremony, prised open the lid with a pair of scissors belonging to the absent Norris. There was an alarmingly loud crack as the lid came in half, but the noise had apparently not been heard outside the dormitory, for no Jephson broke in upon our revels.

A short struggle with the other half of the lid, in which Norris's scissors suffered severely (Benson said thoughtfully that if we bent them back again he *might* not notice anything was wrong), and the way to the fruit was clear. There were six of the pineapples, beauties, all of them, and there were just a dozen of us. A rapid calculation revealed the fact that we should each get half of one. We shared them righteously, one to every two beds, and two to the four visitors from the other dormitories. I was just dividing mine with Nicholas, when a curious thing happened.

Perkyn, who slept across the way, suddenly sprang up with a wild shriek, rushed to his jug, and plunged his left arm into it. It was now about twelve-thirty.

'Look here, young Perkyn!' said Benson, savagely.

'Ow!!' cried Perkyn.

'Shut *up*, you ass; do you want to wake the house?'

'I'm bitten!' shrilled Perkyn.

'You're *what?*' cried Inge.

'Bitten. OW!!!'

He danced painfully, still keeping his arm deep in the jug.

'Perhaps it's only imagination,' suggested dear old Blenkinsop in his good, hopeful way.

Perkyn suspended his Terpsichorean exhibition to throw a piece of soap at the speaker.

The discussion might, and probably would, have been prolonged indefinitely, but for an interruption which switched our attention off Perkyn and his real or imaginary bites in a flash.

'Great Scott, you chaps,' cried Lucas, 'look out. There's a centipede! Look out, Nick, it's coming towards you!'

And sure enough, there, on the floor, simply sprinting for Nicholas's bed in a purposeful manner that seemed to say that, having done with Perkyn, it considered the time had come for the second course, was a genuine centipede. It was three feet long – no, I am allowing myself to be carried away in the enthusiasm of the moment. I scorn to palter with the truth. Subsequent inspection proved that it was only two and a half inches long. But still, even two and a half inches of centipede is quite enough for one dormitory, especially if one has neither shoe nor sock to protect one's feet. The most grasping person will admit this.

I don't think I have ever moved quicker than I did then. I jumped up in bed. My soap was reposing in its place. As the centipede passed over a patch of moonlight on the floor, I let fly. It was a superb shot.

Smack it went less than an inch in front of the beast's nose. The happy result was that it slewed round, and scuttled, still with the same purposeful air, in the direction of Inge.

Inge was out of bed and on the floor – a position fraught with peril. He gave it a nail-brush at three yards' range, and missed. He tried with a second barrel, a sponge, and missed again. The centipede was but a yard from him when he leaped on to Blenkinsop's bed, and at the same moment Blenkinsop, that calm strategist, enveloped the reptile from above in a blanket.

It was the turning-point of the battle.

Up till now the centipede had ranged where it listed, a thing of fear. Now we had it in a corner, and proposed, wind and weather permitting, so show it exactly who was who, and precisely what was what.

Each armed with a trusty slipper, we surrounded the blanket, and waited for the enemy to show up. The minutes passed without a sign of it. Apparently the reptile found it warm and comfortable under the blanket, and meant to stay there.

'Now then,' said Lucas, in the language of the man on the

touchline, 'have it out there, Beckford.' And it *was* rather like a football match. I felt just as if I was playing half behind a pack that wouldn't heel. The suspense was something shocking.

'Look here,' said Inge, after five minutes, 'I'm going to switch the blanket off, and then you chaps go in hard with your slippers. Ready? Now then.'

For intense excitement the next minute beat anything I have ever experienced or wish to experience. We forgot what time it was and how vital it was to keep quiet, and egged each other on with shrill shouts. Perkyn, still with his arm in the jug, danced wildly, and impressed on us the necessity of bucking up.

Off went the blanket. Ten slippers rose into the air. Then whack! down they came, and from the centre of the inferno out scuttled the centipede, calm and unmoved as ever. Excitement ran higher.

'Beck-*ford*!!'

'Coming out your side, Nick.'

'Get to it, get to it.'

'Look out your end, Inge.'

'Coming over.'

Ten slippers crashed down again, and even as they crashed an icy voice spoke from the door.

'What is the meaning of this noise?'

We jumped up from where the late centipede lay flattened on the boards. At the door stood Jephson. He was simply but tastefully clad in pyjamas and a dressing-gown, and didn't look a bit pleased at being woke up at one in the morning.

'Please, sir,' said Inge, 'a centipede.'

'A *what*?'

Inge pointed to the corpse.

'Where did it come from?'

'A case of pineapples, sir,' admitted Inge, reluctantly.

Jephson raised his candle and inspected the debris of the feast in silence.

'Has anybody been stung?' he asked at last.

'I have, sir,' said Perkyn.

'Then dress and go across to Dr Fletcher's.' Dr Fletcher was the school doctor. He lived about a hundred yards from Jephson's.

'And I should like to see you all in my study tomorrow,' he concluded, 'directly after breakfast.'

'And after all,' said Benson, philosophically, on the following day, when Mr Jephson had done with us, 'I'd rather get touched up than more lines. And I think we may say we gave Blenk a fairly decent send-off.'

And the Blenkinsop Society, having admitted that his statements were justified, adjourned for light refreshments.

A cricket story

I should like to start by saying that all this happened two days after my sixteenth birthday, when my hair was still down, so that I hadn't anything to live up to, and it didn't matter what I did – or not much, at any rate. That's how it was.

It all began at breakfast on the Saturday. We were going to play Anfield that afternoon. Anfield is a town a few miles off, and the match is one of the best that Much Middlefold plays. So that I wasn't surprised that Father was annoyed when he got the curate's letter. He opened it at breakfast, just after I had come down. I was pouring out the coffee when I heard him snort in the way he always does when anything goes wrong.

I said, 'What's the matter, Father dear?'

'Here's a nice thing,' he said, waving the letter. 'Morning of match – most important match – team not any too strong – wanting everyone we can possibly get, and here's Parminter writing to say that he can't play!'

'Can't play?'

Mr Parminter was our best bowler. He had nearly got his blue at Cambridge. Father once told me that the Vicar advertised for a curate, and said that theology didn't matter, but he must have a good break from the off; and I thought it was true till I happened to find an old number of *Punch* with the same thing in. But, anyhow, Mr Parminter had got a break from the off.

Whenever we won a match it was nearly always through his bowling. He bowled very fast. A man we know once said that there was much too much devil in his bowling, considering that he was a clergyman.

'Why can't he play?' I asked.

'The wretched man,' said father, 'was at the school treat yesterday, and fell out of the swing and sprained his right wrist. Would have let me know last night, he says, but thought it might be better in the morning. Finds it impossible to move his arm without considerable pain; is dictating this letter to his housekeeper, and hopes that I shall be able to fill his place without difficulty, even at such short notice. Fill his place, indeed! And I hear that Anfield are strong in batting this year, though weak in bowling.'

'What are you going to do?'

'I suppose we must play young Hardy. He's quite incompetent, but he is the only one. Unless you can think of anybody else, Joan?'

I thought.

'No,' I said, 'I can't, Father.'

And it was not till the end of breakfast that I did. And even then I wasn't sure that he would be able to play. The person I thought of was my cousin – or, rather, he's only a sort of cousin, about twice removed. His name was Alan Gethryn, and he was at school at Beckford, which is quite near to us, if you bicycle. He had sometimes been to stay with us on Visiting Sundays. I knew he was good, because he had taken a lot of wickets for the Beckford team in matches. So I suggested him.

Father brightened up.

'That's an uncommonly good idea, Joan,' he said. 'Beckford always have a pretty useful sort of side – they coach 'em well there – and if Alan's in the team he ought to be a decent player.'

'He's in the team all right,' I said. 'He was top of the bowling averages last year.'

'This is excellent. I wonder if we could get him.'

'And I could easily bike over and ask him, Father,' I added. 'Shall I? And if he can play, I could wire to you, so that you would know in time. If he can't play, you can always get Hardy.'

Father said, 'Very well,' so I got my bicycle, and, after sending off a wire telling Alan to meet me outside the school gates during the quarter of an hour interval in the morning, I went off. I got to the school at twenty to eleven, and rode up and down outside, and presently Alan strolled out.

'Hullo!' he said.

'I say, Alan,' I said, 'would you like a game this afternoon for Much Middlefold?'

'A what?' he said.

'A game. Father sent me over to ask you if you'd play. Mr Parminter has sprained his wrist, so we want a bowler. It'll be an awfully jolly match, and you could have tea with us, and get back afterwards.'

He looked thoughtful.

'Difficulty is, you see, the corps are going off on a field-day this afternoon, and I shall be in charge here. Got to take roll-call, and so on.'

'When's roll-call?'

'Four.'

'Oh, I say. Then you can't come?'

'Wait. Let's think the thing over. Reece would take roll-call all right if I asked him, so that disposes of that. It would be out of bounds, of course, going to your place, but I don't see who's to know. So there goes that, too. I could change here and bike over. There wouldn't be any difficulty about that. And I happen to know that Leicester is going to be out of the way all the afternoon. So it's all right. I shall be able to come.'

'Oh, good!' I said. 'Who's Leicester?'

'My Housemaster. Under ordinary circs he'd be at roll-call while I ticked off the names, and I'd have to hand the list to him then. But he was telling us this morning at breakfast that he was going to spend the afternoon looking at an old church somewhere. He's keen on antiquities, you know, and brass-rubbing, and all that sort of thing. So he won't be on hand. All I've got to do is to get back here by about six or half past and give him the list then.'

After lunch Alan came.

'Ah, Alan, my boy,' said Father. 'Glad you were able to turn up. Had lunch? That's right. I've got to go down to meet these Anfield fellows. You come on later. We don't start till two-thirty. You know your way down to the ground, don't you? See you there.'

He went out of the room, carrying his cricket-bag, and returned almost at once.

'Pretty nearly forgotten it, by gad!' he said. 'I say, Joan, there's something I want you to do for me. It won't make you miss more than an over or two of the game. I met a man at the Burley-Greys' some time back, and we got talking about antiquities – seems he's keen about them – so I gave him a general invitation to come over here and let me show him over our church. He has rather unfortunately chosen today for his visit. I had his letter at breakfast, only this Parminter business put it out of my mind. I wish you would just show him the way to the church when he comes, Joan. He will arrive here at about three on his bicycle. Just explain that I can't possibly get away. You needn't stay with him, of course. Simply take him to the church, and leave him. He won't want conversation. He is going to rub brass, or some such thing. I don't know what he means – it doesn't sound a very amusing way of spending a fine summer's afternoon – but that is what he said. Just tell him there will be tea here at about half past four if he cares to turn up for it. But I should not think he would.'

I looked at Alan in a perfect panic. It could not be a coincidence.

'What is his name, Father?' I asked.

Father actually had to think before he could tell me. I could have told him at once.

'Leinster? Leicester – that's it, Leicester. Mrs Burley-Grey introduced him to me.'

Father went out again, and Alan and I were alone. I waited till I heard the front door shut.

'This,' Alan said, 'wants thinking out. Ginger beer may help.' He poured some into a glass and drank it, but it didn't seem to act. He offered no suggestion.

'Oh, do say *something*, Alan,' I said. 'What *are* we going to do? Will you go back?'

'And leave your father in the cart? Not much. I'm a fixture for the afternoon if the place was crawling with Leicesters. Am I downhearted? No ... On the other hand, it's rather a brick, this happening. The thing we want to do is to keep him off the field altogether, if possible, at any rate as long as we can. I don't see why he shouldn't be perfectly happy rubbing brass all the afternoon. Why not leave him there and risk it?'

'I couldn't. We *must* think of something better.'

'Well, you have a shot. I'm getting a headache. I'll tell you one thing I'll do. I'll ask your father if he wins the toss to put them in first, as I have to leave early. That'll help a bit. Hullo, it's twenty past! I shall have to rush. I leave you in charge of this thing. Knock him on the head and tie him up. Lock him in the church and bag the keys.'

I saw him to the door, and watched him bike off in the direction of the field. Then I went back to the dining-room to think it all over.

There was a ring at the front door about three o'clock, and I thought it was bound to be Mr Leicester. A bicycle was against the pillar at the front of the steps, and a thin, elderly man was standing on the top one, leaning down and picking trouser-clips off himself. He stood up when I opened the door, and looked at me enquiringly through a pair of gold-rimmed glasses. He had a very mild, kind face, rather like a sheep.

'Oh, are you Mr Leicester?' I said. 'Because Father's very sorry he's had to go off to the match – we're playing Anfield today – and I'm going to show you to the church.'

'I shall be very much obliged, if it would not be giving you too much trouble. I fear I have called at an inconvenient time.'

He had, of course, but I couldn't say so.

I said, politely, 'Not at all.'

We put his bicycle in the stables and set off across the fields to the church, about half a mile away.

Mr Leicester didn't talk much while we were walking. I think he didn't quite know what to say to me. And I was wondering so much what I was to do to keep him from meeting Alan that I didn't talk much either.

When we got in sight of the church he brightened up.

'How very beautiful!' he said, standing quite still and pointing, like a dog when it smells a bird. 'How picturesque! That grey stone has a delightfully soothing effect against the green of the trees, with the white road winding behind it. How truly picturesque!'

I said, 'Yes, isn't it top-hole!'

He said, 'I beg your pardon?'

I said, 'Not at all.'

And we went on.

As soon as we got inside he pointed again. I saw that he was looking at the old brass tablet at the end of the aisle, the one that was put there by the widow of a man who died in Edward III's time. He put a large piece of paper, which he had been carrying, on it, and knelt down and began to scratch at it with something black. I locked the door, and came and sat in a pew near, and watched him. He scratched and scratched away, and I sat and sat till I heard the clock strike four. I almost wished I had gone and left him, for I was dying to see the match, and I was pretty sure that he would have stopped there.

At about a quarter past four it suddenly occurred to me that there wasn't any need for me to go on sitting there, because the door was locked and I had the key, so he couldn't get out without my knowing. So I got up and began to explore. I had never been anywhere in the church except in our pew, and in the vestry, at a christening, so there was lots to see. I wandered about, and at last I saw a little door with some steps behind it. I went up and up, till I found myself looking into a great sort of loft place full of ropes, which I knew must be the belfry. The steps went on round the corner. I started off again, and came to a trap door. I pulled this down, and there I was on the roof of the tower, with the loveliest view in front of me you ever saw.

I could see the cricket-field, with little specks of white on it. If I had had some glasses I could have watched the match beautifully.

I sat there looking at the view till I heard a scraping on the steps, and Mr Leicester's head bobbed up through the trap door. He beamed at me, panting rather hard, and then pulled himself up.

'Ah! the roof!' he said. 'What a delightful view! I suppose that is the cricket-field, with the little white figures beyond the stream. How delightfully cool the breeze is up here! Really one is almost sorry to have to descend into the heat below.'

I didn't like this. It sounded as if he were going.

'Why not stop up here?' I said.

'It would certainly be pleasant. But I should like to see your father before I return to Beckford. I must thank him for the great treat he has given me this afternoon in allowing me the privilege of seeing this beautiful old church.'

I said, in a hurry, 'Oh, it doesn't matter about Father, really. I mean, of course, he may be batting or anything. He'll probably be very busy.'

'I should like very much to see him bat,' said Mr Leicester benevolently.

'Aren't you going on doing the brass?' I asked.

'I think not today – not today. I find the continuous stooping a little trying for the back, and I have obtained a very satisfactory impression. I think that we had better be going down, if you have no objection.'

So I dropped the keys over the parapet, and they fell with a rattle on the gravel path. It was a desperate measure, as they say in the books, but I couldn't think of anything else.

'What was that?' asked Mr Leicester.

'Oh, I say,' I said, 'I'm awfully sorry. I've dropped the keys!'

'We had better go down and recover them.'

'But don't you see? We can't get out. The door's locked.'

Mr Leicester's mouth opened feebly.

'We must sit here and wait for someone to come and let us out. The worst of it is everybody's at the match. Still, we can't stay here for ever, because when Father finds I don't come in to dinner—'

'Dinner! In to dinner! My dear young lady, it is imperative that I should be back at Beckford at half past six!'

'I'm awfully *sorry*,' I said, 'but unless somebody comes along—'

'Is there no other way out?' he asked.

'I'm afraid not,' I said. 'It *was* careless of me to drop them.'

'Pray, pray do not distress yourself. These accidents happen to everyone.'

I have always thought it awfully nice of him not to be angry, because he might easily have been. I know I should have been if somebody had kept me locked in a place when I wanted to get out.

We sat and waited there for about another quarter of an hour. It was jolly awkward. I didn't know what to say. It was no good talking about the view, because he was too worried by the thought of not being able to get back in time to care much about anything else.

'I really think,' he said at last, 'that we had better shout for assistance.'

It is all very well to make up your mind to shout for assistance, but it isn't easy to think what to shout. We both began at the same time. He cried, 'Help!' I shouted 'Hi!'

We didn't make very much noise really, because he had a weak voice and I didn't shout my loudest, as I was afraid of making myself hoarse. But it sounded quite loud in the stillness.

'I fear it is hopeless,' said Mr Leicester. 'The neighbourhood appears completely deserted.' But just then, as I was hoping that it was all right and that we shouldn't be let out till Alan had got safely home, I heard somebody shuffling along in the road, and singing. It was like the bit in *The White Company* where they're on the burning tower and can't get down and hear the archers singing the Song of the Bow in the distance. Only they were pleased, and I wasn't.

Mr Leicester jumped up and leaned over the side and shouted quite loud. The singing stopped.

''Ullo! 'ullo!' said a voice, and the gate clicked. I looked over Mr Leicester's shoulder, and saw a tramp standing below shading his eyes with his hand.

'My good man,' said Mr Leicester, 'I should be very much obliged if you would let us out.'

'Wot's the little gime?' said the man.

'We are locked in, and cannot get out. You will find the key a little to your left, lying on the gravel path. Take it and unlock the door.'

The tramp was a man of business.

'Wot do I make outer this?' he wanted to know.

'I will give you a shilling,' said Mr Leicester.

''Arf a dollar, guv'nor, 'arf a dollar. Liberty, the bloomin' 'eritage of the bloomin' Briton, thet's wot I'm going to give yer. It's cheap at 'arf a dollar.'

'Very well,' said Mr Leicester.

We went down the steps, and presently we heard the key in the lock and the door opened.

I wasted as much time as possible walking home, and we did not get to the field till about half past five. I was faint for want of tea. Father and Thoms, the son of the vicar's gardener, were batting. Just as we came on to the ground Father hit a beautiful four to leg. I raced on ahead of Mr Leicester to warn Alan. I found him in the pavilion – at least, we call it a pavilion; it's really only a sort of shed. There are two floors. On the one the scorer sits, but not often anybody else. Alan was there, with his pads on.

'Hullo!' he said, 'what a time you've been. What have you been doing? Where's Leicester?'

I told him all about it in a whisper, that the scorer couldn't hear. He seemed to think it funny, but he remembered to thank me. If he hadn't, after all I had been through, I don't know what I should have done.

'Where's he now?' he asked.

'He would come here with me. He's somewhere on the ground.'

'That's rather awkward. Half a second! I'll go down and spy out the land.'

He went down the ladder, but came up again almost at once. He shut down the trap door very quietly, and came and sat at the back of the room.

'That was a close thing,' he said, grinning. 'He's sitting on a bench down there, watching the game. I nearly charged into him.'

'What are you going to do?'

'Sit tight. That's the programme at present. I say, though, this is about the tightest place I've ever been in. I'm in next! Bit awkward, isn't it? If either Thoms or your pater gets out, I'm pipped; I must go down. But perhaps he won't stop.'

'He will,' I said miserably. 'He's waiting to see Father, to thank him for asking him to come to the church.'

Alan grinned again. I really believe he enjoyed it.

'Well, I don't see that we can do anything. It's just possible that your pater may knock off the runs. He's playing a ripping game. It's the other man I'm worried about,' said Alan. 'He's a rabbit from the old original hutch. Look at him scratching away at the fast man.'

I looked at him and wondered why they could not get him out. Every ball seemed to go just above or just to one side of the wicket. Then it was the end of the over, and Father had the bowling. The first ball was a full pitch, and he hit it right into the shed. We could hear it bumping against things down below.

'Well hit, sir,' said Alan. 'Let's hope that's killed Leicester.'

Somebody threw the ball back. The bowler bowled again, and Father drove it over his head. They got three for it.

'Oh, don't run odd numbers,' said Alan. 'Now the rabbit's got the bowling, and he'll be shattered to a certainty.'

Every ball looked as if it was going to bowl that wretched Thoms. The first two hopped over his wicket. The next was to leg, and he swiped at it but missed. The last of the over was a half-volley. He mowed at it, and it hit the top of his bat and up it went into the air, the easiest catch for point you ever saw.

Alan got up with a resigned expression, and began to take off his blazer.

'He can't miss *that*,' he said. 'The young hero will now walk with a firm step to his doom.'

Point was standing with his hands behind his back and a smile on his face, waiting for the ball to come down. It came, and he – missed it. I was quite sorry for him, especially as all the village boys shouted and jeered. (They *will* do it. We can't get them not to.)

'I shouldn't have thought,' said Alan, sitting down again, 'that a man could drop a sitter like that if he'd been paid for it. Now it ought to be all right.'

'What are you going to do about getting back?' I asked. 'If you both start at the same time he's sure to see you.'

'That's true; I'd forgotten that. This business seems to develop difficulties while you wait. Where's his bike?'

'In the stables.'

'Mine's just round behind the pav. So I shall get a sort of start. Can't you keep him hanging about a bit, till I've got well off?'

'I'll try.'

A ripping idea suddenly occurred to me. I got up.

'Where are you off to?' asked Alan.

'The stables,' I said. 'Goodbye. I shan't see you again before you go. Thanks awfully for playing.'

'Thanks for the game. Jolly good game. There's another four. Only six to win now.'

I went down the ladder and ran across the ground. When I got to the gate I heard tremendous yelling from the village boys, and I saw them all going back to the pavilion, so I knew that we had won.

After I had been to the stables, I went back to the field, and met Father and Mr Leicester coming to our house. They had just passed the lodge gates.

'Well, Joan,' said Father, 'we won, you see, thanks to—'

I said, quickly: 'Thanks to you, Father dear. Didn't he bat well, Mr Leicester.'

'Exceedingly vigorously. But I must really hurry away. We left the bicycle in the stables, did we not?'

But when we got to the stables we found the back tyre absolutely flat.

Mr Leicester's face lengthened.

'How very unfortunate,' he said.

'Great nuisance,' said Father.

I said, 'What an awful pity!'

'Particularly,' said Mr Leicester, 'as I omitted to bring my repairing outfit with me. It was a deplorable oversight.'

'Oh, that's all right,' said Father. 'My daughter has whatever you will want. Run along and get the things, Joan.'

It was about ten minutes before I got back. I found them looking at the bicycle in silence. I put down the repairing stuff. Then I said, 'You know it may not be a puncture, after all. Perhaps the valve has worked loose. Mine sometimes does.'

'I hardly think,' said Mr Leicester, 'that that can be the— why, yes, you are perfectly right: it is quite loose. I wonder how that can have happened?'

I said, 'I wonder.'

Eckleton

In his Sunday suit (with ten shillings in specie in the right-hand trouser pocket) and a brand-new bowler hat, the youngest of the Shearnes, Thomas Beauchamp Algernon, was being launched by the combined strength of the family on his public-school career. It was a solemn moment. The landscape was dotted with relatives – here a small sister, awed by the occasion into refraining from insult; there an aunt, vaguely admonitory. 'Well, Tom,' said Mr Shearne, 'you'll soon be off now. You're sure to like Eckleton. Remember to cultivate your bowling. Everyone can bat nowadays. And play forward, not outside. The outsides get most of the fun, certainly, but then if you're a forward, you've got eight chances of getting into a team.'

'All right, father.'

'Oh, and work hard.' This by way of an afterthought.

'All right, father.'

'And, Tom,' said Mrs Shearne, 'you are sure to be comfortable at school, because I asked Mrs Davy to write to her sister, Mrs Spencer, who has a son at Eckleton, and tell her to tell him to look after you when you get there. He is in Mr Dencroft's house, which is next door to Mr Blackburn's, so you will be quite close to one another. Mind you write directly you get there.'

'All right, mother.'

'And look here, Tom.' His eldest brother stepped to the front and spoke earnestly. 'Look here, don't you forget what I've been telling you?'

'All right.'

'You'll be right enough if you don't go sticking on side. Don't forget that, however much of a blood you may have been at that rotten little private school of yours, you're not one at Eckleton.'

'All right.'

'You look clean, which is a great thing. There's nothing much wrong with you except cheek. You've got enough of that to float a ship. Keep it under.'

'All right. Keep your hair on.'

'There you go,' said the expert, with gloomy triumph. 'If you say that sort of thing at Eckleton, you'll get jolly well sat on, by Jove!'

'Bai Jove, old chap!' murmured the younger brother, 'we're devils in the Forty-twoth!'

The other, whose chief sorrow in life was that he could not get the smaller members of the family to look with proper awe on the fact that he had just passed into Sandhurst, gazed wistfully at the speaker, but realising that there was a locked door between them, tried no active measures.

'Well, anyhow,' he said, 'you'll soon get it knocked out of you, that's one comfort. Look here, if you do get scrapping with anybody, don't forget all I've taught you. And I should go on boxing there if I were you, so as to go down to Aldershot some day. You ought to make a fairly decent featherweight if you practise.'

'All right.'

'Let's know when Eckleton's playing Haileybury, and I'll come and look you up. I want to see that match.'

'All right.'

'Goodbye.'

'Goodbye, Tom.'

'Goodbye, Tom, dear.'

Chorus of aunts and other supers: 'Goodbye, Tom.'

Tom (comprehensively): 'G'bye.'

The train left the station.

Kennedy, the head of Dencroft's, said that when he wanted his study turned into a beastly furnace, he would take care to let Spencer know. He pointed out that just because it was his habit to warm the study during the winter months, there was no reason why Spencer should light the gas-stove on an afternoon in the summer term when the thermometer was in the eighties. Spencer thought he might want some muffins cooked for tea, did he? Kennedy earnestly advised Spencer to give up thinking, as Nature had not equipped him for the strain. Thinking necessitated mental effort, and Spencer, in Kennedy's opinion, had no mind, but rubbed along on a cheap substitute of mud and putty.

More chatty remarks were exchanged, and then Spencer tore himself away from the pleasant interview, and went downstairs to the junior study, where he remarked to his friend Phipps that Life was getting a bit thick.

'What's up now?' enquired Phipps.

'Everything. We've just had a week of term, and I've been in extra once already for doing practically nothing, and I've got a hundred lines, and Kennedy's been slanging me for lighting the stove. How was I to know he didn't want it lit? Wish I was fagging for somebody else.'

'All the while you're jawing,' said Phipps, 'there's a letter for you on the mantelpiece, staring at you.'

'So there is. Hullo!'

'What's up? Hullo! Is that a postal order? How much for?'

'Five bob. I say, who's Shearne?'

'New kid in Blackburn's. Why?'

'Great Scott! I remember now. They told me to look after him. I haven't seen him yet. And listen to this: 'Mrs Shearne has sent me the enclosed to give to you. Her son writes to say that he is very happy and getting on very well, so she is sure you must have been looking after him.' Why, I don't know the kid by sight. I clean forgot all about him.'

'Well, you'd better go and see him now, just to say you've done it.'

Spencer perpended.

'Beastly nuisance having a new kid hanging on to you. He's probably a frightful rotter.'

'Well, anyway, you ought to,' said Phipps, who possessed the scenario of a conscience.

'I can't.'

'All right, don't then. But you ought to send back that postal order.'

'Look here, Phipps,' said Spencer plaintively, 'you needn't be an *idiot*, you know.'

And the trivial matter of Thomas B. A. Shearne was shelved.

Thomas, as he had stated in his letter to his mother, was exceedingly happy at Eckleton, and getting on very nicely indeed. It is true that there had been one or two small unpleasantnesses at first, but those were over now, and he had settled down completely. The little troubles alluded to above had begun on his second day at Blackburn's. Thomas, as the reader may have gathered from his glimpse of him at the station, was not a diffident youth. He was quite prepared for anything Fate might have up its sleeve for him, and he entered the junior day-room at Blackburn's ready for emergencies. On the first day nothing happened. One or two people asked him his name, but none enquired what his father was – a question which, he had understood from books of school life, was invariably put to the new boy. He was thus prevented from replying 'coolly, with his eyes fixed on his questioner's': 'A gentleman. What's yours?' and this of course, had been a disappointment. But he reconciled himself to it, and on the whole enjoyed his first day at Eckleton.

On the second there occurred an Episode.

Thomas had inherited from his mother a pleasant, rather meek cast of countenance. He had pink cheeks and golden hair – almost indecently golden in one who was not a choirboy.

Now, if you are going to look like a Ministering Child or a Little Willie, the Sunbeam of the Home, when you go to a public school, you must take the consequences. As Thomas sat by the window of the junior day-room reading a magazine, and deeply interested in it, there fell upon his face such a rapt, angelic expression that the sight of it, silhouetted against the window, roused Master P. Burge, his fellow Blackburnite, as it had been a trumpet-blast. To seize a Bradley Arnold's Latin Prose Exercises and hurl it across the room was with Master Burge the work of a moment. It struck Thomas on the ear. He jumped, and turned some shades pinker. Then he put down his magazine, picked up the Bradley Arnold, and sat on it. After which he resumed the magazine.

The acute interest of the junior day-room, always fond of a break in the monotony of things, induced Burge to go further into the matter.

'You with the face!' said Burge rudely.

Thomas looked up.

'What the dickens are you doing with my book? Pass it back!'

'Oh, is this yours?' said Thomas. 'Here you are.'

He walked towards him, carrying the book. At two yards range he fired it in. It hit Burge with some force in the waistcoat, and there was a pause while he collected his wind.

Then the thing may be said to have begun.

Yes, said Burge, interrogated on the point five minutes later, he *had* had enough.

'Good,' said Thomas pleasantly. 'Want a handkerchief?'

That evening he wrote to his mother and, thanking her for kind enquiries, stated that he was not being bullied. He added, also in answer to enquiries, that he had not been tossed in a blanket, and that – so far – no Hulking Senior (with scowl) had let him down from the dormitory window after midnight by a sheet, in order that he might procure gin from the local public-house. As far as he could gather, the seniors were mostly tee-totallers. Yes, he had seen Spencer several times. He did not add that he had seen him from a distance.

'I'm so glad I asked Mrs Davy to get her nephew to look after Tom,' said Mrs Shearne, concluding the reading of the epistle at breakfast. 'It makes such a difference to a new boy having some-body to protect him at first.'

'Only drawback is,' said his eldest brother gloomily – 'won't get cheek knocked out of him. Tom's kid wh'ought get's head-smacked reg'ly. Be no holding him.'

And he helped himself to marmalade, of which delicacy his mouth was full, with a sort of magnificent despondency.

By the end of the first fortnight of his school career, Thomas Beauchamp Algernon had overcome all the little ruggednesses which relieve the path of the new boy from monotony. He had been taken in by a primeval 'sell' which the junior day-room invariably sprang on the newcomer. But as he had sat on the head of the engineer of the same for the space of ten minutes, despite the latter's complaints of pain and forecasts of what he would do when he got up, the laugh had not been completely against him. He had received the honourable distinction of extra lesson for ragging in French. He had been 'touched up' by the prefect of his dormitory for creating a disturbance in the small hours. In fact, he had gone through all the usual preliminaries, and become a full-blown Eckletonian.

His letters home were so cheerful at this point that a second postal order relieved the dwindling fortune of Spencer. And it was this, coupled with the remonstrances of Phipps, that induced the Dencroftian to break through his icy reserve.

'Look here, Spencer,' said Phipps, his conscience thoroughly stirred by this second windfall, 'it's all rot. You must either send back that postal order, or go and see the chap. Besides, he's quite a decent kid. We're in the same game at cricket. He's rather a good bowler. I'm getting to know him quite well. I've got a jolly sight more right to those postal orders than you have.'

'But he's an awful ass to look at,' pleaded Spencer.

'What's wrong with him? Doesn't look nearly such a goat as you,' said Phipps, with the refreshing directness of youth.

'He's got yellow hair,' argued Spencer.

'Why shouldn't he have?'

'He looks like a sort of young Sunday-school kid.'

'Well, he jolly well isn't, then, because I happen to know that he's had scraps with some of the fellows in his house, and simply mopped them.'

'Well, all right, then,' said Spencer reluctantly.

The historic meeting took place outside the school shop at the quarter to eleven interval next morning. Thomas was leaning against the wall, eating a bun. Spencer approached him with half a jam sandwich in his hand. There was an awkward pause.

'Hullo!' said Spencer at last.

'Hullo!' said Thomas.

Spencer finished his sandwich and brushed the crumbs off his trousers. Thomas continued operations on the bun with the concentrated expression of a lunching python.

'I believe your people know my people,' said Spencer.

'We have some awfully swell friends,' said Thomas. Spencer chewed this thoughtfully awhile.

'Beastly cheek,' he said at last.

'Sorry,' said Thomas, not looking it.

Spencer produced a bag of gelatines.

'Have one?' he asked.

'What's wrong with 'em?'

'All right, don't.'

He selected a gelatine and consumed it.

'Ever had your head smacked?' he enquired courteously.

A slightly strained look came into Thomas's blue eyes.

'Not often,' he replied politely. 'Why?'

'Oh, I don't know,' said Spencer. 'I was only wondering.'

'Oh?'

'Look here,' said Spencer, 'my mater told me to look after you.'

'Well, you can look after me now if you want to, because I'm going.'

And Thomas dissolved the meeting by walking off in the direction of the junior block.

'That kid,' said Spencer to his immortal soul, 'wants his head smacked, badly.'

At lunch Phipps had questions to ask.

'Saw you talking to Shearne in the interval,' he said. 'What were you talking about?'

'Oh, nothing in particular.'

'What did you think of him?'

'Little idiot.'

'Ask him to tea this afternoon?'

'No.'

'You must. Dash it all, you must do something for him. You've had ten bob out of his people.'

Spencer made no reply.

Going to the school shop that afternoon, he found Thomas seated there with Phipps, behind a pot of tea. As a rule, he and Phipps tea'd together, and he resented this desertion.

'Come on,' said Phipps. 'We were waiting for you.'

'Pining away,' added Thomas unnecessarily.

Spencer frowned austerely.

'Come and look after me,' urged Thomas.

Spencer sat down in silence. For a minute no sound could be heard but the champing of Thomas's jaws as he dealt with a slab of gingerbread.

'Buck up,' said Phipps uneasily.

'Give me,' said Thomas, 'just one loving look.'

Spencer ignored the request. The silence became tense once more.

'Coming to the house net, Phipps?' asked Spencer.

'We were going to the baths. Why don't you come?'

'All right,' said Spencer.

Doctors tell us that we should allow one hour to elapse between taking food and bathing, but the rule was not rigidly adhered to at Eckleton. The three proceeded straight from the tea-table to the baths.

The place was rather empty when they arrived. It was a little earlier than the majority of Eckletonians bathed. The bath filled up as lock-up drew near. With the exception of a couple of infants splashing about in the shallow end, and a stout youth who dived in from the springboard, scrambled out, and dived in again, each time flatter than the last, they had the place to themselves.

'What's it like, Gorrick?' enquired Phipps of the stout youth, who had just appeared above the surface again, blowing like a whale. The question was rendered necessary by the fact that many years before the boiler at the Eckleton baths had burst, and had never been repaired, with the consequence that the temperature of the water was apt to vary. That is to say, most days it was colder than others.

'Simply boiling,' said the man of weight, climbing out. 'I say, did I go in all right then?'

'Not bad,' said Phipps.

'Bit flat,' added Thomas critically.

Gorrick blinked severely at the speaker. A head-waiter at a fashionable restaurant is cordial in his manner compared with a boy who has been at a public school a year, when addressed familiarly by a new boy. After reflecting on the outrage for a moment, he dived in again.

'Worse than ever,' said Truthful Thomas.

'Look here!' said Gorrick.

'Oh, come *on!*' exclaimed Phipps, and led Thomas away.

'That kid,' said Gorrick to Spencer, 'wants his head smacked, badly.'

'That's just what I say,' agreed Spencer, with the eagerness of a great mind which has found another that thinks alike with itself.

Spencer was the first of the trio ready to enter the water. His movements were wary and deliberate. There was nothing of the professional diver about Spencer. First he stood on the edge and rubbed his arms, regarding the green water beneath with suspicion and dislike. Then, crouching down, he inserted three toes of his left foot, drew them back sharply, and said 'Oo!' Then he stood up again. His next move was to slap his chest and dance a few steps, after which he put his right foot into the water, again remarked 'Oo!' and resumed Position 1.

'Thought you said it was warm,' he shouted to Gorrick.

'So it is; hot as anything. Come on in.'

And Spencer came on in. Not because he wanted to – for by rights, there were some twelve more movements to be gone through before he should finally creep in at the shallow end – but because a cold hand, placed suddenly on the small of his back, urged him forward. Down he went, with the water fizzing and bubbling all over and all round him. He swallowed a good deal of it, but there was still plenty left; and what there was was colder than one would have believed possible.

He came to the surface after what seemed to him a quarter of an hour, and struck out for the side. When he got out, Phipps and Thomas had just got in. Gorrick was standing at the end of the coconut matting which formed a pathway to the springboard. Gorrick was blue, but determined.

'I say! Did I go in all right then?' enquired Gorrick.

'How the dickens do I know?' said Spencer, stung to fresh wrath by the inanity of the question.

'Spencer did,' said Thomas, appearing in the water below them and holding on to the rail.

'Look here!' cried Spencer; 'did you shove me in then?'

'Me! Shove!' Thomas's voice expressed horror and pain. 'Why, you dived in. Jolly good one, too. Reminded me of the diving elephants at the Hippodrome.'

And he swam off.

'That kid,' said Gorrick, gazing after him, 'wants his head smacked.'

'Badly,' agreed Spencer. 'Look here! did he shove me in? Did you see him?'

'I was doing my dive. But it must have been him. Phipps never rags in the bath.'

Spencer grunted – an expressive grunt – and, creeping down the steps, entered the water again.

It was Spencer's ambition to swim ten lengths of the bath. He was not a young Channel swimmer, and ten lengths represented a very respectable distance to him. He proceeded now to attempt to lower his record. It was not often that he got the bath so much to himself. Usually, there was barely standing-room in the water, and long-distance swimming was impossible. But now, with a clear field, he should, he thought, be able to complete the desired distance.

He was beginning the fifth length before interruption came. Just as he reached half-way, a reproachful voice at his side said: 'Oh, Percy, you'll tire yourself!' and a hand on the top of his head propelled him firmly towards the bottom.

Every schoolboy, as Honble Macaulay would have put it, knows the sensation of being ducked. It is always unpleasant – sometimes more, sometimes less. The present case belonged to the former class. There was just room inside Spencer for another half-pint of water. He swallowed it. When he came to the surface, he swam to the side without a word and climbed out. It was the last straw. Honour could now be satisfied only with gore.

He hung about outside the baths till Phipps and Thomas appeared, then, with a steadfast expression on his face, he walked up to the latter and kicked him.

Thomas seemed surprised, but not alarmed. His eyes grew a little rounder, and the pink on his cheeks deepened. He looked like a choirboy in a bad temper.

'Hullo! What's up, you ass, Spencer?' enquired Phipps.

Spencer said nothing.

'Where shall we go?' asked Thomas.

'Oh, chuck it!' said Phipps the peacemaker.

Spencer and Thomas were eyeing each other warily.

'You chaps aren't going to fight?' said Phipps.

The notion seemed to distress him.

'Unless he cares to take a kicking,' said Spencer suavely.

'Not today, I think, thanks,' replied Thomas without heat.

'Then, look here!' said Phipps briskly, 'I know a ripping little place just off the Ledby Road. It isn't five minutes' walk, and there's no chance of being booked there. Rot if someone was to come and stop it half-way through. It's in a field; thick hedges. No one can see. And I tell you what – I'll keep time. I've got a watch. Two minute rounds, and half a minute in between, and I'm the referee; so, if anybody fouls the other chap, I'll stop the fight. See? Come on!'

Of the details of that conflict we have no very clear record. Phipps is enthusiastic, but vague. He speaks in eulogistic terms of a 'corker' which Spencer brought off in the second round, and, again, of a 'tremendous biff' which Thomas appears to have consummated in the fourth. But of the more subtle points of the fighting he is content merely to state comprehensively that they were 'top-hole'. As to the result, it would seem that, in the capacity of referee, he declared the affair a draw at the end of the seventh round; and, later, in his capacity of second to both parties, helped his principals home by back and secret ways, one on each arm.

The next items to which the chronicler would call the attention of the reader are two letters.

The first was from Mrs Shearne to Spencer, and ran as follows –

My Dear Spencer – I am writing to you direct, instead of through your aunt, because I want to thank you so much for looking after my boy so well. I know what a hard time a new boy has at a public school if he has got nobody to take care of him at first. I heard from Tom this morning. He seems so happy, and so fond of you. He says you are 'an awfully decent chap' and 'the only chap who has stood up to him at all'. I suppose he means 'for him'. I hope you will come and spend part of your holidays with us. ('Catch *me*!' said Spencer.)

Yours sincerely,
ISABEL SHEARNE

P.S. – I hope you will manage to buy something nice with the enclosed.

The enclosed was yet another postal order for five shillings. As somebody wisely observed, a woman's P.S. is always the most important part of her letter.

'That kid,' murmured Spencer between swollen lips, 'has got cheek enough for eighteen! "Awfully decent chap!" '

He proceeded to compose a letter in reply, and for dignity combined with lucidity it may stand as a model to young writers.

5 COLLEGE GROUNDS,
ECKLETON

Mr C. F. Spencer begs to present his compliments to Mrs Shearne, and returns the postal order, because he doesn't see why he should have it. He notes your remarks re my being a decent chap in your favour of the 13th prox., but cannot see where it quite comes in, as the only thing I've done to Mrs Shearne's son is to fight seven rounds with him in a field, W. G. Phipps refereeing. It was a draw. I got a black eye and rather a whack in the mouth, but gave him beans also, particularly in the wind, which I learned to do from reading 'Rodney Stone' – the bit where Bob

Whittaker beats the Eyetalian Gondoleery Cove. Hoping that this will be taken in the spirit which is meant.

> I remain
> Yours sincerely,
> C. F SPENCER

One enclosure.

He sent this off after prep, and retired to bed full of spiritual pride.

On the following morning, going to the shop during the interval, he came upon Thomas negotiating a hot bun.

'Hullo!' said Thomas.

As was generally the case after he had had a fair and spirited turnout with a fellow human being, Thomas had begun to feel that he loved his late adversary as a brother. A wholesome respect, which had hitherto been wanting, formed part of his opinion of him.

'Hullo!' said Spencer, pausing.

'I say,' said Thomas.

'What's up?'

'I say, I don't believe we shook hands, did we?'

'I don't remember doing it.'

They shook hands. Spencer began to feel that there were points about Thomas, after all.

'I say,' said Thomas.

'Hullo?'

'I'm sorry about in the bath, you know. I didn't know you minded being ducked.'

'Oh, all right!' said Spencer awkwardly.

Eight bars rest.

'I say,' said Thomas.

'Hullo!'

'Doing anything this afternoon?'

'Nothing special. Why?'

'Come and have tea?'

'All right. Thanks.'

'I'll wait for you outside the house.'

'All right.'

It was just here that Spencer regretted that he had sent back that five-shilling postal order. Five good shillings.

Simply chucked away.

Oh, Life, Life!

But they were not, after all. On his plate at breakfast next day Spencer found a letter. This was the letter –

Messrs J. K. Shearne (father of T. B. A. Shearne) and P. W. Shearne (brother of same) beg to acknowledge receipt of Mr C. F. Spencer's esteemed communication of yesterday's date, and in reply desire to inform Mr Spencer of their hearty approval of his attentions to Mr T. B. A. Shearne's wind. It is their opinion that the above, a nice boy but inclined to cheek, badly needs treatment on these lines occasionally. They therefore beg to return the postal order, together with another for a like sum, and trust that this will meet with Mr Spencer's approval.

(Signed) J. K. SHEARNE,
P. W. SHEARNE

Two enclosures.

'Of course, what's up really,' said Spencer to himself, after reading this, 'is that the whole family's jolly well cracked.'

His eye fell on the postal orders.

'Still!—' he said.

That evening he entertained Phipps and Thomas B. A. Shearne lavishly at tea.

Sedleigh

I

It was about four o'clock on a mellow afternoon in early April. The sun was shining brightly, birds sang, and rabbits sported in the undergrowth. Everything, so to speak, in the garden was lovely. At a point some four miles from Sedleigh School, in the direction of Lower Borlock, the scenic arrangements were particularly fine. The sun seemed to shine more brightly; rather more birds were singing; there was a slightly more animated look about the increased number of rabbits that sported in the undergrowth. It was a spot where every prospect pleased, and only man was vile.

Man was represented by W. J. Stone of Outwood's. He was sitting on a rustic stile, enjoying the sun, listening to the birds, and observing the rabbits, but – more particularly – smoking. He had not come to that lovely, lonely spot because it was lovely. He had come because it was lonely. Here, of all places, four miles from the school, a man might enjoy his after-luncheon cigarette in peace. It was a pity that there was no faithful friend on hand to watch him enjoy it. It takes two to smoke properly at school – one to smoke, the other to stand by and remark with unwilling admiration, 'I say, you *are* an ass, you know!' He could have wished that Robinson, also of Outwood's, had been at his side. But Robinson had his duties elsewhere. Robinson had to be at roll-call to answer his name – and Stone's.

So Stone sat on his stile alone, and thought of life, drawing meditatively at his cigarette. He congratulated himself on having chosen not only the ideal spot, but also the ideal time. There was a match on today, School v. Town, and all the masters who were not playing golf would be on the touch-line. Sedleigh, as Mr Downing, the games-master, liked to say, was above all a keen school; and its keenness extended to the staff.

It seemed to Stone that nothing could undo him. But Nemesis was lumbering round the corner, in the person, the stout person, of one Collard, the school Sergeant.

The stile on which Stone sat had just one disadvantage. It was a little far back from the road, so that he could not see pedestrians until they came immediately opposite to him. Also there was a broad strip of turf between the hedge and the road. Also, again, Sergeant Collard suffered from tender feet. Therefore the Sergeant, journeying to the Lower Borlock railway station, walked not on the road but on the turf. Consequently his footsteps were noiseless, with the result – now we come to the point – that he came into view of the stile, Stone, and the cigarette while all three were in conjunction. Stone was, indeed, in the very act of expelling a cloud of smoke.

Stone did what he could. He flung the cigarette into the field behind him, and looked at the Sergeant with innocent pleasure, as one meeting a friend unexpectedly in distant parts.

The Sergeant halted.

'Oo-oo-oo, yes!' he observed.

He generally opened conversation in this way.

'Lovely afternoon, Sergeant,' said Stone. 'Ripping, this sun is.'

The Sergeant eyed him sternly.

'And the birds,' said Stone.

'Oo-oo-yes, you young monkey!' said Sergeant Collard.

'And the rabbits,' said Stone.

The Sergeant continued to eye him with his basilisk stare.

It so happened that Stone was not one of his favourites. Indeed, between Stone and himself there had long been raging guerrilla warfare of a somewhat poignant kind. It was Stone who, to the great contentment of the school, had bestowed upon him the nickname of Boots. And he considered it derogatory to the dignity of an ex-sergeant of His Majesty's army to be addressed as Boots by ribald boys.

It was not, therefore, with pain that he realised that duty compelled him to report to Mr Outwood that he had discovered Stone smoking on a stile four miles from the school in the direction of Lower Borlock. Pleasure, rather.

'Oo-oo-oo, yes!' he said. 'Smoking, eh?'

Stone stared.

'Smoking?' he cried. '*Me*?'

'Smoking. *Contrary* to school regulations, as is well known. Young monkey!'

'Boots,' said Stone, 'you're delirious.'

The Sergeant turned a richer purple at the hated name.

'Never you mind my boots,' he said crisply. 'I shouldn't like to be in yours when I tells Mr Outwood how you was smoking con*trary* to school regulations.'

'You're going to tell him that?'

'I am going to tell him that.'

'Where's your evidence?'

'Hevidence! Didn't I cop yer at it?'

'Cop me at it!' said Stone, amazed. 'If you did, why aren't I smoking now? Dash it!' he moaned, 'it's a bit thick. I come here, miles from the school, simply to get away from you and have a little peace, and I'm blowed if you don't follow me. And not only that, you accuse me, absolutely without evidence, of smoking. I call it rough on a chap.'

'I seen yer throw the cigarette away. There it is behind you.'

'And you mean to say,' demanded Stone, 'that just because I happen by the merest fluke to be sitting on a stile within a dozen yards of a cigarette which may have been there goodness knows how long—'

'Ho! May it? Then why is it alight now?'

Stone looked behind him. A thin spiral of smoke was indeed curling up from the grass.

'What's that, then?' asked Sergeant Collard, pointing.

Stone gave the smoke a careful inspection.

'It looks to me,' he said, 'like a prairie fire. Probably caused by spontaneous combustion owing to the heat of the day.'

'Ho!' said the Sergeant. 'It looks to *me* like a cigarette thrown away by some young monkey because he was copped in the act of smoking it.'

'As a matter of fact,' said Stone carelessly, 'I remember now. It *is* a cigarette. A man stopped here just now to ask the time. I recollect now he threw away his cigarette. So that's how it *was*, you see. *Now* you see how silly it is to jump at conclusions, don't you, Sergeant?'

'Ho!'

'By the way, Sergeant,' said Stone, 'I've been meaning to buy your son Ernie some sweets for days. Suppose you take this, and—'

He fumbled in his pocket.

Sergeant Collard snorted ruthlessly.

'Attempted bribery!' he boomed. 'Thereby haggravatin' the offence. Mr Outwood shall 'ear of that, too.'

Stone gave the thing up.

'Oh, get out, Boots,' he said moodily. 'You're a blot on the landscape.'

For some moments after the Sergeant had trudged off, Stone sat on the stile, pondering. It was uncommonly awkward. There was no blinking that fact. Corporal punishment, worse luck, was rarely administered at Sedleigh, the Headmaster objecting to it on principle. He would not have minded that. It only lasted a few moments, and when it was over, there you were with a clean slate. The punishment for smoking would be either lines to a colossal amount or else detention on three or more half-holidays. To these penalties he objected strongly.

He climbed down from the stile, and started to walk towards the school. Life was very grey. The sun still shone, the birds still sang, the rabbits still sported in the undergrowth, but Stone recked of none of these things. He was plunged in gloomy thoughts.

Now, I could haul up my slacks with considerable vim on the subject of Stone's thoughts; I could work the whole thing up into a fine psychological study, rather in the Henry James style; but it would only be cut out by the editor, so what's the use? Let us, therefore, imagine Stone plunged in gloomy thoughts for about three minutes, or four, and then – make it five – at the end of five minutes hearing the droning sound.

At first the sound was simply like the note of some distant bee (or wasp). Then it came nearer, and Stone knew it for what it was, the noise of a powerful motor-car.

It gave him no idea at first beyond the very sensible one of getting out of the road. He got out of the road, and presently the car shot past – a big, red car with one occupant.

Stone watched it disappearing down the road, and was starting once more on his walk when he observed the machine slow down, stop, and begin to back towards him. In a few moments the motorist, coming within hailing distance, hailed.

'I say!' he shouted.

'Hullo?' said Stone.

The car drew level with him. The driver leaned out.

'I say,' he said, 'can you tell me the way to Limpstone?'

'You're going just in the wrong direction,' said Stone. 'You're coming away from it.'

The driver made disparaging comments on the rustic intelligence.

'An old fossil in a smock told me this was the way a quarter of an hour ago.'

'You ought to have turned at the bend in the road, where the sign-post says "To Sedleigh",— oh!'

He gasped. An idea had come to him.

'I say,' he added tentatively, 'I suppose you couldn't— what I mean is, if you would let me hop into the car, I could show you the way. I'm going to Sedleigh, and it's straight on from there to Limpstone.'

'Hop on,' said the driver briefly. 'You're the man I've been wanting to meet.'

'Same here,' said Stone, hopping.

The car moved off.

'What sort of a road is it from here?' said the motorist, as they turned down the bend.

'Quite good.'

'Then sit tight. I'm going to let her rip. I'm all behind time already.'

He opened the throttle. The next few minutes were almost too exhilarating to Stone's thinking. The car touched the road here and there, but for the most part it seemed to skim through the air like an aeroplane. Every now and then it would turn a corner on the rim of one wheel. At an early point in the proceedings Stone lost his breath. He had to hold on to his cap to keep from losing that too. It was with a feeling of profound relief that he observed the school buildings approaching as if on wings.

'Hi!' he shouted in his companion's ear. 'Stop!' The car gradually lessened its speed.

'This is Sedleigh,' said Stone. 'Will you put me down here? Thanks awfully for the lift. You go straight on now till you get into the London Road. You turn down to the right for Limpstone.'

'Thanks,' said the motorist briefly. 'Goodbye.'

'Goodbye.'

II

From the school grounds, as Stone turned towards them, came an intermittent bellowing, rather suggestive of a dinosaur in pain. This was the school ('we are above all a keen school') stimulating the fifteen in its battle with the Town. Just as Stone went in at the gate the bellowing changed to a howl, which grew in volume till it died away in a patter of clapping. Stone knew what that meant. Somebody had scored for the school.

He mingled with the crowd on the touch-line, and found Robinson.

'Hullo!' said Robinson. 'Are you back?'

'Quick, tell me all that's happened,' said Stone; 'who was that who scored just now?'

'Hammond. Jolly good run. Got the ball from a scrum in our twenty-five and nipped clean through. The back almost had him, but he swerved.'

Stone's lips moved. He wore an air of concentration.

'Hammond, our twenty-five – back – swerve,' he murmured. 'Is that the only score?'

'So far.'

'Anything else happened?'

'The Town nearly got over with a forward rush in the first five minutes. That big chap with red hair started it.'

'Who's been doing anything for us?'

'Hammond's been good all through. Hassall nearly dropped a goal.'

'Any of the forwards do anything?'

'Williams pretty hot in the loose.'

'Thanks.'

A few minutes later the whistle blew for 'No-side', leaving the school winners by a try to nil. Stone joined the crowd that moved towards the houses. His gaze wandered to and fro. At last he discovered the man he was looking for – Mr Downing.

He trotted up.

'Jolly good game, sir,' he said.

Mr Downing was in affable mood. The School had won against a heavier team, and the winning try had been scored by a boy in his house. He beamed upon Stone.

'Excellent, Stone, excellent,' he said. 'The team played a good keen game all through.'

'Fine run of Hammond's, sir.'

'Very fine. Quite brilliant.'

Stone dipped into the coffers of his memory and produced Hassall.

'Good shot at a dropped goal, that one of Hassall's, wasn't it, sir?'

'Very good indeed. It was the only thing to do, and it nearly succeeded.'

'It was an awfully good game altogether,' said Stone. 'I thought they were over in the first five minutes when that red-haired forward started that rush.'

Mr Downing agreed that it had been a very near thing. Stone, after a casual mention of Williams' good work in the loose, went off to his house.

Just before tea, as he expected, he was summoned to Mr Outwood's study. It was quite a small party. Sergeant Collard was there, looking stout and important, but no other representatives of the Sedleigh Smart Set were present.

Mr Outwood, that mild-mannered archaeologist, peered at Stone over his pince-nez. He looked troubled.

'Stone,' he said.

'Sir?' said Stone.

'Er—'

'Yes, sir?'

'Perhaps, Sergeant,' said Mr Outwood, 'it would be better if you told your story again.'

'Oo-oo-oo yes, sir,' responded the man of war, amiably. 'In 'arf a minute, sir.'

He proceeded to relate how he had found Stone seated on a stile near Lower Borlock, smoking.

'Leastways,' concluded the Sergeant, ''e'd flung away the cigaroot prompt hon seein' me. Young monkey! But I spotted 'im, sir. Prompt.'

Stone's face during this recital was a study in injured astonishment.

'I think the Sergeant must be mistaken, sir,' he said with unction. 'Smoking is against school rules, and is bad for you, too.'

'Mistook!' boomed the Sergeant. 'Me! Why, I seen you with my own eyes. Yes, and talked to you, too.'

'Talked to me?'

'Yes, talked to you. Young monkey!'

'What time was it?'

'Yes, what time, Sergeant?' interpolated Mr Outwood. 'That is important. I caught sight of a boy who I am nearly sure was Stone, though I had no reason to impress the fact on my memory, immediately after the conclusion of the football match. That would be shortly after four.'

'And fortunately, sir,' said Stone smoothly, 'I happened to meet Mr Downing just as the match finished. You can ask him, if you like, sir. We talked a lot about the match. I remember, now I come to think of it, that we talked about how nearly the Town scored in the first five minutes.'

'In the first five minutes!' shouted the Sergeant. 'Oo-oo-oo yer, you young monkey; I seen you with my own eyes sitting on the stile at four prompt. I'd just looked at my watch.'

Mr Outwood was plainly puzzled.

'Didn't you have sun-stroke once when you were serving in India, Sergeant?' asked Stone with friendly interest. 'I seem to remember hearing you tell some of the chaps that you had.'

'I 'ad sun-stroke, yes,' admitted the Sergeant. 'But I 'adn't this afternoon when I saw you a-sittin' and smokin' on that stile,' he said doggedly.

Stone looked appealingly at Mr Outwood. The Housemaster, in his motherly way, began to reason with the invalid.

'But really, Sergeant, I think— surely. You follow me? This stile you speak of as having been near Lower Borlock. That village is quite four miles from the school. I know from personal experience. There is a church there, portions of which date back to pre-Norman times. I have frequently bicycled to it.'

'Of course, if I had been there and had had my bicycle sir,' said Stone, as one who insists on being reasonable, 'I might have got back in time for the finish of the game; but my bicycle is being mended. Had the fellow you thought you saw, Sergeant, a bicycle?'

'I didn't see no bicycle.'

'Then I think you will agree, Sergeant,' said Mr Outwood, soothingly, 'that the whole thing must have been a mistake. The effects of sun-stroke frequently reappear in after-life, I believe, and—'

'I saw 'im on that stile a-smokin',' persisted the seer of visions.

'You fancied you did,' said Mr Outwood. 'Probably you were thinking of Stone at the moment—'

'He's always thinking of me, sir,' said Stone with an affection-ate glance at the perspiring warrior.

'That is how it all happened,' beamed Mr Outwood. 'You see, Sergeant, Stone could not possibly have covered the distance in the time on foot, so that—'

He was interrupted by a knock at the door. One of the maids entered.

'Might I speak to you for a moment, sir?'

'Certainly, Jane. Excuse me one instant.'

He went out. There were sounds of a murmured conversation in the passage. During the interval Sergeant Collard and Stone eyed one another in silence, the Sergeant with something of the Gorgon in his gaze, Stone all cheery friendliness. Presently Mr Outwood came back.

'Certainly, Jane,' he said over his shoulder. 'Show him in here.'

Stone was wondering who 'him' referred to, when there came from outside the sound of ponderous footsteps, and into the room walked a policeman, who, having apparently recognised an acquaintance in Sergeant Collard, nodded to him, and stood at ease, breathing heavily.

'Yes, constable?' said Mr Outwood. 'What is it that I can do for you?'

The policeman cleared his throat. 'It's like this, sir,' he said.

Fixing an absolutely expressionless eye on an engraving that hung over the mantelpiece, he began to speak in what was evidently the manner he reserved for giving evidence before magistrates.

'On the afternoon of the – I mean this afternoon, at five minutes after four o'clock. I was on the road between Lower Borlock and Sedleigh, when I heard a sound, and round the corner came dashing a nortermo*bile*.'

'I beg your pardon, constable?'

'A nortermo*bile*, your worsh— sir. A red one, sir, exceeding of the speed limit by a matter of eighty miles a hower. Why,' he went on, dropping the official manner and speaking with a touch of human heat, 'if I 'adn't looked precious slippy it 'ud have knocked me into hash. It was all hover so quick and such a shock I 'ad, that cop his number was more than I could do. He was off in a flash. The only thing I saw was that there was a young gent sittin' beside the shovoor with a red and blue striped cap. One of the young gents from the school, as likely as not, I thinks. And makin' enquiries, I finds that the young gents in your house wears red and blue striped caps, sir.'

'Yes, yes; that is so, constable.'

'Why,' said the policeman, for the first time seeing Stone, 'same colours as this young gent 'ere 'as on his tie. And blow me if I don't think that was the very young gent—'

He looked at Stone. Mr Outwood looked at Stone. Sergeant Collard looked at Stone. Stone looked at the carpet.

The silence was broken by the voice of the man of war, raised in a psalm of triumph.

'Sun-stroke! Oo-oo-oo. Yes! Sun-stroke? Ho! Young monk—'

Mr Outwood was still looking at Stone with eyes from which the scales had fallen.

'Well, Stone?' he said.

THE END

The twenty-five stories collected in *Tales of Wrykyn and Elsewhere* were originally published in the following British magazines:

'Jackson's Extra', *Royal*, June 1904
'Homeopathic Treatment', *Royal*, August 1904
'The Reformation of Study Sixteen', *Royal*, November 1904
'Ruthless Reginald', *Captain*, April 1905
'The Politeness of Princes', *Captain*, May 1905
'Shields' and the Cricket Cup', *Captain*, June 1905
'An Affair of Boats', *Captain*, July 1905
'The Last Place', *Captain*, August 1905
'An International Affair', *Captain*, September 1905
'The Deserter', *Royal*, August 1905
'A Division of Spoil', *Captain*, September 1906
'Educating Aubrey', *London*, May 1911
'The Strange Disappearance of Mr Buxton-Smythe',
    Public School, December 1901
'The Adventure of the Split Infinitive', *Public School*,
    March 1902
'Welch's Mile Record', *Captain*, November 1902
'Pillingshot Detective', *Captain*, September 1910
'Pillingshot's Paper', *Captain*, February 1911

'An Afternoon Dip', *Pearson's*, September 1904
'A Corner in Lines', *Pearson's*, January 1905
'The Autograph Hunters', *Pearson's*, February 1905
'Playing the Game', *Pearson's*, May 1906
'Blenkinsop's Benefit', *Captain*, August 1904
'Personally Conducted', *Cassell's*, July 1907
'The Guardian', *Windsor*, September 1908
'Stone and the Weed', *Captain*, May 1910

TITLES IN THE EVERYMAN WODEHOUSE

This edition of P. G. Wodehouse has been prepared from the first British printing of each title.

The Everyman Wodehouse is printed on acid-free paper and set in Caslon, a typeface designed and engraved by William Caslon of William Caslon & Son, Letter-Founders in London around 1740.